Passionate
Promises

A Legacy

Patricia Marlett

Published in the United States of America
Published by High Tower Publications

First Edition 2009 ISBN: 978-1-60696-866-6
Second Edition 2017 ISBN: 978-0-9854059-7-7

High Tower Publications
2 Samuel 22:3

Passionate Promises

A Legacy

The Story of Sabrina

Dedication

This book is dedicated to my father, Rufus Allen, for always being there for me with love and encouragement in all my endeavors.

Acknowledgement

There is one I will always acknowledge and give thanks to above all others. I honor, praise, and give the glory to my heavenly Father, for it is by His grace that I am blessed.

I also give thanks to my husband, Mark, for his endearing love and support.

*To all the special Aunts
and their Nieces*

Chapter 1

She was going to miss her flight. Five minutes simply wasn't enough time to get from the airport's main lobby to the gated area where the plane awaited. At least, that was what she feared, struggling forward through the maze of people heading in the same direction. Sabrina held a tight grip on the oversized bright floral tote bag hanging from her left shoulder while balancing the bulky black equipment bag on her right. They were weighing her petite five-feet five-inches stature down to more like five-three, or at least she felt as though she was shrinking. She should be used to carrying this kind of weight since she did this for a living, but it never failed to leave her winded with aching shoulder muscles by the time she was on the plane and plopping down in the seat.

Continuing to dodge people pressing forward, Sabrina inadvertently bumped passersby with her extensions but kept marching on as quickly as she could manage. Rushing through the terminal in a sprint, she heard her cell phone playing the Beatles' *Yellow Submarine* tune from somewhere in the depths of the oversized tote. Absently thrusting her hand into the floral bag, Sabrina dug it out and noticed the caller was her sister, Sophie.

"Make it fast Sophie, I'm almost to the plane," Sabrina demanded.

"Listen Sabrina, I need you to come home. We have a family emergency," Sophie solemnly stated.

"What emergency? You know I'm on my way to San Diego for a shoot in the morning."

"I don't want to give you bad news over the phone, Brie, just come home, okay," Sophie pleaded.

"I can't just change my plans, this is my job. Anyway, what is the emergency, and hurry up, I'm almost to the gate."

"Alright, Brie, have it your way. You always do."

"What did you say? I can't hear you. It's very noisy here."

Sabrina pressed the cell phone closer to her ear.

"Aunt Millie was found dead this morning in her kitchen," Sophie stated, on the verge of crying.

Sabrina stopped in her tracks causing a cascading domino effect with the people following behind. Walking around her, some turned back with a stern look for abruptly halting their journey through the terminal.

"That can't be. I was with her a month ago and she was fine. What happened? How could she be dead?"

"I don't have details. I got a call from her neighbor, Bella Stafford, who found her this morning. Apparently, they were going to an interior designing class and when she didn't answer the doorbell, Bella went around and knocked on the side door to the kitchen. Still not getting an answer, she went in and found her lying on the floor in front of the sink. She called the police, and they came and took her away and that's all I know at the moment."

"Okay, I'll take the next flight home. I need to let Joe know of my change in plans. I'll call you later with the flight information," Sabrina said abruptly, before pushing the disconnect button.

Walking to the nearest chair, she plopped down letting the bags slide from her shoulders to the floor. It wasn't possible her favorite aunt was dead. Reeling from the shock, Sabrina sat in a daze staring straight ahead not noticing anyone or anything, trying to maintain her composure while tears welled up in her eyes.

She remained sitting for several minutes hearing the flight

announced over the intercom but unable to move. She was in the San Francisco Airport on her way south to San Diego for another photo shoot. Her job kept her traveling across the country, spending more time in the air than on land.

After several years of snapping pictures, she had finally reached a pinnacle of subdued fame. When Sabrina was twelve years old, having received her first camera from her dad as a birthday present, she knew immediately she wanted to be a photojournalist. From that day on, she was never without her camera which automatically became an additional appendage of her body. Wherever she went her camera went, to the annoyance of family and friends because she was forever taking pictures of them.

Once she started high school, Sabrina's first real photography projects began. Taking on small assignments for the school paper gave her experience which later led into submitting independent work while in college. By the time she graduated, Sabrina already had the strong beginnings of a career, because she was very good at capturing a world through the eye of the camera that no one else seemed to notice. Freezing those moments in time and displaying her work for others to have the same experience was simply a dream come true for Sabrina.

Working for *Nature on the Run* magazine for the past nine years including the part-time stint while in college, earned her the position of senior photojournalist. Along with the ranking position came her own personal assistant who scheduled the assignments directing her from one end of the country to the other. Sabrina was forever grateful that someone else took care of the business matters leaving her to do what she loved best.

Some of her most recent pictures were being categorized in a special edition of the magazine called, *Animals of the Wild.*

She was undoubtedly headed in the direction of making a name for herself since many of her photographs were also appearing in select art galleries displaying the theme of *Nature in the Raw.* Feeling secure her career was established, Sabrina enjoyed a degree of popularity with a modest approach.

Sabrina got up from the seat knowing she had missed the final call for the flight to San Diego, but it really didn't matter because she wasn't getting on that plane. Walking in the opposite direction toward the airline ticket counter, she changed the ticket to a one-way home to Florida. The next flight leaving San Francisco to Orlando wasn't for two hours. She decided to wait in one of the little restaurants near the terminal area.

Ordering a cup of coffee at the front counter of a place called *Grill and Grab*, she struggled to balance the shoulder bags and a steaming cup of liquid. Carefully walking toward a back corner table, she placed the hot cup down first and then unloaded the heavy bags onto a nearby chair. She settled on one of the hard uncomfortable seats and watched the flutter of activity near the entrance.

Sabrina was a people watcher, inheriting that tendency from her mother and considered that was why photojournalism suited her so well. She had the patience to sit, watch, and wait so often required to capture the unexpected shot. Waiting for her flight home, she sipped coffee and tried to come to terms with her heartache.

She reached over rummaging through the tote to locate her cell phone pushing the speed dial button to Joe Morgan, her assistant. Sabrina explained she wasn't boarding a plane to San Diego, but waiting for a flight to Orlando. After declaring the reason, he offered his condolences and assured her he would handle the rescheduling of the photo shoot, knowing there was time to meet the deadline for the upcoming edition in the magazine.

Sabrina was so dedicated to her job, that even a family emergency made her wince a little if it meant she couldn't meet a deadline. Photography was everything to Sabrina. Her entire life revolved around her profession.

Before hanging up, Joe confirmed he would reschedule the shoot at the San Diego Zoo, which was a big relief that another photographer would not be sent in her place. Then she called her sister to give Sophie the flight arrival time at the Orlando International Airport.

Knowing she would be in California for several weeks, Sabrina didn't leave her car at the airport parking garage as she typically would have done, but instead had her sister drop her off. Now, Sabrina would need to be picked up and taken home, and it would be very late when the plane arrived. Sophie would have to drive approximately forty-five minutes to deliver Brie home in Cocoa Beach and then backtrack to her own. Sabrina wished she didn't have to inconvenience her sister, but it couldn't be helped.

When she talked with Sophie there was no further news about Aunt Millie, and not wanting to tie up her sister's phone in case Bella might be trying to get in touch, they kept their conversation short. Sabrina refused to think of Aunt Millie because doing so would surely make her cry, and she knew if she started, she wouldn't be able to stop. Instead, she made a mental list of the things that needed to be done upon returning home. But that direction of thought didn't last long until her mind conjured up a memory of her aunt. She was desperately trying not to collapse into a weeping spectacle.

Less than a month ago, Sabrina was with her aunt and she was fine. They were having a great time together which they always did when she came to visit. Brie, as her family calls her, purposefully planned her schedule whereby she could visit every two to three months. One of the things they enjoyed every time Sabrina visited was to sit on the floor in the den near the fireplace and make floral arrangements to be used for gifts.

It never mattered to Brie what they did. Being with Aunt Millie in her country home was always a special time. It was like stepping into her own private sanctuary away from the everyday life of being on the go, racing from one place to the next, and living out of hotel rooms. Her aunt's home became a haven where she could unwind and relax. It wasn't that she did not enjoy the fast-paced lifestyle, but rather, visiting with her aunt gave Sabrina a short reprieve. She always returned to work feeling refreshed and ready for the next assignment.

Long ago on one of those visits, Aunt Millie took Brie for a slow drive around the countryside pointing out her neighbor's homes. She showed Sabrina where her best friend, Bella, lived which happened to also be her adjoining neighbor to the west. Living in this beautifully landscaped region located in the majestic foothills of Asheville, North Carolina, houses were deliberately located apart, not close enough to borrow a cup of sugar or stick of butter. Stretched about a quarter mile in distance with a forest in between, you couldn't see from one house to the next. Sabrina remembered Aunt Millie would say, *It's not living in the country if you can see population out your window.*

It wasn't possible to think she would never see her again. Aunt Millie was always so full of life, enjoying spontaneous things like walking in the rain or staying up till three in the morning watching old classic movies, crying over the ending. She was a best friend to Brie, and now she realized more than ever how much visiting her aunt in her country home meant, with its solitude and slower pace acting like a balm to her hectic lifestyle. Where would her getaway haven be now? This was all she knew. Her life would never be the same.

Chapter 2

It was nearly midnight when the plane landed in Orlando. Getting off the tram and walking the short distance to the main lobby of the airport, Sabrina immediately spotted her sister. Picking up the pace, she approached a young woman who was a reflection of herself and began to feel tears forming in her eyes when she greeted her twin with a tight hug. When the sisters were together, it was practically impossible to tell them apart. They were very attractive women with their shoulder-length hair the color of wheat, perfectly shaped oval face, and the most unusual shade of golden-amber eyes; a striking color combination.

The only true way to tell the girls apart was by a count of freckles across the bridge of their nose. Sabrina had a sprinkle more freckles than her twin, but you had to be in the presence of both women at the same time and look very carefully to notice that little difference. When they were teenagers, they loved to switch roles with family and friends to see how long it would take them to realize they were with the opposite twin. They had a lot of fun with that trick until getting caught pulling it on their dad. Suffering through a long lecture about their thoughtlessness left them agreeing to never do it again. Of course, Sabrina and Sophie felt they had gotten several good years in before retiring their prank.

With the sisters remaining in an embrace, they could hear the whispers from the people walking past. It was typical when they were together. Reluctant to pull apart, they began walking through the lobby toward the escalators down to the claim area. One little boy in front was pointing a finger at them while pulling on his mother's hand to get her attention. Brie gave him a smile, and he shyly turned his face away hiding a grin in his mother's dress.

It didn't take long to walk the distance to the conveyor belt where variations of luggage were already making the rounds. Spotting her two matching floral pink tapestry pieces, Brie quickly stepped forward and grabbed one with each hand; she was an old pro at this. Sophia took one bag and Brie the other, and with luggage in tow, they proceeded toward the double glass doors to the outside pick-up area.

Sophie's husband, David, was parked, waiting in his black SUV. Spotting them coming through the door, he climbed out of the driver's seat and came around to the back of the vehicle. He gave Sabrina a quick hug and gathered the luggage, tossing it in the back. Brie opened the backdoor, placing the equipment bag on the floor before sliding onto the seat while Sophie sat in the front. David pulled out into the line of traffic leaving the airport toward the Beeline east to Cocoa Beach.

David met Sabrina in college in her junior year when he was admiring her work on display in the campus art museum. He was strolling through the museum on a Saturday afternoon and came upon an exhibit of an oversized black and white photo of four baby chicks in a nest fighting over the single worm being released by their parent. What made the picture so striking was the eagle's nest sat high on top of a street lamppost to a backdrop of skyscrapers; a most unlikely place to see an endangered bird's nestled family.

Not realizing the woman standing beside him was the photographer, he drew this stranger into an impromptu critiquing of the photograph. While David was paying high compliments, Sabrina didn't confess to being the eye behind the camera as they struck up a conversation talking well into an hour, when Sophie walked up.

"Hey sis, looking good," Sophie commented with a smile, nodding her head toward the enlarged photo hanging by two thick chains from a wooden beam in the ceiling.

He turned to see who was speaking and was shocked to be seeing double. Blinking several times to clear his vision, David still couldn't tell them apart. He thought he must have been staring at the photo too long and it was causing his eyesight to temporarily fail.

"Hi, I'm Sophie Fitzgerald, and I see you're admiring my sister's work. She's very good, don't you think?" Sophie asked, beaming with a smile.

"This is your work?" David asked, feeling embarrassed.

"I didn't mean to embarrass you, but I always like to get a person's first reaction. It gives me an honest perspective of my work," Sabrina confessed.

"And besides, I didn't want to stop hearing your wonderful compliments," she teased.

"Actually, it was great talking with you. I have a lot of respect for talented people. Wish I could claim I had a special gift for art, music, or sports, but it wasn't meant to be. This may seem bold of me since we just met, but when you are finished here I would like to buy you both a cup of coffee at *The Coffee Jug* around the corner," David inquired of the twins.

"What do you think, Brie?" Sophie asked, turning to her sister.

"Well, we do have him outnumbered, so I suppose it would be okay," Sabrina said, glancing at David.

"Alright. We'll meet you there in about ten minutes," Sabrina told him.

"That sounds good to me. I'll go hold a table for us," David replied, turning to leave.

"He's cute," Sophie whispered, watching him walk away.

"Yeah, I suppose so," Sabrina remarked absently, still staring at the photograph, critiquing her work.

"Who is he? I haven't seen him around campus," Sophie

asked.

"I don't know. He was studying the photo and started up a conversation," Brie commented, still staring at the picture.

"Well if you aren't interested, I wouldn't mind finding out more about him when we meet at the coffee shop. Do you think he will be interested in me?" Sophie asked her sister.

"Gosh, Sophie, I don't know. Would anyone want to date someone so ugly as you?" Sabrina stated, barely containing her laughter.

Sophie gave her one of her famous stern raised right eyebrow looks while folding her arms across her waist.

"Well, if I'm ugly so are you, twins all the way!" Sophie exclaimed, feeling much better for having the last word.

This was typical bantering between them.

"Okay, let's go meet your Mr. Right," Sabrina said, turning to walk toward the front of the building.

David had reserved a table in the back of the little coffee shop and stood when he saw the twins walk in motioning with his hand so they could locate him. He was a slender man of approximately five-eleven in height with neatly trimmed light brown hair and dark blue eyes. Sabrina thought it was his eyes that captured Sophie's interest.

Sophie went ahead of Sabrina and arrived first at the table sitting closest to David while Sabrina took a chair opposite him. Waiting for their coffee order, the sisters learned he was a senior majoring in education. He wanted to be a high school math teacher and eventually get his masters to continue teaching at college level. Sophie squealed with delight when she heard this and chimed in she was also an education major wanting to be an elementary school teacher. They were curious that they hadn't run into each other before now since they were taking the same classes on campus.

With their common interest in teaching and an instant attraction to one another, they became inseparable after that night. David and Sophie spent all their free time together during the remainder of his senior year, and it wasn't long, they were planning their future. They wanted to be married two weeks after Sophie graduated, which gave them approximately a year and half before she became Mrs. David McKinley.

The remaining days in college passed quickly with David graduating followed later by Sabrina and Sophie. When the newlyweds settled into a small house in Orlando, Sabrina took a full time position with the magazine and chose to relocate across country in Washington state. It had been three years and her apartment lease was up for renewal.

Brie was considering whether to stay another year or move back to Florida to be close to Sophie and David. She often mentioned wanting her to live nearby, and perhaps it was time to make a change. After all, it didn't matter where she hung her clothes, for she was rarely home.

Chapter 3

For several minutes no one spoke, while David maneuvered through traffic toward the Beeline, a straight shot to Cocoa Beach. Sabrina broke the silence from the backseat.

"Anymore news about what happened to Aunt Millie?" Brie inquired of her sister.

"I talked to Bella several times today, and she said when the police arrived they arranged for her body to be taken to the city coroner and from there she would be transported to the funeral home. Bella mentioned she would be glad to help with the necessary arrangements, so everything could be taken care of before we arrived. Apparently, she has connections in the community and could get things done quicker than the usual time frame. Since she offered and was willing to take care of the details, I told her to go ahead and select a funeral home and use her own discretion to the specifics. It seemed best to let her take charge since we don't know anyone in Asheville, and I didn't think you would mind, Brie," Sophie explained.

"No, not at all. It sounds like the best way to handle this, if Bella is okay with it."

"She's been a big help. Bella is having a hard time, though. They were very good friends. She gave us the name of the funeral home, and David talked with the director, Jim Norris, who'll have the death certificate for us when we arrive. He took care of putting an announcement in their morning paper, *The Asheville Chronicle*. I didn't realize a funeral could be put together this quickly. I guess Bella has connections," Sophie continued.

"It's just as well, there's no reason to delay."

"We've already made arrangements to have subs take over our classrooms, and David booked three tickets for tomorrow morning."

David was a mathematics teacher at Colonial High School which was located on the west side of Orlando where he taught tenth grade algebra. Sophie traveled in the opposite direction to Cambridge Elementary School teaching third grade. They truly enjoyed their profession and were favored by all the students in their respective schools. It didn't take either of them long to get employment within the school system, because teachers were in demand in Florida. David had a choice between an elementary or high school classroom and opted for the high school and never regretted the decision. Being a teacher for a year prior to marrying Sophie gave him the opportunity to save money for the down payment on a house.

"I've talked to Joe about taking a few days off. I don't know what assignments he has scheduled other than the zoo in San Diego, which can be put on hold," Sabrina said, holding back tears.

Brie's heart was broken over her aunt's death, but she refused to cry until she was in the privacy of her home. Each remained silent for the duration of the drive to take Sabrina to her condo. Though Brie was accustomed to getting around by herself, she was glad for the company because it had been a long day flying from one end of the country to the other.

Sabrina lived in a condominium right on the beach with the ocean literally at her back door, and though she wasn't home often, one of her pleasures was sitting on the balcony watching the people on the beach chase the tides while the surfers rode the waves to shore. There is a peaceful tranquility living near the ocean which she finds comforting when returning from long assignments and grueling travel schedules.

Brie bought the condo two years ago when Sophie begged

her to return to Florida, and it sounded like a good idea since she felt it was probably time to have a more permanent residence. A condominium suited Sabrina's lifestyle, giving her a place to call her own. She and and Sophie had a great time shopping for furniture and decorative accessories, placing them strategically throughout the apartment with her personal collection of prints and souvenirs. The appealing photographs, appropriately displayed, made Sabrina's condo very warm and inviting, with the enlarged pictures being the focal point throughout the apartment.

Her favorite subjects have always been of nature. Whether animals, the weather, or a beautiful sunset. It never ceases to amaze Brie to be able to capture spectacular performances, such as the unexpected pleasure to preserve a tornado in Kentucky, a blizzard in Montana, and a hurricane in the Florida Keys. These naturally occurring elements are now permanently displayed in her home.

Keeping the décor in soft earthy colors of mocha, greens, and browns makes walking into Sabrina's home like entering into the plush reception area of an upscale art museum. The living room had a soft taupe-colored suede sofa with glass top tables encased in a grey pewter base. A beautiful walnut bookcase sits against one wall holding the television and stereo system, while on the opposite wall displays two matching wingback chairs in a geometric design of neutral colors.

David drove up the driveway to the front of *The Pelican Cove Condominium* building and parked near the lobby entrance. He walked around to the back of the vehicle and gathered Brie's luggage while Sophie and Sabrina fell into each other's arms, hugging tightly for a moment.

"It'll be alright. Get some sleep tonight, and we'll talk in the morning," Sophie whispered softly to her sister.

Sabrina pulled away from the embrace and merely nodded her head when David came around pulling her two pieces of luggage. She reached into the backseat and grabbed her tote and equipment bag.

"Do you want to come in and get something to drink?" Brie asked.

"No it's too late, and we all need to get some rest. Tomorrow will be a busy day, but be sure and call me in the morning before you leave for the airport."

"First thing after coffee," Sabrina replied.

David offered to take Sabrina's luggage to her apartment on the seventh floor of a twelve level building, but she refused being accustomed to toting suitcases around. He grabbed the bags heading for the glass door of the condominium building with Brie walking beside him pulling out the security card. When they reached the entrance door, she swiped the card in the lock and took the bags from David, proceeding inside toward the elevator.

David returned to his wife and gave her a hug before lending his hand to help her into the vehicle. Walking around the front of the SUV, he took a quick glance toward the building before sliding behind the steering wheel, turning the ignition, and heading west toward home. It had been a long and emotionally draining day for Sophie also.

Being a teacher, Sophie didn't have the same open schedule her sister had, making the visits with Aunt Millie typically centered at holidays. She loved her aunt very much and would miss her terribly, but knew Sabrina would take her death much harder; this wasn't going to be easy for Brie to deal with. David drove back to Orlando in silence, respectful of his wife's somber mood knowing she was lost in thoughts of her aunt.

David and Sophie bought their house right after she graduated from college, having spent many a weekend house hunting along with planning their wedding. Their combined savings and the extra money David stashed away from his first year of teaching made buying their first home affordable. It was a small three-bedroom house in a relatively new neighborhood.

The first thing on Sophie's list was to change to color of the walls from white to a spectrum of beautifully bright rainbow colors. Being the complete opposite of her sister, who liked subdued earth tones, Sophie preferred vivid shades such as sunflower yellow, burnt terra cotta, and grassy greens for her haven, and with traditionally styled furniture, it made her home brightly appealing.

Pulling into the driveway, Sophie was still absorbed in mournful thoughts. It had been a very sad day and tomorrow wasn't going to be any better when they would be on a plane to Asheville.

Chapter 4

Sabrina let herself into the apartment, and was suddenly struck by an overwhelming feeling of sadness. She took the luggage straight down the hallway to the master bedroom placing them on the bed, putting the camera bag on a nearby chair, and backtracked to the kitchen for a glass of water. It had been tedious flying from the west to east coast, and it didn't help matters with the delays at the airport. However, now she was alone and thoughts of her aunt were weighing heavy on her mind.

Brie went back to the bedroom and unzipped both pieces of luggage throwing the flaps across the bed. She unpacked her clothes and toiletries, putting the few dirty items into the white wicker laundry basket in the adjacent bathroom. Next, she placed her brushes and makeup on the countertop knowing she would need to repack them in the morning. Doing this necessary chore helped to keep her mind off Aunt Millie. Sabrina knew she would have to repack fresh clothes in the morning and be on another plane, this time to Asheville, but right now she didn't want to think of what was ahead.

With everything put away, she got ready for bed. Slipping between the sheets, Brie laid there thinking about the events of the past twenty-four hours; nothing seemed real. Instead of going to the San Diego Zoo to photograph the newborn lion cub, she would be attending the funeral of her last remaining relative other than her sister. Her world had suddenly turned upside down.

Sophie and David were lifelong companions, but Brie depended on her aunt to be her best friend. Those times where gone forever. The sadness was overwhelming as she finally let the tears she had been holding back all day flow. It was difficult for Sabrina to believe she would never see Aunt Millie again. Rolling over on her side and giving the pillow a few punches, she cried herself to sleep.

Brie's career in photojournalism and Sophie's teaching schedule made their times together infrequent. Thus, long ago, Sabrina began to rely on her aunt to fill the need for companionship. Traveling was one of only a handful of things that made Sabrina and Sophie different. Sabrina enjoyed solitude while Sophie liked having many friends and being around people.

While growing up, Sophie was always labeled the social butterfly and Sabrina was chided for being a hermit. They may look identical, but they definitely expressed their own unique personalities. *Different strokes for different folks*, Sabrina used to say whenever she was reminded of her lack of social grace. Everyone in the family would sit around talking at gatherings, but Brie found that to be boring and wanted to be alone with her camera.

Morning came too soon, but she managed to crawl out of bed at five-thirty. With a fresh cup of coffee in hand, Sabrina dialed Joe's cell phone leaving a message she was flying to North Carolina in a few hours and would contact him later in the day. Next, she phoned Sophie as promised and agreed to meet them at the airport lobby. A couple of hours later, she was parking her car in the long-term parking garage and proceeding straight to the lobby where she immediately spotted David and Sophie standing near the security area. Upon approaching them, David handed her a ticket.

"How did you sleep?" Sophie asked.

"Not well, how about you?" Brie returned the question.

"I didn't sleep much, either."

"We had better get in the security line; our flight leaves in thirty minutes. We're cutting it a little close this morning, but since we weren't checking in luggage I figured we had plenty of time," David remarked, concerned.

It didn't take long to pass through security and onto the tram that would end at the terminal area. The passengers were already in line boarding, so they simply followed everyone onto the plane. Sitting solemnly in their seats waiting for takeoff, Sabrina thought of all the times she spent on an airplane going somewhere. She loved her work and the places it took her because no two assignments were the same, but this was one trip she didn't want to take.

The atmosphere in the plane took on a quietness that made Brie's mood even more solemn. She had the window seat and spent most of her time staring at the cloud formations, reminiscing about the times she had shared with her aunt. Sophie sat quietly reading a magazine while David rested with his eyes closed.

David made arrangements for a rental car when they arrive in Asheville, and they were now making their way out of the airport lobby to the rental area. Sabrina and Sophie walked silently, knowing people were staring at them, but they were accustomed to the commotion they seemed to cause whenever they were together and had learned long ago to ignore the whispers.

"What is the name of the funeral home?" Sabrina asked her sister, while they waited for David at the rental counter.

"*Baterman Funeral Home* and we are supposed to be there at three o'clock. Bella will meet us in the lobby. I have the directions, so it shouldn't be hard to find."

David walked over to where they were standing.

"Stay here while I pull the car around," he told Sophie, handing her the paperwork.

He maneuvered the car close to the glass sliding doors and motioned for them to come out. Tossing their luggage in the car trunk, Sabrina slid into the backseat with her equipment bag while Sophie got in the front and fastened her seatbelt. David climbed behind the steering wheel, and they were officially on their way.

Chapter 5

The weekday traffic was heavy coming from the airport into the downtown district where the funeral home was located. David parked in the back, and they walked around to the front entrance. The historic building with its architectural design of red brick and four large white columns appeared well maintained. Bella was waiting in the lobby not far from the double wooden doors.

Sabrina and Sophie stepped through the entrance holding hands while David walked behind them. It was second nature for Brie to pay attention to her surroundings, and the first thing that caught her eye was how nicely decorated the interior was with colors of burgundy and blues. The walls were covered with pinstriped wallpaper and large Victorian prints and mirrors were appropriately arranged. There was a beautiful floral print sofa against one wall and several traditional wingback chairs in solid royal blue velour hugging various wall space and corners. Brie couldn't miss the beautiful crystal chandelier hanging in the center of the room, majestically above her head.

Large green fern planters stood on either side of the inside entrance while bouquets of flowers were strategically placed around the lobby. There was a podium to her immediate left with a guestbook open for signatures, and an elderly woman standing near the doorway to the viewing room passing out a bereavement card to everyone as they walked past her. She saw Bella coming toward her through the crowd of people standing

31

around. Releasing her hand from Sophie's, Brie stepped forward right into Bella's embrace.

They hugged tightly for a moment before letting go of each other. Having met Sabrina at her friend Mildred's house on more than one occasion, Bella instinctively knew it was Sabrina that approached her first. Releasing each other, Bella turned slightly and stretched out her arms for Sophie who stepped forward for a quick hug. It brought tears to everyone's eyes.

Sabrina grabbed Sophie's hand in her right and Bella's in her left, and the three women went together into the viewing room while David followed behind. They continued to hold tightly to each other making their way toward the front where Aunt Millie lay at rest. With a quick glance, Sabrina noticed the congregation sitting in the pews as they walked past.

When they reached the dark ebony wood coffin, Sabrina closed her eyes briefly and upon opening them, looked down into her aunt's face. Aunt Millie was a striking woman in her early sixties with short black hair trimmed in a chic style and a soft porcelain complexion. *She looks so peaceful lying there,* Brie thought.

Sabrina let go of Bella's hand and gently touched her aunt's cheek, running the back of her fingers over Aunt Millie's smooth skin. Tears welled up in her eyes. She turned to look at her sister and squeezed her hand when she saw Sophie silently crying by her side. David was standing on the other side of Sophie and quietly put his arm around his wife's shoulder and led her to the front row of pews where they sat down together.

Bella also went to sit by Sophie leaving Sabrina standing alone. Brie felt mesmerized staring down at her aunt. Aunt Millie was in perfect health, always walking for exercise, ate the right foods, and even took vitamins. Of course, people do suddenly have a heart attack or stroke, but it seemed so unlikely that it would happen to Aunt Millie. Looking into her face with its serene expression, she felt as though something wasn't right. It just couldn't be possible she was gone forever.

The tiny little hairs on the back of Brie's neck stood up and goose bumps ran down her arms even though she was wearing a pantsuit with long sleeves. Absently rubbing her arms to ward off the chill, she continued to stand by the coffin not ready to join the others at the front pew. Suddenly she felt the presence of someone beside her and lifted her head slightly to see who had approached, but when Sabrina looked up there was no one there. Taking a quick glance over her left shoulder, Brie noticed that everyone remained seated, but she was sure she felt a slight change in the air. Someone was standing next to her as she could *feel* their presence. She continued to remained at her aunt's coffin oblivious to anyone else in the room. Shrugging her shoulders to shake off the feeling, she bent down close to her aunt's face.

"I love you Aunt Millie. You'll always be with me," Sabrina whispered, kissing her softly on the cheek while holding back tears.

Sabrina left her aunt with her head bent low, not wanting to make eye contact with anyone in the room. She went to sit next to Bella, closing her eyes, trying to gain control of her emotions, refusing to cry in front of all these people. When she opened them, Sabrina slowly turned her head in each direction to take a better look around the room, realizing there were more people present than she expected. It seemed her aunt was popular because there must have been over a hundred people attending.

She leaned into Bella.

"Who are all these people?" Brie whispered.

"Your Aunt Millie was very well known and liked in the community," Bella informed her, proudly.

Again, goose bumps popped up on her arms when she felt a slight shift in the air beside her just before the funeral director began the service. Turning to see who was sitting down, she found the space empty, yet it felt as though someone had just sat down next to her. Silently trying to absorb the service, Sabrina was beginning to feel strangely uncomfortable about her aunt's funeral. She didn't understand what was happening but concluded she must be more upset by her aunt's death than first realized.

The only people permitted to continue for the burial were Sabrina, Sophie, and David, but they agreed to include Bella if she wanted to attend. Tears welled up in Bella's eyes at the kind gesture as she followed them to the gravesite. It was decided to have those last few moments alone with their aunt before she was laid to rest. David had talked with the funeral director making their request known before they arrived.

Following the hearse on the grounds behind the funeral home, Sabrina didn't express to Sophie what she recently experienced, thinking if she could keep herself together a little longer; this day would soon be over. *I'm just in a state of shock, that's all it is,* she comforted herself.

It was done. Aunt Millie was securely settled in her burial place. They said goodbye to Bella and drove back to the funeral office to complete the final business transactions and were now backtracking through the lobby toward the front double doors. A man was sitting in one of the chairs alongside the wall and stood when they approached. He had dark brown hair with strands of gray through his mustache and sideburns and wore tortoise-shell glasses.

"Excuse me, I realize this is in poor timing; however, I need to speak to you. Sabrina and Sophie, your Aunt Mildred was a client. She told me about you," he stated as a means of introduction.

"Who are you?" David asked in response.

"I'm George Thomason, Mildred Wilson's attorney," George replied, nonchalantly.

"Our aunt had an attorney?" Sabrina blurted out without thinking.

It was a surprise to Brie to learn their aunt would have any need of an attorney.

"Why would she have an attorney?" Sophie asked, looking at her sister.

"I'm terribly sorry for your loss, but I do need to discuss a few things with you both."

"What might that be?" David asked, skeptically.

Pulling out his business card to show he was who he claimed to be, George encouraged them to take a few minutes of their time to join him at his office down the street, stating he held their aunt's Last Will and Testament. Unbelieving and yet curious, they followed him the couple miles down the road. It seemed they didn't have a choice when he was so insistent to speak with them in a more private place, and it had to be now rather than later.

George's office was already closed for the day, so it took him a minute to unlock the door and turn off the alarm. Once everyone was seated in his office, he pulled a file from the bottom desk drawer and opening it, took out the document lying on top.

"What I have here is your Aunt Mildred's Last Will and Testament," George said, holding the paper in his hand.

Sabrina and Sophie turned to each other.

"What are you talking about? Our aunt wouldn't have a Will. She doesn't have anything but her house," Sabrina spoke up, being the first to recover from the news.

"Well, it seems she has a little more than that," George replied, knowingly.

"It would probably be best if I just read this to you."

David remained silent during the exchange. After all, this wasn't his blood relative that had died.

"To keep this as simple as possible, I'll list her assets and how she wanted them distributed and make sure that you each get a copy of the Will," George stated, getting down to business.

"Sophie, to you she left an insurance policy in the amount of fifty thousand dollars."

Sophie jumped out of her seat.

"What, that's impossible! My aunt does not have the means to have a policy for that amount," she practically shouted at the attorney.

"Well, she does and you are the sole beneficiary of the policy. It states that upon her death you receive said amount of money," he calmly explained to Sophie.

Still standing, Sophie turned and stared at her sister and then her husband in total disbelief. She was so shocked she didn't know what to say and slowly sat back down in the chair.

Seeing that she wasn't about to have another outburst, George continued.

"Sabrina, your Aunt Mildred left the house and all the furnishings to you and stipulates that she would prefer you live in the house as opposed to selling it, but that would be up to you. It is free and clear of any mortgage or liens."

"Her house! I can't take her house," Sabrina exclaimed.

"She knew that Sophie and David were settled, and the money would help them along. And for you, Sabrina, Mildred expressed she would like to see you settled one day and seemed to think you would be happy living here," he said, conveying his client's thoughts.

"I have a home in Florida, and I travel constantly for my job. I don't want to live in the country," Sabrina rattled off reasons to defend her lifestyle.

"Well, you can always sell the house. It's your decision," George proclaimed, having expressed his client's wishes.

Reaching inside the narrow center drawer of his desk, he pulled out a silver keyring with three keys on it.

"Here are the keys to the house," George said, reaching across the desk to hand them to Sabrina.

He turned to Sophie.

"Since the death of your Aunt Mildred, I began the process of acquiring the check from the insurance company. It is at her request that I personally hand you the check without there being any delays, and I have it ready for you. I merely need you to sign the appropriate paperwork," George told Sophie.

"And Sabrina, the house will be deeded over to you. Mildred asked that I handle these final details; however, the house is yours to occupy whenever you want. The paperwork is merely a formality I will take care of."

During this exchange, David remained silent while the attorney went over the details of the Will. Reeling with shock from this latest news, Sabrina and Sophie thanked Mr. Thomason and agreed to meet in the morning at ten o'clock for Sophie to sign the paperwork to receive her inheritance and a copy of their aunt's Will.

It was nearing dusk when they realized they had gone all day on airplane food. David suggested backtracking to the little restaurant they passed earlier. Sitting on a booth at *The Country Kitchen,* each order an iced tea and studied the menu, unsure of what to order. Sabrina and Sophie had lost their appetite, but knew they needed to eat something and finally decided on the special of chicken and dumplings, mashed potatoes, and green beans listed on the today's special board.

"What are you going to do with Aunt Millie's house, Brie?" Sophie spoke first.

"I don't know. I can't believe she would leave me her house and expect me to live in it. Where would she get the idea I would want to live in the country?" Brie asked, rhetorically.

"Well, you can sell it. It doesn't mean you have to live in it," David contributed his thoughts.

"I didn't know Aunt Millie had an insurance policy. Of course, it wouldn't have been my business, anyway. It's so hard to believe," Sophie said, softly.

"I know what you mean. I probably was the closest to her, and she never mentioned having a Will. Mr. Thomason said the house was paid for, so I don't have to do anything right away. I can leave it for now and decide some other time what to do with it."

"That's a good idea, don't make a hasty decision," David suggested.

"I suppose we should go by Aunt Millie's house in the morning before we head home, or I should say *your* house, Brie," Sophie remarked.

"Since I'm sure we'll be up early, let's go by there before we stop at Mr. Thomason's office," Sabrina agreed, somberly.

They ate dinner in silence and then drove a few miles south to the hotel where David had made reservations. After checking in, they took the elevator to the third floor to adjacent rooms. It had been an emotionally draining day, and no one seemed in the mood to discuss the events further, so with a quick hug they said good night.

Sabrina went into the room and placed the suitcase on the rack next to the window. She sat down on the edge of the bed staring into space overwhelmed with grief. She leaned back and rolled her body into a fetal position letting the tears flow down her cheeks. After lying there for what seemed like eternity, Sabrina got up and prepared for bed. All she wanted to do was fall into a blissful sleep, and perhaps when she woke up in the morning this will have all been a bad dream. That was her last thought as she fell into a deep slumber.

Chapter 6

The next morning the weather was unexpectedly chilly. Sabrina had forgotten how cool the fall days could be in the mountains. After checking out of the hotel, they went back to *The Country Kitchen* for a large breakfast that could hold them until they returned home. The aroma of pancakes filled the air, and Sabrina couldn't resist ordering them when she saw stacks on plates being delivered to nearby tables. Along with her full plate of eggs, hash browns and grits, she ordered a tall stack of multi-grain and nut pancakes. Sophie and David, likewise, enjoyed a hardy meal before driving to their aunt's house.

Bella was standing in the driveway when David pulled up and walked over to the girls as they were getting out of the car and gave each a hug.

"I'm so sorry for your loss. I miss her, and I can't believe she's gone," Bella announced, bursting into tears.

"I thought you might come by so I stopped to see if you needed my help with anything," she continued, drying her eyes.

Bella was a tall, slender woman who always wore dark polyester slacks with white blouses. Rarely would she change the color of her top. With her short, auburn hair kept brushed back from her face, it gave her a matriarchal look. She simply didn't like to fuss over her appearance. Sabrina's observant eye focused on her light olive skin tone and thought about how pretty she would look wearing a soft peach blush and coral lipstick and adding a touch of brown mascara to her hazel eyes. It would give a softer look to her complexion.

"Thanks Bella, but there isn't anything to do at the moment," Sabrina said sadly.

"Will you be staying long?"

"No, we all have to get back to work. In fact, we're catching a plane home this afternoon," Brie volunteered the information.

"If you need me to keep an eye on the house, or anything else I can help with, let me know. You have my number."

"Thank you for everything you've done, Bella. My sister and I appreciate your taking care of the funeral arrangements for us. It was a tremendous help."

"It was the least I could do. She was my best friend. I figured you girls could use a helping hand with the arrangements since you aren't from this area."

"I'll leave you girls alone; I'm sure you want to go through the house. You know where I live so come by anytime," Bella continued, turning to leave.

"Come in with us," Sabrina invited her to join them.

"No, I'm not comfortable going into the house right now."

"I understand. I'll be in touch, Bella," Sabrina told her.

Sabrina guessed it had to do with Bella finding Aunt Millie's body. She took the ring of keys from her purse, walked to the front door, unlocked it, and went in with Sophie and David following behind. The house was a two-story English Tudor with the outside structure a combination of gray brick and dark stained wood. Along the front were four large tinted windows surrounded by brown wooden shutters. The front door was painted a dark chocolate brown with two narrow panes of glass on either side and above the door was a small crescent shaped window.

Walking into the foyer gave the option of turning left into the living room or right into a formal dining room. Straight ahead through a small hallway beside a staircase brought them into the kitchen located at the back of the house. Sabrina went directly for the kitchen, remembering Bella stated that was where she found Aunt Millie.

It was a large room divided by a long counter that separated the actual kitchen area from the dinette. The cabinets were whitewashed oak with light gray marble countertops. The appliances were all stainless steel. There was a large window over the kitchen sink and another wider one along the same wall on the opposite side of the counter with a contemporary glass top table with four chairs situated for a nice view of the landscape.

Plantation style white wooden blinds were on the windows with custom-made checkered-box navy and white pleated valances. On the far wall in the dinette area was a matching whitewashed open-faced china cabinet holding all types of miscellaneous collector's plates and knickknacks that her aunt had collected over the years.

"It seems strange to be in the house without her here. I feel like I am trespassing," Sophie confided, following behind her sister.

"I know what you mean. I'm not exactly comfortable myself," Sabrina admitted, even though she had spent more time in the house than Sophie.

They looked around for a minute, not touching anything as though it were off limits. They walked back through the hall to the foyer and up the stairs to the second floor where the bedrooms were located. Stepping into the master bedroom felt strange to Sabrina. She walked toward the bed and sat on the edge looking around the room. This was her aunt's bedroom, yet now it was her room, her house. It left her with a very unsettled feeling.

David left the girls alone, deciding to sit in the living room and wait while Sophie roamed from room to room unsure of what she was expecting to find. She finally drifted back to the bedroom where Sabrina remained sitting on the bed.

"What are you going to do with all of Aunt Millie's things?" Sophie asked.

"I think I will leave everything the way it is for now. I'm not comfortable going through her clothes and stuff."

"Well, what about the house? I can't believe Aunt Millie left it to you. Oh, I don't mean that the way it sounded! What I'm trying to say is that it appears she thought you would live here. Why would she think something like that when she knows your job keeps you on the road?" Sophie asked, trying to explain herself.

"I know it's strange. I don't understand it either, and I can't live here."

"You could come back when your work schedule isn't so hectic. Maybe when you are ready to take some vacation time you might want to return and sort through her things. Perhaps put the house on the market and sell it and invest the money," Sophie advised.

"I suppose so, but I'm not sure that's the right thing to do," Sabrina confided.

"I'm going downstairs to sit with David. Take your time. We can leave whenever you're ready," Sophie said over her shoulder giving her sister some time alone.

Sabrina closed her eyes thinking of the happy memories she shared with her aunt in this house. She didn't know how much time had passed when she felt a light tap on her right shoulder. Not opening her eyes thinking Sophie had come back upstairs, she easily responded.

"Okay Sophie, give me another minute, and I'll be right down," Brie stated, softly.

"You must stay," she heard a whisper close to her right ear.

"Sophie, you are confusing me. First, you tell me I should lock up the house, and now you think I should stay. Make up your mind," Sabrina said with her eyes still closed.

She felt the tap again, and this time she opened her eyes expecting to see her sister standing in front of her, but there was no one there. Quickly jumping to her feet and swirling around to view the entire room at a glance, Sabrina could see she was alone. But she knew she wasn't alone. Someone had someone had tapped her on the shoulder. Thinking that Sophie had gone into the master bathroom, she called out to her.

"Sophie, are you in there?"

No answer. She went to the walk-in closet and looked in the doorway, but no one was there. Brie knew she had been tapped on the shoulder not once, but twice, and she heard someone say, *you must stay*. Feeling uneasy, Sabrina went downstairs where David and Sophie were sitting on the sofa talking quietly.

"Sophie, were you upstairs just a minute ago?" Brie asked, cautiously.

"No, I've been here with David. Why would you ask me that?"

"Oh nothing. I just thought I heard you."

"Are you two ready to go?" David asked.

"Sure, just give me a minute. I want to go back into the kitchen,"

Sabrina responded, before turning in that direction.

"Take your time, I don't mean to rush you."

Sophia got up and followed her sister.

"What is it Brie? Why did you think I was upstairs a minute ago?" Sophie asked with concern.

"It's nothing. I thought I heard you talking to me when I was upstairs," Brie replied, quickly brushing it off.

Sabrina was already feeling uneasy about the house and wasn't sure what to say to her sister. She noticed Sophie was looking down at the floor in front of the kitchen sink.

"I guess this is where Bella found Aunt Millie. How awful that she was all alone," Sophie said quietly.

Sabrina came around the counter and stood beside her sister.

"I can't believe this has happened. I was here less than a month ago, and she was so full of energy and laughter. I want to know what happened," Sabrina stated, moving to stare out the kitchen window.

She looked towards the ten acres of woods attached to the

back of the property. *What am I going to do with all of this*, she wondered. Remaining at the window, Sabrina felt the slightest breath on her cheek and the word *stay* whispered softly in her ear.

"I can't," Brie answered, continuing to look outside.

"What? I didn't hear you," Sophie replied.

Sabrina turned, noticing her sister had walked over to the counter that separated the kitchen from the dinette area.

"I said I can't," Brie repeated herself.

"You can't what?" Sophie asked.

"I was merely answering your statement to stay. I said I can't," Sabrina replied in exasperation, feeling like they were talking around each other.

Sophie looked at Brie as though she had grown another head.

"Brie, I didn't say anything."

"Yes, you did. You were standing over here and whispered in my ear to stay," Sabrina told her with more conviction than she felt.

"Brie, what is going on? First, you think I was talking to you upstairs, and now I'm whispering in your ear. What's happening to you? Are you having a nervous breakdown or something?"

"No, I'm not having a breakdown, and you know better than to suggest such a thing," Brie answered in a huff, feeling hurt her sister would say that.

"I'm sorry Brie. You're right. I take it back, but obviously you are having some kind of a weird experience, and I'm just trying to understand."

"I know that I just heard a voice softly say in my ear that I should stay and felt a whisper of breath on my cheek, and I didn't imagine it," Sabrina said with assuredness.

"Okay, I believe you, but this is so like the *Twilight Zone*. Did you recognize the voice?"

Sophie couldn't believe she was asking such a question.

"I thought it was you. So no, I can't say I recognized the

voice," Brie said, feeling foolish for having this conversation in the first place.

"Maybe the shock of Aunt Millie's death has increased your stress level a notch or two," Sophie stated, trying to come up with a logical explanation.

"Perhaps my mind is playing tricks on me," Brie admitted.

"This is too weird. What are you going to do? Are you going to stay?" Sophie asked, worried for her sister.

"No, I'm not staying. I don't know what Aunt Millie was thinking by leaving me her house. Besides, I don't have time for a house and all the work that goes into keeping one up. I'm not home long enough to enjoy my apartment."

"Well, you can't leave it unattended forever, but it doesn't mean you have to decide this very minute either. Are you ready to leave? David's probably getting anxious, and we have to be at the attorney's office soon."

"You're right, let's go. I have plenty of time to think about what to do."

They left the kitchen and walked back into the living room where David was still sitting on the sofa.

"You girls ready? We still need to go to the attorney's office, and I thought you might want to stop at the gravesite," David remarked.

"We're ready," Sophie answered her husband.

David got up and followed his wife while Sabrina lagged behind pulling the keys from her jeans pocket. Still feeling uneasy about the voice, she hesitated for a moment on the threshold quietly listening for any sound, but the house stood in silence. Shrugging her shoulders, Sabrina locked the door and headed down the front walk toward the car where David and Sophie were already waiting.

Sabrina looked out the side window of the car at the house that was once her haven. David took off down the road in the direction of the attorney's office. Brie turned and gave a final glance through the rearview window. A strange feeling came over her as though she was leaving someone behind. Of course,

45

that was impossible. No one lived there anymore.

Chapter 7

It didn't take long to reach Mr. Thomason's office. Sophie signed the necessary legal papers and was handed an insurance check for fifty thousand dollars, and a copy of the Will. Wishing Sophie well, George turned to Sabrina.

"Sabrina, I was a friend to your aunt and her attorney. Giving you the house meant a lot to her. She hoped one day you would settle here and make this your new home. I realize you can't make that kind of a life-altering decision overnight, but give it some serious thought. Mildred believed in time you would come to understand why it was important to her."

"I would suggest keeping the utilities on so the temperature in the house can be regulated during the summer and winter months, and you can have the utility bills transferred to your Florida mailing address. I'll drive by periodically to make sure no one has vandalized the property," he continued.

Handing Sabrina a copy of the Last Will and Testament, George extended his arm to shake Sabrina, Sophie, and David's hand.

"Thank you, I would appreciate that," Sabrina said, feeling uneasy.

Completing their business with the attorney, they left his office right at the noon hour traffic. Their flight to Orlando was in three hours, and they needed to get to the airport so it wasn't possible to return to the cemetery. Sabrina felt a pang of regret but had already decided to return in a couple of months. Something she couldn't explain was drawing her back to the house. Perhaps it was the unexplainable voice that seemingly nagged at her subconscious.

Making a quick decision to spend the holidays in her aunt's country home, Sabrina hoped she could convince Sophie and David to join her. She had a two-week break at Christmas, and if she was able to finish all scheduled assignments for the remainder of the year early, she could possibly take the entire month of December off. She decided to voice her idea to Sophie about spending Christmas in Asheville.

"Sophie, I think I'm going to come back here for Christmas. Why don't you and David join me, and we can spend the holidays here in the country?" Sabrina asked her sister.

"Oh Sabrina, we can't. David and I are going to his parent's house this year. We just made the plans while you were gone to San Francisco. I meant to tell you, but then we got the news about Aunt Millie. Why don't you come along with us? It'll be fun," she countered the offer.

"I think I'll come back here for Christmas, but thanks for the invite."

Sabrina felt an urgency to return, and the holidays provided her the freedom to stay awhile and explore.

"Are you sure that's a good idea to return by yourself?"

"Of course, why wouldn't it be? I've spent many a night in that house."

"I was hoping we could spend Christmas together and you'd join us in Pittsburgh," Sophie declared, feeling sad knowing she wouldn't be with her sister for the holidays.

"I'm sorry and I do wish we could be together, but you'll have a good time," Sabrina said, regretfully.

The remainder of the trip to the airport was in silence. The atmosphere in the car was solemn with each absorbed in grief. David pulled the car into the rental section and removed three pieces of luggage from the trunk, motioning the sisters to go inside the building and wait for him. When he joined them, they rushed through the lobby to get in line for boarding passes and on through security which was backed up. Someone at the front of their line was upset about losing a key while emptying his pockets.

Understanding the stress involved in traveling, Sabrina glanced at her watch and they had exactly twenty minutes to get on the plane. She was accustomed to this, but David and Sophie looked worried.

"We'll make the plane, don't fret. They make sure all scheduled passengers are accounted for before taking off," Sabrina said to Sophie, hoping to alleviate some of her worry.

"I'm sure you're right. It's just been a long day, and I'm tired and want to get home."

"I'm glad I have the weekend off before going back to California," Sabrina confessed, wanting some down time.

David was so absorbed in the man with the lost keys. He didn't hear the conversation between the sisters. Finally, the security guard pulled the man out of the line so others could proceed. They made it through the gate, down the terminal and onto the plane with two minutes to spare. Sabrina took her usual window seat with Sophie to her right and David on the aisle. She couldn't wait to be home to have some time alone to think and grieve. Everything happened so fast once she received the call from Sophie. Sabrina closed her eyes resting her head back against the headrest while David and Sophie quietly watched the last minute boarders try to find a seat.

"Do you think we should go back to work, or maybe have subs takeover our classes for another day?" Sophie asked her husband.

"If you feel up to it, I really think we should go back to work. We probably have some catching up to do with the class assignments," he replied.

"I suppose so. I do miss my kids, but I feel so drained at the moment. The thought of doing anything right now doesn't appeal to me," Sophie admitted to her husband.

The plane took off on time and once in the air, David fell

asleep.

"When are you going back to California?" Sophie asked her sister.

"I probably will be flying out on Monday. I need to call Joe in the morning to make the arrangements."

"David thinks we should go back to school tomorrow even though it's Friday, but I feel like I need a long weekend. It's so sad, but I guess we all have to get back to our lives," Sophie declared with a sigh.

"You were closer to Aunt Millie than I was. I just didn't have the opportunity to get away and visit with her like you did, and I don't mean that derogatorily, it's just a fact. Getting married right out of college then settling into a teaching career, I simply haven't had the opportunity to make as many trips as you have, but Brie I am glad that you could. I want you to know I'm happy she left her house to you. You are the only one who should have it," Sophie confided.

"Do you really mean that?" Brie asked, hoping there would be no ill feelings between her and Sophie over their respective inheritance, because obviously the house with the acreage was worth a lot more than the cash settlement Sophie received.

"Brie, how could you think I would protest over something that wasn't mine to begin with? I still don't understand how Aunt Millie could leave me any money. Not expecting anything and then getting something was a real surprise, and I'm totally content. In fact, I would still be content if you got the house, and I received nothing. It would still be fair in my mind," Sophie explained her feelings.

"You were the one who spent the most time with Aunt Millie so you are the one she should rightfully leave her belongings to."

"I'm so glad you aren't upset about the will," Sabrina stated, thankful there would be no ill feelings between them over their inheritance.

"Of course, I meant every word."

Feeling there wasn't much else to talk about at the moment,

they sat in silence the remainder of the flight. Sabrina closed her eyes and rested, while Sophie flipped through the magazine she found in the pocket of the seat.

Landing in Orlando when the sun was setting seemed to exacerbate the fatigue that was plaguing Sabrina and Sophie. Not wanting to delay getting to their respective homes, they hugged each other in the parking lot and went separate ways to find their cars. For once, Sophie was glad they arrived at the airport in their own vehicles because she was simply too tired to drive her sister home.

Driving on autopilot, Brie let her mind drift to the visit they made earlier to the house. She recalled the feeling that came over her when she heard the soft whispers. Sabrina knew she hadn't imagined it, but what did it mean? Surprisingly, she wasn't afraid or anxious about the incidences, but rather a strong need to know who and why someone was reaching out to her. *Why is this happening to me,* she questioned.

She pulled into the side garage of the condo building and parked. Grabbing the luggage from the trunk, Brie made her way inside the building. It didn't take long after leaving the elevator to walk down the hallway to her apartment. Once inside, she headed to the bedroom, dropping the suitcase on the bed. Retracing her steps to the kitchen for a glass of water, she went to sit in the living room.

Brie remembered how hesitant she was to invest in buying a condo knowing she would be gone most of the time, but Sophie seemed so desperate for her to come back home and settle close. Once Sabrina got over the buyer's remorse, she and Sophie began painting walls and decorating, watching everything fall into place. Sabrina was pleased to have her own home, and not a rental.

Curled up on the corner of the sofa, she leaned her head back and fell asleep. Later, she unraveled from the slumped position and stumbled into the bedroom noticing the alarm clock on the nightstand beaming two-forty five in the morning. Pulling the piece of luggage off the bed, it dropped to the floor near her feet. Sabrina swiftly yanked the comforter back and crawled between the sheets. She was simply too tired to change into pajamas or wash the makeup off her face. Her last remaining thought was recalling something her mother told her when she started wearing makeup in her teens, *Don't go to bed with makeup on your face, you'll wake up five years older in the morning*. Waking up five years older didn't hold a whole lot of urgency at the moment. Brie couldn't move a muscle even if she wanted to, and on that thought, she fell asleep.

"You must stay," she heard the voice.

"Who are you? Why can't I see you? I don't understand what you are trying to tell me," she pleaded.

Sabrina was dreaming. She was back in her aunt's house sitting on the bed looking straight ahead at the doorway feeling drawn toward the wispy figure that she couldn't see clearly. She knew someone was there, she could *feel* their presence but who was it, and what were they trying to tell her? She walked slowly toward the door but the soft transparent figure faded in mid-air. Brie stopped, quickly turning around to search the room, but she was alone again.

"Where are you? You have to be here somewhere. Why did you leave? I don't understand," Brie cried out, practically in tears.

She felt a soft tap on her right shoulder and choking on a scream woke up startled panting for air. Did someone just tap her on the shoulder, or was it merely the dream? Sitting quietly trying to get her racing heart under control, Sabrina's mind stressed to figure out what just happened. The alarm clock stated it was four o'clock. Had she only been asleep over an hour? What was happening to her? To be hearing and feeling a presence was just a bit unnerving. Was she so upset at the loss of her aunt that she was imagining things? These experiences felt very real to her. *What is going on here,* she questioned.

Sabrina got up and went into the kitchen for a drink of water. She couldn't fall to sleep after a dream like that. Taking the glass, Brie went into the living room, drew open the blinds and unlocked the patio door, and stepped out on the balcony. From her lounge chair, she listened to the ocean waves rolling onto shore and felt the salty breeze brush across her skin. She could see the neighboring condominium buildings to either side of her complex with their lights showing off a misty glow toward the ocean.

Sabrina replayed the events since her sister's phone call. It didn't feel right her aunt would die this way when she appeared so vibrant a month ago. Something was nagging at Sabrina, but she didn't believe it was Aunt Millie trying to communicate to her from the grave. So who was it and what did it mean? How could she find out? Brie watched the sun rise over the ocean, unusually content to simply enjoy the beauty instead of grabbing her camera and recording the glorious introduction to the day.

Chapter 8

Sophie called at seven in the morning to let Brie know they were going into work since David thought it best to get the kids back on track with weekend homework. After hanging up the phone, Sabrina called Joe to let him know she would be ready to go to San Diego on Monday and to make the necessary arrangements. This would give her three days alone to mourn her aunt's death before getting back to work.

Momentarily, Sabrina's thoughts drifted to the dream. She didn't know what to think of all that had happened since the funeral, or how to find the meaning behind what she was experiencing. Brie felt the only logical thing to do was to forget it and get on with her life. She took a quick shower, dressed, and was ready to face the day.

She sat at the small glass-top table in the kitchen making a list of what to do over the weekend. Brie began feeling more in control of her emotions and decided to go out and buy something new for the trip back to California. Shopping always made her feel better, and while at the Merritt Square Mall perhaps she would have her hair trimmed. A little pampering always boosted her spirit.

Several hours later, Sabrina returned with two new outfits. It was still early enough to do some household chores, so she started by putting laundry in the washing machine located in a closet next to the kitchen and dragged out the vacuum cleaner for a quick run over the carpet. She considered that enough work and made a sandwich, taking it along with a glass of fresh brewed iced tea to sit on the balcony and watch the people on the beach.

Sabrina spent the remainder of the weekend at home taking long walks along the shoreline in the evening and watching old movies until late at night, needing this time to mourn privately. When Joe called with the flight time to leave on Monday, Brie discussed her plan to take the month of December off. She wasn't asking to be relieved of any scheduled assignments, but rather to be able to complete them ahead of schedule. Joe informed Brie he would take a look at the bookings and let her know what he could do. With that accomplished, she called Sophie Saturday afternoon to let her sister know she would be flying out.

The rest of the weekend was uneventful. She pulled out photo albums filled with pictures taken over the years, but it only deepened her sadness seeing photos of the past with her parents and Aunt Millie. Going through them made her cry, so she put them away.

By Sunday afternoon, it was time to pack. She was feeling better and ready to get back to work. There had been no more dreams, and Sabrina was sure it had been stress induced. Packing with a few new items of clothing was a treat, and she knew to take a variety of seasonal clothes to be prepared for wherever she would be sent next.

Early Monday morning, Sabrina was on the Beeline traveling toward the airport. She called Sophie before she left for work.

"Hi sis, I called to tell you after the zoo shoot I'm off to Montana," Brie explained.

"What's in Montana?"

"A horse ranch."

"That should be interesting. When you get back, let's plan for dinner one night," Sophie requested of her sister.

"Sure, that's sounds good. I shouldn't be gone more than a couple of weeks, but I'll keep you posted."

"Brie, have you given anymore thought to those strange occurrences?" Sophie probed her sister.

"Yes, I have been thinking about that. And since you mentioned it, I had a very weird dream the first night I was back home."

"When did you plan to tell me about it?" Sophie asked a bit miffed.

"I'm trying to put it behind me, so it didn't enter my mind to say anything."

"What was the dream about?"

"It was a replay of what I was experiencing when we were in Aunt Millie's house."

"It's probably just you being upset about Aunt Millie's death."

"I'm sure you're right."

"I wouldn't give it too much thought. Have fun and be careful," Sophie added, ready to end the call.

"You know, I always do."

"Love you, sis," Sophie chimed.

"Love you, back," Brie dittoed.

She threw the phone on the passenger seat. Sabrina had driven the Beeline to the Orlando International Airport so often she felt she could do it blindfolded. Her thoughts returned to Aunt Millie; so many unanswered questions over the nature of her death. Would she ever be able to find out the cause? *I really want to know what happened,* she pondered.

Sabrina reached the airport in plenty of time; checked in two pieces of luggage, retrieved a boarding pass, and headed for the nearest coffee shop for a large mocha latte. Sitting at a small round table near the entrance, she watched a little boy who wanted his daddy to take him into the *Animal World* store, where displays of every known animal sat proudly waiting for its new owner to claim him.

She saw the boy pointing toward a big giraffe that was standing proudly at the entrance of the store. Though she didn't hear the conversation between the father and son, Sabrina just imagined the father was explaining that the giraffe was too large to take on a plane. She continued to watch while they went inside and came out with the little boy holding a much smaller giraffe. He seemed delighted with his present and quickly took off in a sprint toward a young woman sitting on a nearby bench.

Brie turned away from the scene. After tossing the unfinished drink, she gathered the camera bag and tote to make her way toward the security area where the line was already stretching into the lobby. She had approximately thirty minutes before boarding the plane. There was a two hour layover in Houston which would give her plenty of time to have lunch before arriving in San Diego at three o'clock Pacific Time. She made a mental note to call Sophie while in Houston.

Arriving on schedule, Sabrina's prearranged rental car was ready for pick up at the airport. This wasn't her first trip to San Diego, so she quickly maneuvered her way through traffic to the Radisson she always stayed at when in the area. Brie was to report to the zoo at six o'clock in the morning. This was a very easy assignment that would take only a couple of days.

Sabrina was greeted by a young man in uniform who came around the front of the car to open the door. With purse in hand, she got out and opened the backdoor to retrieve the equipment bag. Another uniformed valet pulled the two pieces of luggage out of the trunk, placing them onto a garment dolly, and followed Sabrina toward the sliding glass doors. Once checked in, he accompanied her to the fifth floor and deposited her luggage into the room. After unpacking her clothes and toiletries, Sabrina decided to go down for an early dinner at *The Flamingo* restaurant inside the hotel.

The restaurant was located on the main floor to the right, and when she entered the dining room, Brie was seated by the hostess at a table with a window view. Simultaneously, a waiter came over with a menu and glass of water. She perused all the meal choices and selected the marinated salmon, roasted garlic potatoes, green beans, and a fresh garden salad with a sweet iced tea, a rare find in most California establishments. They only served unsweetened.

She became absorbed in the fantastic view of the marina with the setting sun showing a brilliant rainbow reflection off the water as the sailboats bobbed along the dock. A couple was sitting on deck of a yacht anchored a short distance away, but Sabrina didn't think they could spot her in the restaurant because the windows were tinted and the sun was to her advantage. A natural instinct was to grab a camera and snap a picture; however, not having one with her she simply enjoyed the view.

The meal arrived and Sabrina ate leisurely enjoying the peace and quiet. She thought about the morning shoot. She excelled at delivering better than life pictures, always wanting to give the magazine a great presentation of photographs to choose from for each new edition. Brie was always thorough in her work and wanted to provide several different backgrounds so the editors would have options for their layouts.

The first thing Sabrina did upon returning to the room was check the equipment bag which was a routine performance she did easily. Always carrying three cameras; each serving a specific task, made her bag heavy to lug around along with the additional supplies.

Pulling out her favorite camera, the Canon EOS Mark II SLR, Brie checked it carefully. This was her baby with its 2.0 inch LCD and interchangeable lens. It rendered a pure as life picture having a magnificent 16.7 mega pixel capacity. Next she took out the Nikon D40x SLR with its two accompanying lens, and last was her Olympus SP-550UZ which she used mostly for carefree shots.

After carefully placing them back in the bag, Sabrina proceeded to get ready for bed. She didn't bother to turn the television on because whatever was happening in the world didn't matter at the moment. She went to bed and fell asleep.

Chapter 9

Something woke her. Sabrina opened her eyes and lay perfectly still listening for a noise, but all she heard was the hum of the air conditioning fan. Turning her head to the left, the alarm clock read two-thirty in the morning. Brie continued to remain perfectly still while her mind raced to figure out what disturbed her sleep. Not hearing any suspicious sounds, she propped herself up on one elbow and scanned the room. She could clearly see all the features, and there was no one there. Sabrina was in the habit of keeping the bathroom light on and the door cracked to allow a stream of illumination. It gave her a sense of comfort.

Uncertain of what woke her, Brie slipped back down under the covers and eventually fell asleep. She was startled awake again, but this time she heard a voice whispering near her ear. Sitting bolt upright ready to attack, Sabrina searched the room noticing the clock declared only an hour had passed.

"This is crazy. I know I'm not losing my mind," Sabrina spoke aloud.

"Alright, maybe I am since I'm sitting in the middle of the bed in a hotel room talking to myself," she mused.

It was as though someone was trying to get her attention, but she didn't understand who, or for what reason. She got out of bed and made a cup of coffee with the courtesy coffeemaker. While it was doing a slow brew, Brie went into the bathroom to splash cold water on her face. Looking in the mirror, she could see dark purple smudges under her eyes. *Whoever invented eye concealer is a genius,* Brie spoke to her reflection.

She left the bathroom to pour a cup of coffee adding the complimentary powdered cream and sugar. She went to sit on the recliner near the window opening a slit in the curtain allowed her a fabulous view of the parking lot. Brie settled into the chair sipping on the coffee letting her mind explore the events of the previous month. She realized this all began with Aunt Millie's death, for it was at the funeral home standing by the coffin when she had the first brush with this sensation or awareness of a presence.

Closing her eyes, Brie drifted into a light sleep and dreamt of Aunt Millie. In the dream, she was looking down into her aunt's face while she lay in a coffin and bending to place a kiss upon her cheek; Aunt Millie opened her eyes and stared right into Sabrina's. Pulling back with a start, she woke spilling the coffee in her lap.

Sabrina glanced at the clock and noted it was nearly four-thirty in the morning, which would make it seven-thirty on the east coast. She thought of calling her sister, but what would she say? Sophie would just tell her she was under too much stress and needed a vacation.

Sabrina decided to get ready for the morning photo shoot. She took a long shower and then quickly did her hair and makeup. She went downstairs for the continental breakfast which was already open to guests. While enjoying a second cup of coffee, she phoned Sophie.

"Good morning," Brie said warmly into the phone when she heard her sister's voice.

"Hi sis, I was just thinking about you. The weirdest thing happened. I kept waking up during the night with you on my mind. I don't think I was dreaming of you, but all of a sudden I would wake up and my first thought was of you. How weird is that?" Sophie asked.

"Well, perhaps not as weird as you may think. I kept waking up during the night. Remember when we were in Aunt

Millie's house the day after the funeral, and I thought you were whispering to me? I woke up last night to the same thing again, not just once but twice. I don't know what to make of it," Sabrina confessed.

"Oh my goodness Brie, are you scared? What do you think it is? Maybe your mind is playing tricks on you."

"At first, I considered that, but I'm sure now that it isn't in my head," Sabrina replied calmly, taking no offense to her sister's inference.

"Brie, what are you going to do? How can you find out what this means?"

"I don't know yet. All I do know is that this began with Aunt Millie's death. The first time I had this happen was at the funeral, so I'm thinking it has something to do with her."

"What do mean at the funeral? You never said anything to me about that. I thought the first time was at the house? Is there anything else you aren't telling me?" Sophie asked a bit too sharply.

"Sophie, don't get upset. I'm not keeping anything from you, at least not intentionally. I was very upset about Aunt Millie's death, so at the funeral home I merely brushed the incident aside, not giving any significance to the matter. All that happened was while I was standing at the coffin alone, I thought I felt someone come up beside me. When I turned to see who it was, there wasn't anyone there. This is why I am calling you first thing this morning to talk to you about last night."

"If you think this is about Aunt Millie, what does it mean? Do you think she is trying to talk to you from the grave?"

"No, of course not. Dead is dead."

"What are going to do?"

"When I go back to the house in December, I'll have time to do a little investigating. I want to go through her papers and see if she has any medical receipts that might explain what really happened to her. Maybe she was sick, and we didn't know it. I want to find out what caused her death," Sabrina spoke with conviction.

"You know they put on the death certificate unknown cause probable cardiac arrest but you're right, we really don't know."

"Listen Sophie, I've got to run, or I'm going to be late, We'll talk more about this later," Sabrina remarked, getting up from the table.

"Okay, have fun with the baby cub, and we'll talk soon."

Sabrina dashed back to the room, freshened up, grabbed her tote and camera bag, and backtracked to the main lobby. The valet brought the rental car to the entrance and she was on her way to the zoo.

Time always went quickly for Brie when she was engrossed in an assignment. The cub was adorable snuggled next to his mother, and she was able to capture some great shots. She took pictures from morning until dark using each change in the natural lighting to her advantage. This was an easy assignment since the animals were contained within their habitat.

By early Wednesday afternoon, Brie was sitting at her laptop emailing the photos to Joe. She checked out of the hotel and was headed to the airport to return the rental car and catch the five-thirty flight to Montana.

Sabrina had the option of flying out on Wednesday evening or first thing Thursday morning giving her an additional night in San Diego. However, anxious to get to Montana, she told Joe to book the evening flight, keeping in mind her personal plans for the month off.

Chapter 10

Returning the car and checking the luggage went smoothly since the airport wasn't overly busy, and Brie found herself with some time to spare. She sipped on a mocha latte in a chair at the terminal and called Sophie letting her know she was on her way to Montana. Sabrina wondered how long this photo shoot might take, which was not typical of her nature while on an assignment, but found herself wanting to hurry and finish so she could begin her vacation. She felt a pressing need to return to her aunt's house believing the answer to what she was experiencing lay there.

Joe called *The Wildrose Ranch* to make arrangements for someone to meet Sabrina at the airport. The assignment was to capture daily life on a ranch. He had already discussed the business details with Victor Robinson, the owner, and secured the signing of all necessary legal documents allowing Sabrina the freedom to photograph whatever she deemed appropriate for this particular spread in the magazine. This photo shoot was for a special segment entitled, *Life on the Wild Range,* to be published in the spring edition.

She never knew from one assignment to the next if it required a day, a week or longer. By Sabrina's calculations, this one might take a couple of weeks, and though she was ready for a vacation, she also felt excitement for her work. It was November, and Brie knew the weather would be much colder in the mountains of Montana and was ready for the change.

Sabrina found her assigned seat on the plane. Joe knew to always book flights near a window because she preferred to not have someone sitting on either side of her. She didn't like feeling claustrophobic. As the plane was taking off, Brie rested her head against the window closing her eyes, hoping to get a short nap before landing in Montana.

Sabrina was picked up at the airport by the ranch foreman, Jesse James, who spotted her immediately from her photograph in the magazine and started walking toward her while she made her way through the lobby. Noticing a tall, muscular man wearing a black Stetson headed in her direction, Brie stopped when he was within two feet of her.

"Miss Fitzgerald, I recognized you from your photo. I'm Jesse James, *The Wildrose Ranch* foreman," Jesse claimed, extending his hand for a shake.

"Hello, yes, I'm Sabrina Fitzgerald," Brie said confidently, accepting his right hand.

"This is quite an honor to have a celebrity at the ranch. We don't get celebrities our way," Jesse confessed.

"That's a very nice thing to say; however, I'm not a celebrity, just a photojournalist on assignment."

"Well, that may be so, but to us cowboys you are a refreshing guest," Jesse commented, candidly.

Not responding to his compliment, Sabrina began to walk toward the baggage claim area. Jesse reached for the black equipment bag that was slung over Brie's shoulder noticing it was heavy.

"Oh, no need to bother. I always carry my equipment bag and please don't take offense. I won't even let a family member handle it," Sabrina offered as an explanation.

"None taken."

Jesse walked quietly by Sabrina's side as they made their way to get her luggage. Brie felt compelled to ask him about his name.

"I bet you are teased a lot about your name," Sabrina said, already feeling comfortable with this tall cowboy.

She felt an instant camaraderie which often occurred in her travels. Sabrina met a lot of people in her line of work, and not too often did she come across someone she didn't like. Though she wasn't social like her sister, she knew how to be receptive to people and make them feel at ease in her presence.

"Yep, all the time. My parents had a sense of humor, so I'm not surprised by my name," Jesse replied with a chuckle.

He was much taller than Sabrina, so she found herself straining her neck to look upward to glimpse his face. He looked down at her with a silly grin, and she couldn't help but smile right back. Arriving at the baggage claim area, she spotted her suitcases traveling around on the conveyor belt.

"Those are my bags coming around the corner, the two floral tapestry ones," Sabrina told him, pointing in their direction.

Jesse grabbed the two pieces of luggage, one in each hand and nodded toward the opposite direction to the parking garage. He led the way while Sabrina scurried alongside trying to keep pace with his long-legged stride. They approached a shiny, black Dodge Ram truck, and Jesse tossed the bags in the back before opening the door for Brie. She quickly unloaded her tote and equipment bag on the floorboard just as Jesse took her elbow to help her step up into the cab.

The *Wildrose Ranch* was located about an hour northwest of Missoula. Once they left the city, they fell into a comfortable conversation. Jesse found himself answering Sabrina's trail of questions about life on a ranch. She explained this was her first trip to a horse ranch. They continued a light banter making the time go by quickly during the drive.

It was sundown when he pulled into the circular driveway of a typical two-story ranch-styled house. The home was made of stained wood siding with a wrap-around porch of roughened planks. The banister along the perimeter of the porch was notched-pine logs making the house look very rustic.

Jesse stopped parallel to three wide-planked steps leading to the front door. Large bare flowerpots were situated along the sides of each step ready for spring planting. On one side of the entrance were matching dark oak-stained rockers and on the other an old-fashioned wooden glider. Additional empty flowerpots were situated around the porch. *I imagine this is a pretty sight in the spring when flowers are overflowing in these pots,* Sabrina thought.

He jumped out of the cab, walked around the front of the truck to open the door, and extended his hand to Sabrina when she stepped down. Brie turned to retrieve the camera bag, and Jesse reached over the back of the truck and grabbed the luggage. Again, she followed his lead through the entrance into the foyer. *He must be right at home, because he didn't knock first,* she thought.

Hearing the commotion of them entering the house, Victor and his wife, Betty, came into the foyer to find Jesse putting Sabrina's luggage by the staircase. When he turned toward them, Jesse made the appropriate introductions.

"Welcome Sabrina, it's good to meet you," Victor bellowed in a deep voice, extending his large hand to shake hers.

He was a husky man with jet-black hair, bushy black eyebrows, and the deepest blue eyes Sabrina had ever seen. His tanned skin showed wear from years in the sun. *In his younger days, he must have been a very handsome man,* she thought. She guessed him to be probably early fifties and wondered if that was his natural hair color.

"We are so delighted to have you here," Betty spoke next, also extending her hand to shake Sabrina's.

"Thank you. It is my pleasure to be selected to do this photo shoot. I am very excited about it," Sabrina informed them both.

"Well, you'll probably find life on a ranch a lot different than what you may have expected, but we certainly hope you enjoy your time with us," Victor assured her.

"I've seen your picture in magazines alongside your work, and I have to say it is a pleasure to have you here. I think your photographs capture the essence of your subjects," he said.

"I appreciate the compliment."

"I'm expecting a call shortly, so if you will excuse me, I need to return to my office. Please make yourself at home, and if you need anything don't hesitate to ask," Victor declared, turning to leave Sabrina standing alone with Betty and Jesse.

"Jesse, would you please take Miss Fitzgerald's luggage to the guest room before you leave? I don't think we'll be able to manage that on our own," Betty asked.

"Not a problem. I'm glad to help," Jesse stated, moving from behind Sabrina.

Effortlessly, he picked up the luggage and started up the stairs.

"First, let's get you settled into your room, I'm sure you must be hungry. We've already eaten since supper time is early around here, but I will have Leanne prepare you a plate, and afterwards, if you like, I'll take you on a brief tour of the house, so you'll know your way around," Betty told her.

"That would be nice, I'ld appreciate it. And, yes, I'm very hungry," Sabrina admitted.

Just when Betty was turning to lead Sabrina up the stairs, Jesse was making his way down and headed for the door.

"Thank you, Jesse, and we'll see you tomorrow. Have a good evening," Betty said, softly.

"Mr. James, thanks for picking me up at the airport and for the great conversation," Brie said with laughter in her voice.

"You bet, and call me Jesse," he said with a twinkle in his eyes.

Victor's wife was a petite woman with beautiful red hair that cascaded in waves to her shoulders and a soft complexion lightly tanned from time spent outdoors.

Her green eyes sparkled when she laughed, making her look much younger than her fifties. Dressed in jeans and a blue plaid shirt, she was a striking woman.

Betty took Sabrina up a spiral staircase to the second floor and down a long hallway to the end. The door opened into a spacious room with a huge knotty-pine canopy bed located on one wall and a tall matching armoire on the opposite. The furniture seemed massive, but then the room was very large. Setting the camera bag and tote on a nearby barrel-backed chair, Sabrina stepped into the center. Noticing a door in the far left corner, she approached and walked into a very modern bathroom with marbled countertops, gold plated fixtures and a large, dark blue mosaic tiled shower. It was beautiful.

This room surpassed any five star hotels Sabrina had ever stayed at. It was elegant, and yet, at the same time very homey and comfortable with the oversized furniture. She walked to a window that showed off the entire back stretch of land. As far as Sabrina could see, there were green pastures quartered off with perfect white fencing. Straining her head a bit to the right, she could barely see a large, bright red building with white doors and matching shutters. It looked like a picture of a Norman Rockwell calendar. Brie knew she and couldn't wait to get started.

Chapter 11

Betty left Sabrina alone to unpack and get settled in, stating she would return in fifteen minutes to show her to the kitchen for supper. Sabrina pulled out her cell phone and called Joe to let him know she had arrived. Next, she punched the speed dial number to her sister.

"Hi sis, I just got in and this place is spectacular. You would love it," Brie exclaimed, walking around in the room.

"Beautiful, you say. Wish I were there, too."

"I'll take extra pictures of the landscape and send them to you," Sabrina offered.

"Great, I'll have to get my excitement vicariously through you. Did everything go well for you in San Diego?" Sophie questioned, already knowing her sister would say what she always said after a shoot.

"Absolutely, I always get a good picture."

Sabrina loved to tease her sister.

"I know you wouldn't have left without them being perfect."

"Oh sis, you know me so well."

"You bet! Always and forever," Sophie chimed.

"I expect to be here for about two weeks. That should give me plenty of time to get what I need, but I'll keep you posted. Got to run," Brie said, ready to end the call.

"You've always got to run. Have lots of fun, sis," Sophie

told her with a giggle.

Sabrina tossed her phone onto the bed and unzipped her suitcase, pulling out clothes and hanging them in the armoire. The bottom drawers were perfect for her remaining things. This would be her final assignment for the remainder of the year, and for the first time in Sabrina's career, she was taking a month off. She headed for the stairs and was met by Betty.

"Good timing. Let's get you some supper," she stated, cheerfully.

After a homemade chicken casserole and vegetables, Betty gave Sabrina a quick tour of the house, returned her to the guest room, and excused herself to retire for the evening. Ranch life started in the dawn hours so it was customary to end the day early, and that was fine with Sabrina. She was ready to settle in also.

Brie was so exhausted when she crawled between the satin sheets she immediately fell into a deep sleep and, once again, dreamt she was back in her aunt's bedroom being confronted by an invisible being. Sabrina didn't awaken until she felt the sunlight on her face the next morning. Rolling over to see the clock on the nightstand, she was shocked to discover it was ten o'clock. Sabrina jumped out of bed and ran into the bathroom, showered, dressed, and quickly worked her hair and makeup. She grabbed her bags and ran down the stairs to the kitchen and walked in cautiously to find Leanne, the housekeeper and cook, standing alone, preparing lunch.

She was a short, slightly plump woman with a round face and small hazel eyes. Her nose appeared large in proportion to the rest of her face. She wore no makeup, and her skin showed the wrinkles that appear with time. Her hair was smoothed back into a gray bun at the base of her neck. Brie guessed her age to be late sixties.

Leanne turned when she heard Sabrina enter the kitchen. Feeling completely embarrassed, Brie asked the whereabouts of the Robinson's. Leanne explained that Betty was at the stables and Mr. Robinson went into town, and she then insisted that Sabrina have a seat at the table while she prepared her breakfast. Brie ate eggs and toast with her cup of coffee and thanked Leanne for the meal before heading toward the stables with her camera bag, prepared to work.

The walk across the yard was invigorating with the cold air blowing in her face. Sabrina entered the stables and was hit with the strong smell of horse flesh and manure. The stables were lined with approximately twelve stalls and all were occupied. She walked toward Betty and Jesse who were standing outside a stall near the back. They appeared to be having a serious discussion and turned to greet Sabrina when they heard her approach.

"Good morning, how did you sleep?" Betty inquired.

"Apparently, to well. I can't believe I overslept," Brie confessed with embarrassment.

"Not a problem. We don't expect you to get up at the crack of dawn like us ranchers."

"Thank you, but I do need to start my day much earlier than this."

"Good morning, Jesse James."

"Good morning to you, Sabrina," he said with a smile.

"If you don't mind, I'll just do some exploring on my own, but I'll make sure I stay out of everyone's way, and hopefully they won't even know I'm around," Brie remarked.

"That's fine. If you have any questions, just let Jesse or me know," Betty said in a soft voice.

Sabrina left and walked outside the stables. Standing for a moment in the doorway, she saw some activity at a fenced area to the right and decided to go over and check it out. She approached a couple of men bent down and noticed they were examining a foal.

"Good morning," she said to their backs.

Startled, both men stood and turned to greet Sabrina. She learned that the infant was only a month old and sick, so they had to separate him from his mother. She stepped back and snapped a few pictures knowing she was on the job; however, photographing a sick animal wasn't how Sabrina imagined she would start this shoot.

Everyone was very helpful at the ranch. Sabrina established a routine and kept pace with the ranchers in the days that followed. She would take candid shots of the men doing their daily chores such as mending fences, repairing the stable doors, and exercising the horses. This was one of those assignments that made it hard to see the end.

Brie was fascinated with these large beautiful animals and loved being around the fenced areas watching them graze. Sometimes the horses would become frisky with one another, and she captured some of her best shots during these times. She declined the invitation to go horseback riding, having fallen off a horse when she was a teenager left her too afraid to try again.

On her second day, Brie was introduced to two teenage children as they entered the house from school. Betty explained they had their children later in life compared to most. A seventeen year old son named Justin and a fourteen year old daughter named Gabrielle. Each day after school, Justin would run upstairs to change his clothes, come down to the kitchen for a snack, and head out to the stables. Brie usually didn't see him again until supper. He was a quiet young man; an obvious younger version of his father. He even had the same handsome features of dark hair and blue eyes. The respect between father and son was very apparent. Often they discussed openly at the dinner table issues regarding the ranch. Victor listened intently when his son spoke of matters needing attention.

Gabby showed no interest in the daily functions of the ranch; however, she did engage her father in conversation about her prized possession, her horse, Sassy Mae. She was forever expounding on something new Sassy Mae did each day. Gabby believed her horse had human qualities.

The bantering that took place at the table each evening was like being in the middle of a live play, watching the love and respect for one another flow. This was all so new and fascinating to Sabrina that each day she could hardly wait for dinner just to sit back and listen to the conversations shifting from subject to subject in the blink of an eye. She knew she would miss this.

Gabby was fascinated by Sabrina's profession and spent a great deal of time hanging out with her, and it was a mutual enjoyment of each other's companionship. She shared with Gabrielle how she began taking pictures when the was about her age. When Gabrielle wasn't in school or working with Sassy Mae, she could be found with Brie, toting her equipment bag.

The two weeks that followed were very enjoyable for Sabrina. They treated her like family which would made it much harder to leave. Brie was pleased with the results of this assignment and upon returning home would email the disk to Joe. Sad to see it come to an end and yet ready for her vacation, she phoned Joe that she was finished and to book a flight home. Later that day, he called to confirm a morning flight.

Sabrina informed everyone at dinner that evening that the assignment was complete and she would be taking the morning flight back to Florida. They were sorrowful to see her leave. Early the next morning, Leanne made a big breakfast and instead of everyone leaving the house before the break of dawn, when Brie came downstairs she was greeted by the entire family, including Jesse, in the dining room. They were all waiting for her to come down for a final meal together. It brought tears to her eyes when she realized what they had done. She knew chores started early and the kids should be in school. Betty came over to where she stood in the doorway and putting her arms around her shoulder, led Brie into the dining room to sit for breakfast.

"I'm going to miss you all so much. You have so graciously welcomed me into your home," Sabrina said, holding back tears.

"Consider this your home away from home. Anytime you want to come back, the door is always open to you," Victor remarked.

"Absolutely, you must visit with us, Sabrina," Betty confirmed her husband's statement.

"Thank you so much. I may take you up on the offer."

"We'll hold you to that," Victor stated, assuredly.

Having finished breakfast along with a second cup of coffee, Sabrina knew she couldn't delay departing any longer. Jesse was taking hero the airport, and they had an hour's drive ahead of them. She had put together a special disk of family photos and gave it to Betty before leaving.

Standing at the front door, Sabrina gave each a hug while Jesse put the luggage into the back of the truck. She had never become so attached to a family, but then her job didn't typically require spending time in someone's home. She promised to stay in touch as she stepped up into the truck.

The drive back to the airport was quiet since Sabrina wasn't in the mood for light conversation and Jesse didn't try to encourage her into talking. When they reached the airport, she suggested he leave her at the airline check-in point outside, and she would leave the luggage there and proceed to the terminal. She was used to navigating her way through airports.

Jesse lifted the bags from the back of the truck, and Sabrina retrieved her tote and equipment bag from the floorboard and stacked them on top of the suitcases. She turned and gave Jesse a quick hug thanking him for bringing her to the airport. Taking a handle in each hand, she dragged the pieces and stood at the check- in line. It would be several hours before she would be home.

Chapter 12

Sabrina couldn't wait to get back to Asheville because for the first time in her life, photography wasn't the only thing that motivated her. How strange to want to go to the country knowing it wouldn't be the same without Aunt Millie. And these sporadic dreams were beginning to bother her. *Why am I having them in the first place,* she questioned.

Brie had stayed in touch with George throughout the following weeks and knew the deed to the house had been changed and she could pick it up upon her return. *What an unusual twist in life,* she thought.

The plane was due to arrive in Orlando mid-afternoon, and having promised Sophie she would stop by for dinner upon her return from the Montana assignment, she called her sister from the airport before boarding the flight home.

"Hey Sophie, I'm getting on the plane soon and should be at your house by five o'clock," Brie told her sister.

"Great, dinner will be ready."

"We're boarding now so got to go. See you in a little while."

"See you soon."

The flight was uneventful, the way most were to Brie and arrived on time. She collected her luggage, loaded them in the trunk of the car, and left the airport headed west into Orlando. Traffic coming out of the airport was busier than usual this time of day, so it took Sabrina longer to arrive at her sister's house.

Hearing the car in the driveway, Sophie went to greet her sister. They fell into each other's arms for a long embrace and held tight before turning to walk into the house. David came from the kitchen, meeting his sister-in-law in the foyer and gave her a big hug. When Brie noticed the large apron he was wearing, she knew he was in charge of preparing dinner.

"What's on the menu, David?" Sabrina asked teasingly, stepping back from the embrace.

"I made your favorite," he stated proudly, with a smile.

"That would be pot roast. Oh, David, how did you know I have a taste for your pot roast?" Brie said, comically.

"That's easy, you always like pot roast," David replied with a grin.

"Did you make a lemon meringue pie, too?"

"Of course, nothing but the best for my two girls," he declared.

David was actually a very good chef and enjoyed preparing meals for Sophie. Often he would do the cooking on the weekends when he had more time to concentrate on trying new recipes.

Dinner was enjoyable as they caught up on each other's news. Feeling very much at home in her sister's house, Brie began telling stories of her experience at the ranch. She told them about Gabrielle and how she followed Brie everywhere when she wasn't in school. After dinner, Sophie and Sabrina went to sit in the living room, while David stated he would clean the kitchen.

Brie told Sophie about Jesse James, the tall, dark, and mysterious man she rarely saw the entire time she was there but wished she could have gotten to know better. She was disappointed that it wasn't possible to make a connection with him. It had been a long time since Sabrina met someone she would have liked to have known better, but the timing seemed off, or perhaps he simply wasn't interested in her.

"Wow, Brie, you actually met someone. I think this is a first for you," Sophie said, teasing her sister.

"Not a first, but close. I don't have time to cultivate a relationship when I'm working," Sabrina defended her lifestyle.

"Are you going to contact him?"

"No, I have no reason to. If he were interested in me, he would have made the effort while I was there, so obviously the feeling wasn't mutual."

"Not necessarily. He could have been extremely busy just like you were with the shoot. Things aren't always as they seem," Sophie declared with sisterly insight.

"Well, I would say he had more than one opportunity to pursue me if he was interested. After all, it was Jesse who drove me to the airport. He could have made his move if he wanted to. I think he didn't find me attractive, or I wasn't his type," Sabrina explained.

"I can't imagine anyone not finding you attractive. As far as his type, maybe he thought you were out of his league. You know, country boy meets city girl."

The conversation was dropped when David walked into the room bringing a tray of three coffee mugs and three large slices of pie. He put it down on the table in front of the sofa where the sisters were curled up talking.

"David, you are spoiling me," Sabrina told him with a smile.

"My pleasure, I love to spoil my two favorite girls," he winked at Brie, handing her a mug.

"Sophie, you have yourself a really good man."

"Oh, I never forget that, and to think he is all mine," Sophie replied, batting her eyelashes at David when he handed her a cup of coffee.

"Okay you two, you're going to make me want to flex my muscles, but because I don't have any, that would not be very impressive," David declared with a chuckle.

Having been teased enough for one evening, David started telling stories about the kids in his classroom and the numerous mischievous pranks they try to pull during the day. You would think high school students would consider themselves too mature for such antics, but apparently not, which David's stories testified. Before long, Sabrina and Sophie were matching with tales of their own teenage antics.

Being with Sophie and David made Brie realize how much she missed times spent together. In the past, Sabrina wasn't concerned in the least about family events. She preferred to be off with her camera but after all these years, she could now understand why this was so important to Sophie. Maybe it was the melancholy she was experiencing since their aunt's death that made her think of Sophie and what she would do if she didn't have her sister. It was a frightening thought.

It was late when Brie left to go home. She thanked David for the fabulous meal and entertaining evening, giving him a hug before leaving the house. Sophie walked her sister to her car.

"That was a lot of fun. Thanks, sis. I think I needed this evening more than I realized. It's been a long time since I have laughed that hard," Sabrina confessed.

"We need to do this more often. This is what I miss most about you traveling and being gone so much; the time we could have together, and I'm not trying to put a guilt trip on you," Sophie said, solemnly.

"I understand and I miss you, too. I need to put more personal time into my schedule, and I promise you I'll work on it."

"I would love that."

"Sophie, I had another dream when I was at the ranch. I can understand one time due to the circumstances, but more than that is a bit much," Sabrina told her sister.

"That's for sure. This is getting to be too strange. I don't know what to tell you."

"There isn't anything you can say or do. I just wanted to let you know."

"Are you okay? I mean how are you handling this?" Sophie

asked.

"It bothers me. It can't be normal to have the same dream repetitively. It has to mean something, but I don't know what."

"Let me know if it continues. I can't do anything about it, but I want to know."

She felt badly for her sister, but didn't know what to say to comfort her.

"I'm probably being a bit melodramatic about it. I just wanted to tell you," Brie remarked.

"And you're right to tell me."

They hugged and Brie climbed behind the wheel of her bright red Mustang convertible. She gave one last wave to her sister before pointing her car east toward the beach. It would take an hour to get home.

Sabrina was feeling a need to alter the way she had been conducting her life. Maybe the experience, or lack thereof, with Jesse James sparked these feelings. It wasn't everyday she found someone interesting enough to want to get to know better. It made her feel sad and lonely.

She always thought she had her life in order, but found it disheartening to think she was missing out on a very important aspect. Brie realized she wanted more than a career and being with Sophie and David this evening only magnified her desire to make some changes.

Chapter 13

One of the first things Sabrina did upon returning home was to book a flight to Asheville. She would be flying out on Tuesday, allowing herself only a few days to get everything in order at home. Brie was anxious to begin her vacation and the less time at home meant more time in the country. She called Sophie to give her the flight information because they would be leaving soon for Christmas in Pittsburgh.

Both sisters were saddened that they would not be together for the holidays, but neither wanted to change their plans. They promised to make it up to each other when they returned home. Sabrina called Joe to give him the dates she would be in Asheville because if there was an interesting assignment over the holiday she wanted to know about it. He agreed to keep her informed but didn't foresee anything spectacular happening in her absence.

After securing her condo for the month and parking her car at the airport garage, Brie was back at the terminal waiting for a plane. It was delayed coming in, but the passengers boarding were assured they would not miss their connecting flights. She had been doing this for years, so why did sitting in the airport suddenly make her feel alone and lonely? On the plane Sabrina concentrated on making a mental list of things to do. Though she was excited to have an extended vacation, Brie wondered if she would get bored with so much free time.

The plan made one stop in Atlanta for additional passengers

which went smoothly. There weren't any delays and the flight arrive on time. Sabrina had a rental car waiting and was now merging with the evening traffic, pulling into her aunt's driveway just when the sun was setting. She unpacked the car placing the luggage by the staircase. She remembered to bring an extra suitcase with winter sweaters, scarves, and gloves knowing the weather would be cold.

Sabrina went straight to the thermostat to set the heat and then into the kitchen. She found a lot of moldy food along with a quart of sour milk in the fridge and began tossing everything into a plastic trash bag until there wasn't anything remaining but a couple sticks of butter and a carton of expired eggs.

Brie made peanut butter crackers discovered in the pantry and brewed a cup of tea in the microwave for supper. She didn't feel like going back out to a restaurant for dinner. There would be plenty of time in the morning to get settled in and go to the grocery store.

She retrieved her purse by the staircase, pulled out her phone and called Sophie.

"Hi sis, I'm here," Sabrina wanted to assure her sister.

"How was your flight?"

"It was fine. The rental car was ready when I got to the airport so no problem there. I had to clean out the refrigerator, something we didn't think to do when we were here for the funeral."

"Your right, I didn't think of that, either. Find anything with fur on it?"

"A few things were covered in green. After all this time, nothing could possibly be any good, but I did find some saltines and peanut butter in the pantry and that was supper."

"Yummy. I won't tell you what we had."

"That's okay. Whatever you had, I know it was better than crackers. I'm going to the store in the morning after I have some of those pancakes at *The Country Kitchen* restaurant."

"There you go."

"How does it feel to be in Aunt Millie's house? I know it's

yours, but does it feel strange or uncomfortable being there alone?"

"No, it doesn't seem strange. I'm used to being in this house. I keep thinking that she is out running an errand and will be walking through the door at any moment."

"I'm going to unpack now that the house is beginning to warm up. The neon sign at the bank said it was forty-five degrees outside. I'll call tomorrow."

"Okay, talk to you then. Sleep tight and remember to lock up."

"Already did."

"I love you, sis," Sophie said in farewell.

"Don't worry about me, and I love you too," Brie signed off.

Sabrina grabbed the suitcases and dragged them one at a time up the stairs. She wasn't ready to stay in her aunt's master bedroom so she took her things into the guest room facing the front of the house. Lining the luggage side by side near the bed, Brie unpacked clothes and hung them in the closet, putting the smaller items in the cherry-wood dresser on the opposite wall. This was the room she always used when visiting her aunt, so this felt like a normal routine.

Brie always used the bathroom across the hall so she took the toiletry bag and laid out the cosmetics on the counter top near the sink. Beginning to feel more at home, she walked through the upstairs flipping on lights in each bedroom and then went downstairs and did the same in the formal living room, den, and dining room. By the time she had made a complete circle on the first floor area, the house was lit top to bottom. No mistake that someone was living in the house.

Roaming from room to room and lightly touching items on tables with her fingertips made Sabrina think of Aunt Millie. With tears in her eyes, she walked into the den, her aunt's favorite room, the one they spent the most time in, and sat down in her usual chair. It was a glider-rocker made of dark green corduroy fabric, identical to the rocker placed across the room with a matching ottoman that floated between the two chairs. Her aunt usually got dibs on the ottoman to prop up her feet. They would sit here in front of the fireplace talking, reading, watching television, or sit on the floor doing crafts.

Gently rocking, she rested her head on the backrest and closed her eyes, not realizing she had fallen asleep until she felt the light tap on her shoulder. Brie woke up startled and sat straight up expecting to find her aunt standing in front of her telling her to go on up to bed, but there was no one there. Sabrina knew she was alone in the house so it must have been a dream, again.

Too tired to give it any thought, she got up from the chair, and walked upstairs to quickly prepare for bed, leaving all the lights on except the one in the bedroom. She climbed under the comforter to fall fast asleep, and it wasn't until nine in the morning with the sun shining through the front window that she woke up.

Sabrina always slept peacefully when she was at her aunt's house. In that split second upon awakening, Brie thought this was an ordinary visit and her aunt would be downstairs having a second cup of coffee. When she came fully awake, the realization that she was alone gave her a sad feeling. Deciding not to dwell on the emptiness of the house, she quickly showered and dressed in a comfortable pair of jeans and red turtleneck sweater. Sabrina walked through the house turning off the lights, not sure why she left them on the previous night. In the light of day, Brie felt a little foolish.

Her first order of business today was to have a huge breakfast and buy some groceries. She wanted to stop by Bella's house and let her know she was in town and also pay a visit to George to get the deed to the house. Grabbing her handbag and cell phone on the kitchen counter, Sabrina went out the front door. It took a few minutes for the car to warm up before she drove down the road to *The Country Kitchen* for a large stack of pancakes.

After breakfast, Sabrina drove to Bella's house. Standing at the front door rubbing her arms against the cold, she waited for her to open the door.

"Hey, Sabrina, good to see you. Come in and have a cup of coffee. Just made a fresh pot," Bella commented.

"Hello to you too, Bella, and I would love a cup," Brie replied.

Sabrina followed Bella into the kitchen toward the table tucked in the corner, while Bella grabbed two Christmas mugs from the cupboard and poured coffee into each. She put them along with cream and sugar on a tray and brought it over to the table.

"Well, I sure am glad to see you. When did you get in? How long will you be staying?" Bella asked as she sat down at the table.

"I got in last night, and I have a month off. I want to go through my aunt's things and not be rushed."

Sabrina didn't want to reveal the real reason for returning so soon.

"If you need any help, just let me know. I always have plenty of free time these days and would be glad to lend a hand."

"Thanks for the offer, and if I get overwhelmed, I might take you up on it."

"How are you and Sophie doing?" Bella asked.

"We're okay."

They chatted for awhile, and Brie excused herself to do her errands, promising to stay in touch. On her way to the grocery store, she stopped at the attorney's office. Though she didn't make an appointment to see George, he wasn't with a client at the time of her arrival and motioned Brie to come into his office.

"How've you been, Sabrina?" George asked.

"I'm okay and looking forward to spending the holidays here," Brie answered.

"That's good. If you need any help while you're here, please let me know. I've been driving by periodically to keep a close check on the house."

"I appreciate that. I stopped by to let you know I was in town and to pick up the deed."

"I have it right here," George said, reaching into the desk drawer.

"Thank you. I'll stay in touch," Sabrina told him, accepting the envelope.

"Be sure you do."

Next, Brie headed towards the grocery store. This was her last stop before returning to the house to start on some chores. Cleaning the kitchen and restocking the pantry and refrigerator was a good place to begin. *Food first*, she thought.

Chapter 14

Sabrina cleaned the refrigerator with hot soapy water before putting away the fresh food items and then tackled the pantry. All the groceries were put away before she continued to clean the remainder of the kitchen including mopping the floor. Content with the kitchen in order, Brie went upstairs.

She approached each bedroom standing in the doorway for a moment before entering. Sabrina wasn't sure why she felt so uneasy. She was very familiar with this house and there shouldn't be this uncomfortable feeling she was experiencing. She continued down the hallway to the master bedroom and felt she was trespassing when she stepped into the spacious room. She wanted to call out to Aunt Millie but knew there wouldn't be a response.

Feeling an overwhelming sadness, Brie went downstairs toward the back of the house and into the den. It was already dark outside, and remembering hearing on the car radio the temperature would be dropping to the low thirties, she lit the fireplace. It brought to mind many memories of sitting in front of the fire making home crafts.

Feeling a bit lost in the big house, Brie called her sister. Sophie answered on the first ring.

"Hi sis, I'm settled in, if you can call it that."

"I'm glad you called. I was thinking about you being all alone in that big house," Sophie told her.

"I know."

"You spent the most time with her, and I know you miss her very much. Besides, the two of you had a very special relationship."

"It's strange to be in the house without her. It leaves me with an odd feeling that something isn't right. I don't know how to explain it," Brie confessed.

"What do you mean?"

"I don't know. I can't really explain it, exactly."

"So what are you going to do? If you've a bad feeling, then maybe you should reconsider staying during the holidays and come stay with us for Christmas. Catch a flight straight into Pittsburgh, and we'll pick you up at the airport. You can spend the holidays with us at David's parent's house; I know they won't mind," Sophie pressed her point.

"Thanks for the offer, but I really want to be here."

"Well, the offer stands if you change your mind."

"I know, and I do appreciate it."

"You've only been there a day, but are you really sure you want to stay an entire month by yourself? You're used to being there with Aunt Millie. This will be different."

"You're right. This will certainly be different, but I still feel it's the right thing for me at this time."

"Alright, it's your decision."

"I'll call you in a day or two," Brie told her, hanging up.

Christmas was three weeks away and she was determined to stay. She had already given some thought to putting up a tree because Aunt Millie did every year. Her aunt loved the holidays and always had a fresh tree cut from the *Cooper Christmas Tree Farm*. She thought of going over in about a week and getting one. That was where everyone in the community bought their Douglas Fir. Tomorrow she would get the boxes of decorations from the closet under the stairs and go through them.

While looking out the kitchen window into the back acreage while her coffee brewed, Brie felt a light breeze blow over her shoulders. Instinctively, it made Sabrina turn around to see if someone was behind her, though she knew there would be no one. What did this mean? Who was trying to get her attention? She would have to start investigating for answers, but wasn't even sure where to begin. *Why isn't this scaring me out of my wits,* she asked herself.

"I know you are here. Who are you, and why am I not afraid of you?" she spoke aloud.

There was no answer, not even a shift in the air around her. Brie hoped if she voiced her thoughts, she could draw this apparition to reveal itself, but it didn't work. Somehow, she sensed it was the same *being* that whispered in her ear the day of her aunt's funeral.

Sabrina poured a cup of coffee, took two sips, and headed for the stairway closet. Pulling out two large boxes and dragging them into the den. She unpacked the Christmas decorations positioning them around the house. She found several candles tucked in the bottom of one box and after placing them on tables and in the kitchen, lit each one. The aroma of cinnamon quickly filled the air.

The house was beginning to look and smell as it should during the holidays. She played Christmas music from the collection of compact discs her aunt kept. With the fireplace crackling and the music filling the silence, she sat in her favorite rocking chair to decide what her new household chore would be.

Brie was rethinking the tree idea seeing all the decorations set out around the house would be enough to satisfy her holiday spirit, but for some unexplainable reason she wanted the house decorated exactly like Aunt Millie would have done.

Sabrina called Bella for directions to the *Cooper Christmas Tree Farm*.

"Oh, no need for directions. I can take you there since I have to pick out a tree myself. Why don't you drop by tomorrow morning and we'll go together," Bella suggested, delighted to hear from Sabrina.

"Sounds like a plan. Is nine o'clock to early?"

"Nine is perfect. I look forward to it."

"Thanks, Bella. I'll see you then."

The remainder of the day was uneventful for Sabrina. She walked around inside the house lightly inspecting items on tabletops. When the sun went down, she retired early. The next morning, she was ready to purchase a Christmas tree.

They shared a cup of coffee and drove out to the tree farm. Bella explained that the farm had been in the family for three generations. The timber was grown in designated rows on the backside. They hire extra people to cut the trees and take truckloads into town to sell under a large white canopy, but many come out to the Cooper's place to select their own tree. Sabrina wasn't sure what to expect when they arrived.

After parking in front of a large building which resembled a barn, Brie could hear the whine of a large saw. There was activity around the entrance as she and Bella made their way toward the door. A man approximately six feet tall and wearing a baseball cap walked out toward them.

"Hello, Bella, here for your Christmas tree?" he asked.

"Of course, and I want a big one this year," she replied.

This was their customary banter every year when Bella came to pick out a tree. She always asked for a tall tree.

"Ben, this is Mildred's niece, Sabrina Fitzgerald. This here is Bennaird Cooper," Bella said, introducing them.

"Hello Sabrina, I knew your aunt and I'm so sorry to heart of her passing. She came here every year to pick out a tree," Ben told her.

"Sabrina is staying at the house this holiday. We came to pick out a couple of trees."

"Great, that's two Douglas Fir Christmas trees coming right up. If you want to start down that pathway, I'll get a chain saw and meet you there," said Ben, pointing in the direction to the right of the building.

Bella and Sabrina walked toward the field of trees and were quickly swallowed by the masses while they made their way through the maze. It was making Brie feel very claustrophobic, and she wasn't sure how much longer she could hold out.

"I'll stick to a small tree. One I can handle," she told Bella. Wanting to find a tree and leave, Sabrina spotted a small one no taller than herself and seeing Ben walking toward her, pointed to her choice.

"I like this one," Sabrina said too quickly.

"Alright, this one it is. Step back, and I'll cut it down for you."

"Doing as she was told, Sabrina retraced her steps but not by much considering there were trees all around her. In just a few seconds, the tree was down and Ben dragged it out into open space with Sabrina following behind. He glanced at Brie to notice she was breathing too fast.

"Are you okay? You're looking a little pale," he asked, concerned.

"Give me a minute, and I will be. I get claustrophobic," Sabrina confided, breathing rapidly.

"Take some deep breaths and you'll be fine."

"I'm better now, thanks."

"If you'll wait here, I'll get Bella's tree."

Sabrina nodded. Feeling much better, she waited patiently, looking around the acreage of trees as far as the eye could see. She had never given any thought before to where Christmas tress came from. Of course, she knew someone had to grow them, but she always had an artificial tree that she pulled out of a box and assembled.

She noticed Bella following Ben dragging a tree. He dropped it next to Sabrina's and pulled out a yellow tag from his back pocket and tied it around the base of Bella's tree. Seeing the confusion in her eyes, he explained this was to identify who had which tree.

"I'll deliver the trees this afternoon."

"Wonderful, how much do I owe you?" Sabrina asked.

"Nothing, this one is on me. I really liked Mildred, so it's my tribute to her, if I may?"

"That is very thoughtful. Thank you," Brie told him.

She was practically in tears.

"Ben, bring the bill when you deliver my tree, and I'll settle with you then," Bella requested.

"Sure thing, and I'll see you later this afternoon."

Bella and Sabrina said their goodbyes and within minutes were pulling into Bella's driveway. Sabrina thanked Bella for taking her to get a tree and instead of following her into the house, walked toward her own car. She had some things to do at home and was anxious to get started.

Chapter 15

She had been putting it off long enough. Now that Brie was settled in the house, it was time to do a little sleuthing. Sabrina knew there had to be a reason for hearing voices and sensing a presence when no one was there. She could no longer ignore it.

Near the window in the master bedroom was an old-fashioned cherry wood secretarial desk with a matching chair that held her aunt's important papers. Aunt Millie was a very organized person so it wasn't a surprise to find the papers in exact stacks according to importance. Brie began rummaging through them, finding nothing unusual at first glance, but then, she wasn't sure what she was looking for.

She opened the middle desk drawer, pushing papers and miscellaneous things around until her fingers touched the edge of an envelope stashed in the back right corner. She saw her name written across the front and underlined. *How strange,* she thought. *Why would Aunt Millie have a sealed envelope with my name on it,* she wondered.

Playing with it in her hand, Sabrina was at a dilemma to open it, afraid it may have bad news. Perhaps Aunt Millie had a serious health condition that she didn't want revealed until after her death. There was a small part of Brie that wasn't sure she wanted to know what took her life. That would mean that during the visits Aunt Millie was pretending to feel good for her sake. All those times they laughed and did crazy things, her aunt could have been slowly dying. It was a thought that was hard to deal with at the moment.

Brie took the envelope downstairs into the den and sat in the rocker. Should she call Sophie first and tell her what she had discovered, but then the envelope was addressed to her, so technically she could open it without feeling as if she was betraying her sister. Brie ended the suspense and very methodically opened the envelope finding a single piece of paper. The stationery was a soft shade of pink with a border of dark rose petals. She recognized her aunt's handwriting and read:

My Darling Sabrina,

I have always felt like you and Sophie were the daughters I never had. Though you were my sister's children, I carried you both close to my heart and loved you with more of a mother's love than an aunt. I think you know this to be true.

There were many times in the past few years I debated how to present the following news to you. Should I reveal this in person during one of your visits, or present it after I was no longer with you. You can see, I opted for the latter. By now, you are aware of my Last Will and Testament and the division of my estate. Though you may not realize it at the moment, Brie, there will come a time in your life when you will understand the reason why I did this in such a manner. I wanted to leave you and Sophie a legacy that exceeds materialistic things, if you will accept it.

In these past years, I have felt deeply inspired to help others in a manner that would be beneficial to the recipient. Being settled comfortably in my lifestyle with plenty of spare time, I wanted to make an impact of some kind with my remaining days. I set out on a personal quest to spend time with individuals who didn't have the companionship of family or friends and to help those truly in need. I realize what I did was not unique by any means; however, it became unique to me. In a short time, I came to secretly call my mission Passionate Promises. What began as a simple task to sit one day with someone recouping from an illness and the next day run an errand for another, revealed to me the need to show compassion toward others. I became very passionate deep within my soul about doing this and made a promise to my heavenly Father that I would help others in whatever capacity I was able because I knew in my heart that He was leading me. He strengthened and guided me along the path of His choosing.

I gave my time freely to sit with individuals despondent with the outcome of their life. I would visit, listen to their stories, and try to explain that they could overcome their present hardship no matter how bad it may have seemed. I tried to encourage them to not let the circumstance they were in dictate the outcome. The more I visited people, the more I felt a calling to do so on a greater level.

It became my own personal crusade to help those who felt they no longer had a reason for living. Spending time with people who were confined to their homes, even if only temporarily, let them know that someone out in the world cared about them; they were not alone. We all need encouragement from time to time. I believe my visits played a part in helping them get back their passion for life. It requires patience and understanding without harboring judgment. You and Sophie have the qualities that would make you ideal candidates for this endeavor.

I can imagine the shocked expression on your face while you read this. I believe the impact of Passionate Promises will become more understandable in time to come. It would mean a great deal to me if you would carry on my personal legacy to help others by demonstrating the compassion that I know lies within your heart. I have not meant to burden you with something you may believe you have no interest in, but rather to challenge you to continue what I started by searching your heart. The answer lies there. Sabrina, please give this serious consideration.

I hope one day you might come to enjoy the community of

Asheville, and leaving my home to you will give you the opportunity to explore. I realize it is a completely different lifestyle, but I believe someday you will be ready for a change, and you will think about the legacy I have left for you. Share this with Sophie because I would like for both of you to seriously consider taking Passionate Promises to a new level in whatever capacity you are led. Don't be too hasty to turn away from the idea because you might be very surprised by the opportunities that will be opened to you.
Love,
Aunt Millie

Sabrina let her hand fall into her lap, allowing the letter to drop from her fingers to the floor. She was stunned by this new revelation of her aunt's life and for some odd reason, found it disheartening. *Why didn't Aunt Millie tell me of this long ago, since apparently it had been going on for a while? Didn't she trust me with this part of her life? Why was it kept a secret,* she asked herself in bewilderment. Brie felt betrayed. While deep in thought, she heard the doorbell ring and getting up from the chair, she picked up the fallen letter and placed in on the table.

Looking through the peephole, she could see Ben standing with a Christmas tree in one hand. She had forgotten he would be delivering the tree this afternoon. Brie opened the door to let him in and directed Ben into the den to place the tree alongside the fireplace. Obligingly, he took the tree and gently laid it on the floor and then retraced his steps back to the truck to get the stand. It didn't take long before the tree was in place.

"Thanks Ben, it looks great. I should pay for this beautiful tree."

"No need, this one is for Mildred."

"Would you like a cup of coffee before you leave?" she asked, casually.

"Right now, I would enjoy a cup; however, I have five more trees to deliver before dark. Otherwise, I'd definitely take you up on the offer. Can I take a raincheck?" he asked.

"A raincheck it is," Brie said with a smile.

"Be sure and put a cup of water in this pail every four or five days so the tree won't dry out too fast."

"Glad to know that. I wouldn't have thought of it."

Ben straightened the tree and made sure it was secure in the pail and wouldn't topple over. Then he wiped up the miscellaneous needles that had fallen on the floor and walked toward the kitchen. Sabrina showed him where the garbage container was located.

"You're all set. I hope you enjoy your tree," he stated, walking toward the foyer.

"Oh, I will."

"I'll call in a couple of days for that cup of coffee."

"I hope you do," Sabrina replied, watching him walk toward his truck.

She was looking forward to it. He seemed like a very nice man and wasn't hard on the eyes, either. She noticed how his hair was long enough to curl up around the edge of the beige baseball cap he was wearing with an embossed logo imprint of a Christmas tree in green and the company name in red lettering. *How appropriate,* she thought.

Sabrina studied the bare tree, anxious to begin decorating it. Sliding the two boxes close to the tree, she began placing ornaments on the beautiful Douglas Fir, meticulously situating each one in just the right spot. Two hours later, she stood back to examine her work and was pleased with the results. No flickering lights or streamers, just uniquely made ornaments her aunt had collected throughout the years.

Brie stashed the empty boxes back under the staircase and backtracked to the kitchen to retrieve her cell phone. She went into the den and curled up in the rocker. Before calling her sister, she sat for a few minutes with her eyes closed resting her head against the back of the chair. Sabrina wondered how her sister would react to the news she was about to tell her. Finally, she hit the speed dial button.

"Hey Brie, I was just thinking about you. How are things in

the country?" Sophie asked.

"Things are going well. I got a tree and decorated it this afternoon, and it really looks festive in the house," Sabrina told her.

"I'm glad you decorated. It makes the holidays fun. David is enjoying being with his dad; they are inseparable."

They had arrived in Pittsburgh two days prior.

"Sophie, I came across a letter in Aunt Millie's desk. It was addressed to me so I opened it. The letter was about something she called *Passionate Promises,* where she would help people in need," Sabrina explained.

"I don't understand. What is *Passionate Promises?*"

"Apparently it was a name she gave her endeavor to helping people. She called it her personal crusade to help others by running errands, or sitting with someone recouping from an illness."

"Isn't it strange she would keep something like this to herself? So what else did she say about it?"

"She wants us to continue it."

"No kidding. This is a real surprise. What do you think?"

"I don't know what to think. I'm shocked, actually."

"What exactly did you say *Passionate Promises* is?" Sophie inquired again, uncertain if she understood what Sabrina was telling her.

"Aunt Millie would sit with people who were home recovering from illnesses and spend time with them because they didn't have family or friends nearby to do it."

"You spent the most time with her; did you know she was into helping the helpless?"

"No, she never mentioned it, nor implied that she was into anything like this."

"Why do you suppose she didn't tell us? I mean she waits until she is dead to reveal her good neighbor routine. I don't get it."

"I know, I've thought the same thing but obviously she had her reasons. I'll read the letter to you."

After finishing, she paused for her sister's reaction.

"It seems to me Aunt Millie was addressing this to you, so what are you going to do, Brie?"

"I don't know. I have to give it some thought. I think she was meaning for both of us to consider carrying on her crusade. She did mention you also."

"I can't exactly see you spending what free time you have sitting with the helpless," Sophie stated a bit too strongly, ignoring her sister's implication that she be a part of it too.

"Let's just sit on this for a while. We can talk about it again after the holidays," Sabrina suggested.

"That's a good idea. Are you feeling lonely, yet?"

"No, I'm used to being by myself, but I didn't realize how much I enjoyed coming here until now. I'm beginning to understand why she felt compelled to leave the house to me. It wasn't just the house, but rather her home with all its warmth."

"Aunt Millie wanted you to be happy, and she knew exactly what she was doing when she left her home to you."

"How is everything in Pittsburgh?" Sabrina inquired, changing the subject.

"We're having fun, and it looks like we'll be seeing snow for Christmas. To us Floridians, that is a real treat," Sophie proclaimed, anxious to see some white.

"I'm holding out for snow here, but it doesn't look promising."

"In that case, I'll make a snow angel for you," Sophie giggled.

"Sounds good. I'll call you in a few days. Love you, sis."

"Love you back," Sophie said before hanging up the phone.

Feeling better for having called her sister, Sabrina decided to put the letter on hold. She didn't intend to ignore her aunt's request, but at the same time, she had no experience with what Aunt Mille was asking of her. She intended to give it some serious thought. It was upsetting to Brie to discover a side to her aunt's life that she had not been aware of. *Why would she have kept this from me,* she questioned.

For the remainder of the holiday, Brie wanted to enjoy her country home, and besides, she had some sleuthing to do on a different matter. She wanted to find the cause of her aunt's death, believing the root to her unusual experiences lie there.

Chapter 16

The days before Christmas became a blur for Sabrina. She shopped for David and Sophie, mailing a large package of gifts to them in Pittsburgh. Visiting the quaint little shops in Asheville became an adventure and she found wonderful presents. Brie sent a package to Joe, her assistant, and bought a cashmere scarf and glove set for Bella. She also spotted a uniquely designed brass business card holder shaped in the form of a deer with antlers and purchased it for George.

Sabrina had the gifts wrapped and placed them under the tree along with the presents received from Sophie. With her shopping done, the house decorated and two weeks remaining till Christmas, she wanted to make her deliveries and then settle into doing some research. She could have easily accepted what the death certificate stated had it not been for the continuing occurrences that nagged at her. Was it an act of nature, or was there more to Aunt Millie's death? Sabrina wanted to know the truth.

She called Bella on her cellphone.

"Hi Bella, it's Sabrina. I wondered if I could stop by for a few minutes."

"You don't have to call first, come over anytime."

"Thanks, I'll be there shortly."

"I'll make a fresh pot of coffee."Bella told her.

Sabrina ran up the stairs to the guest bathroom where she had her toiletries. Putting on a touch of peach blush and putting lipgloss on her lips took away the paleness of her porcelain skin. She quickly ran a brush through her hair pulling it back into a ponytail and went back down to the den to retrieve the gifts and her cell phone.

She also took the Olympus SP-550UZ from the equipment bag she kept in the foyer wanting to take a drive through the downtown area and take some pictures later in the day. She also planned to stop by the gravesite and take a few shots of Aunt Millie's headstone.

When Sabrina pulled up, she noticed the smoke curling into the cold air from the chimney. Bella was holding the front door open as she rushed inside to the warmth of the house.

"You look cold. Come in."

"This is for you," Sabrina remarked, handing the gift to Bella.

"What is this? Tell me you didn't go out and buy me a gift? Darling, Sabrina, you didn't need to do that," Bella exclaimed, delighted for the present.

"It's just a little something. I hope you like it."

"You're so sweet. Thank you. Let's go to the kitchen."

Sitting at the small dinette table, they sipped on their coffee served in Christmas mugs.

"Your Aunt Mildred was always talking about you. She loved those times when you came to visit. They were very special to her. She adored you, Sabrina, but I think you know that," Bella stated, reminiscing about her friend.

"Oh, it was mutual. I miss her so much, especially during this holiday. That's what compelled me to decorate her house and get a tree."

"She would have loved the fact that you came."

"I felt a need to be here this year."

She had no intention of revealing to Bella the incidents that occurred at the house which was the real reason Brie returned. She wanted to ask Bella about her aunt's activities, but concerned how to bring the subject up.

"Bella, can I ask you a question about my aunt? You were

good friends, and I thought you could shed some light on what she did with her time. I noticed there were a lot of people at her funeral. I always thought my aunt was more of a recluse, and to see so many attend was a surprise," Sabrina declared.

"Oh, Mildred liked her privacy, which perhaps appeared that she was a loner, but truth be told, your aunt had a heart of gold. She was always helping someone," Bella spoke proudly of her friend.

"What do you mean?"

"She would go sit with the elderly or run errands for anyone who couldn't get out. I think it made her feel useful; gave her a purpose in life."

"In all the years I have been coming here to visit her, she has never once mentioned this to me. Why do you suppose she kept it to herself? Why wouldn't she tell me she did good deeds and helped people?" Sabrina asked, not knowing if she wanted to tell Bella about the letter she had discovered.

"I can't answer that, but I'm sure she must have had a reason. Sometimes when we help others through the goodness of our heart, it isn't a matter that we want to brag about, or feel a need to explain to anyone. Perhaps that's the way Mildred felt about it. I do know this, it made her feel good to help others."

"I understand what you are saying, but I thought our relationship was close enough that she would have share this with me. It's upsetting not having known about it when she was alive. I feel like I've lost something that I never really had in the first place. I'm probably not making any sense," Sabrina declared with a sigh.

"You're making perfect sense, Sabrina. Don't hold it against your aunt for not revealing how she spent her time when you weren't here. Knowing Mildred, she would have a very good reason for not telling you. It may be she wanted you to learn about this after she was gone because it would have more meaning to you then. I do believe in time you'll discover the answers to your questions."

"I'm sure you're right."

Both women fell silent, each contemplating the meaning behind their conversation. They changed the subject to the holidays which reminded Bella to invite Sabrina to her Christmas Eve party. Bella wanted Sabrina to meet her closest friends. Brie said she wouldn't miss it.

"Well, I'd better go. I have a couple errands to run before I go home. I just wanted to stop by and give you your present."

"I'm glad you came over and thank you for the gift. Reminds me of what Mildred would have done; thinking of others. You have a good heart, Sabrina, just like her. I know one thing about my dear friend, she never did anything without a purpose. Think of what her reason might have been in withholding this information rather than condemning her for doing so."

"I understand. What you're saying is that it didn't have anything to do with our relationship, but rather something she wanted me to discover on my own."

"Exactly."

Bella pulled Sabrina into a hug when she stood up from the table. Brie gathered her coat and bag and walked to the front door. She turned to give Bella another quick embrace before stepping out into the cold air.

"Thanks, Bella. I'll call you in a couple days."

She glanced toward the house while backing out of the driveway and saw Bella standing, waving goodbye. Throwing her hand up, she waved back and drove into town toward George's office. She was playing Santa Claus today and had another gift to deliver.

George was with a client when Sabrina arrived. After checking in with the receptionist, Brie sat on the tanned leather sofa to the right of the entrance door. Two print high-backed chairs were located on the opposite wall with a small table between them. While she waited, she had the opportunity to study the décor of his office. The area was large and nicely decorated with dark walnut wood furnishings including the receptionist's desk and matching credenza that held a printer and other office equipment. The carpet was a plush soft gray. *Very nice,* she thought.

Brie picked up a magazine to read but found her mind replaying the conversation she had earlier with Bella. What she said made sense and seemed to confirm what Aunt Mille wrote in her letter. It didn't occur to Brie to ask Bella if she was aware that her aunt had a name for her cause, she wondered if she knew the crusading her aunt did was called *Passionate Promises.* Maybe she would ask her sometime. Sabrina looked up to see George standing at the front desk shaking hands with his client. He motioned her to follow him.

"Sabrina, it's good to see you. What have you been up to?" George inquired, stepping behind his desk to take a seat in the oversized leather chair.

She noticed his office was a duplicate of the reception room with the exception of a wooden bookcase situated behind his desk packed full of books. Sabrina took the familiar chair.

"I've decorated the house and put up a tree. I don't want to take up a lot of your time, but stopped by with a Christmas present. Something I saw in a shop and it made me think of you."

She stretched over the desk to hand the wrapped present to George.

"Why, Sabrina, how thoughtful," he replied, accepting the gift.

George began to chuckle, shaking his head back and forth. Sabrina stared at him wondering what was so funny, but kept silent.

"Sabrina, this is the very thing Mildred would be doing right now if she were here. Ever year, about this time in fact, she would come by with a present, just as you have done, and literally say the same thing you just said. She saw something in a shop. The irony that the two of you would do something so identical, and yet I'm sure unbeknown, is amazing," George explained.

"Really. My aunt bought you a Christmas present?" Sabrina asked, amused.

Of course, when she thought about it, she could see her aunt doing that. After all, George was her attorney and a friend as well. Brie always knew her to be a loving person, but it was interesting to discover that loving nature extended beyond the family to friends and even strangers.

"Your aunt was a kind person. I have been her attorney for many years, and I can tell you she always talked about you and Sophie. She would get so excited when you were due for a visit. Mildred would call to tell me when you were coming into town."

"Coming here to see her was the highlight of my days. Being with Aunt Millie was like coming home. Can I ask you a question? You said you knew my aunt for years. Do you know anything about her helping people in the community?" Brie dared to ask.

"Yes, I do. Mildred was forever helping someone. She liked to be low-keyed about it. Sometimes she'd stop by and tell me about an individual she had been visiting, or ask me to let your know if I knew of anyone needing assistance. She was very generous in donating her time to help others. Why do you ask?"

"I couldn't help but notice the number of people attending her funeral. For all the times I have been here to visit, I've never heard her talk about having many friends, so to see such a large attendance was quite a surprise. I wondered who they were and how they knew my aunt. Do you know how long she has been helping people?" Sabrina asked, hoping George could fill in some of the missing pieces.

"I've known your aunt for about seven years, and it seems she first mentioned this to me about five years ago. Sometime around then."

"Wow, five years and she never once mentioned it to me," Sabrina said, feeling deflated.

"Sabrina, don't be discouraged by what I've said. Your aunt

was a woman of purpose. I can't think of one time she didn't know exactly what she wanted to do and would carefully implement the necessary action. This is no different. She had a motive for leaving you to discover her life interest this way. Personally, I think she enjoyed leaving a puzzle for you to solve, because that would be just like her," George stated with conviction.

Finding this conversation interesting and running somewhat parallel to what Bella had told her, Sabrina knew she had a lot of serious thinking to do. What was Aunt Millie trying to tell her?

"I'm beginning to understand my aunt had a life I wasn't privy to. Everyone is entitled to their privacy, but it has come as a shock to think there is a big gap in what I thought I knew. Anyway, it wasn't my intent to take up a lot of your time. I merely wanted to stop by for a minute and drop off this present in case I didn't see you before Christmas. Thank you for the conversation," Sabrina stated, standing and reaching across the desk to shake George's hand before leaving his office.

"Thank you, Sabrina and enjoy your new home. Be sure to stay in touch."

"I will," Brie replied.

Sabrina left his office and passing the receptionist wished her a Merry Christmas. Having completed her errands, Brie drove around the downtown district and snapped a few pictures from the car window using her zoom lens. It wasn't her style to take pictures of old buildings, but she found herself fascinated by the history and heritage of the area. Next, she went to the cemetery and took some photos of the gravesite.

She was now ready to return home. She needed to get back to discovering what really took Aunt Millie's life. On the drive back to the house, her mind replayed both conversations. George only confirmed what Bella had told her about Aunt Millie having a lifestyle that she kept private. Brie planned to find out why Aunt Millie handled this the way she did.

It was daunting to discover her aunt's crusade, but Brie was developing a respect for Aunt Millie. She was definitely going to give this matter serious consideration since apparently it meant so much to her. Maybe this wasn't as foolish as Brie first thought when she read the letter. It appears there is more to *Passionate Promises* than she first realized. *This I can't ignore,* she told herself.

Chapter 17

Sabrina picked up her aunt's letter and reread it. Okay, Aunt Millie made herself useful by helping people in need, ran errands, sat and talked to the lonely. There wasn't anything special about doing that, she rationalized. Surely there are a lot of people in the world that help their neighbors and friends and probably even went so far as to help total strangers, she continued to think this through. What made Aunt Millie any different from others, and why did she call it a crusade, giving her good deeds a name? Most of all, why would she expect me to continue it, she wondered. *Aunt Millie, what were you thinking? What is this all about?* Sabrina asked aloud.

Leaving the letter on the table, Brie took a walk through the house starting with the first floor, slowly passing through each room, realizing there wasn't anything she would change. The furniture was Early American mixed with some Traditional making the décor warm and inviting, blending golden pine with dark oak, and the result was perfect for a country house.The second floor bedrooms were done with a Victorian flair in the accessories and decorative furnishings. Sabrina couldn't imagine removing one single item and decided to leave everything as it was.

Stepping into the master bedroom gave Brie a feeling of sadness. This was her aunt's second favorite room. Sabrina didn't enter the master bedroom often because it was in this room she still felt a strong presence. *Strange I feel this way,* she thought.

The king-sized mattress was encased in a huge sleigh-bed of dark cherrywood. A beautifully designed comforter covered the bed with a scatter of brocade throw pillows of all sizes and shapes. Large porcelain print lamps with tasseled shades were on either side atop nightstands. On the opposite wall was a cherrywood armoire which held the television behind two bi-fold doors and three drawers below packed with winter clothing.

Pulling open the first drawer, Sabrina found it stuffed with sweaters. She realized she wasn't ready to give away her aunt's clothes. Brie walked over to the walk-in closet noticing the clothes hanging neatly organized by color and item. This made Sabrina smile because she did the exact same thing; all the blouses, dress slacks, jeans, jackets and so forth.

Sabrina sat on the bed letting herself fall backward, closed her eyes, lying perfectly still listening to any sounds the house might make, but it remained silent. Why did this make her feel so uncomfortable? Being alone was a part of Sabrina's life. It never crossed her mind to question her lifestyle, until now. Why was she feeling she was missing something important? What was causing these feelings of emptiness? Was it the death of her aunt, the mysterious sensation of someone's presence, or perhaps the bombshell letter? She didn't know what to think of everything that had happened since her aunt's death, but it was causing a very unsettled feeling. A moment later, she fell asleep.

"Stay," she heard the voice whisper softly.

"Sabrina, you must search within," the voice continued.

Was she dreaming? She tried to see who was talking to her but the vision was a blur. The voice was softly spoken and there was no shape to the image before her.

"What am I searching for?" Brie asked.

"Dear Sabrina, The answers lie within you. Search deep within your heart and all things will be revealed to you," the wispy voice insisted.

"But I'm not understanding any of this," Brie replied.

"I can only give you guidance, dear one," said the voice.

"Guidance for what? Who are you? Why can't I see you? You keep coming to me, but I don't understand," Sabrina declared to the wispy figure before her.

"In due time, Sabrina, patience. You will come to understand soon," the voice faded.

"Wait, you can't leave me, come back," Sabrina demanded as she watched the figure slip away.

"No, come back! Come back! Wait!" Sabrina woke up shouting into the air.

Rolling over on her side and tucking her hands underneath her cheek, she began to cry, feeling alone and uncertain of what was happening. Sabrina believed what she had just experienced was more than a dream. It was very real to her and though she should be frightened, she didn't feel threatened. She had never been so lonely as she was at this moment. *Did things like this happen to other people? I'm not losing my mind, I'm not losing my mind,* she chanted.

"What is it that you expect me to understand? How can I know, if you don't tell me? Why won't you show me who you are?" she asked aloud.

Knowing there wouldn't be any answers forthcoming, she remained still as the tears slid down her cheeks. If she felt any fear from these encounters, Sabrina knew she would not be able to handle what was happening to her. But because there was a peace that surrounded her during these experiences, she believed it had to be for good.

Sabrina remained there for a long time watching the sun setting through the window. Finally collecting her composure, she walked into the bathroom to splash cool water on her face. She went downstairs to the kitchen to find her cell phone and called her sister.

"Hey sis, how's everything up north?" Sabrina asked with more cheer than she felt.

"Hi Brie, we're having a great time. David is enjoying him-

110

self. I've been doing some shopping with his mom and baking cookies. What have you been doing lately?"

"Lots of things. I've put up a tree, decorated the house, shopped, and visited with Bella. Things like that and it keeps me busy," she told her.

"Aren't you lonely yet?"

"Maybe just a little."

"The offer still stands to join us. There's plenty of room for you and I know that David's parents wouldn't mind," Sophie encouraged her sister.

"I know and thanks, but I plan to stay put."

"Sophie, remember those episodes of my hearing a soft whispering voice? Well, I had a dream and saw a shadowy figure telling me to have patience that everything will be revealed to me soon. I don't know what to make of it," Sabrina told her, solemnly.

"You said it was a dream. That's all it was, Brie, just a dream. I don't think it means anything. Why, do you?"

"Honestly, I don't know. I've read that things can be revealed to people through dreams, and I think it is possible for someone to have a dream foretell of a future event. What I don't understand is why me? What does this have to do with my life?" Sabrina declared on a sigh.

"The only thing you can do is wait it out, but you don't sound afraid. If that was happening to me, I'd be freaking out," Sophie chuckled.

"If I didn't think this had something to do with Aunt Millie's death, I might be joining you. However, I feel strongly this has to do with her since it began at the funeral."

"Maybe whatever it is will be revealed to you while you are there."

"Actually, I hope it does. I want to get to the bottom of what is going on. It's starting to annoy me that I don't know, like trying to put a puzzle together when all you have are the border pieces. Anyway, I wanted to know what your thoughts were. Hope you have fun in the snow when it arrives. I'm still waiting to see some down here," Brie said, changing the subject.

"Try not to put to much thought into this. I know it's really weird, but what can you do but wait and see what happens. Stay in touch, especially if you get anymore encounters of the creepy kind," Sophie said, laughing.

She was trying to cheer her sister.

"You'll be the second to know after me," Sabrina replied, laughing too.

"Talk to you soon, love you, sis."

"Love you back."

Feeling better having talked with her sister, Sabrina went upstairs, turning on lights as she walked toward the master bedroom. She sat down at the desk and stared at the miscellaneous papers piled on top. *Is the answer to the cause of my aunt's death lying somewhere in drawers of this desk,* she contemplated.

Brie skimmed through papers in the large file drawer on the bottom right but found noting out of the ordinary, just typical repair receipts for the car, roof cleaning, lawn service, and so forth. Sabrina didn't know what she was looking for, but was hoping something would surface to explain it.

She came across a folder with the word medical handwritten across the tab. Sabrina took it over to the bed, spread the opened file across the comforter and began reading each page carefully. So far she had uncovered nothing more important than receipts for her annual doctor visits. The recent dates showed her aunt had been for an eye exam and also for a dental check-up. And there were a couple of trips to the doctor for the flu.

Feeling disappointed, she closed the file and replaced it in the desk drawer. She was hoping this folder in particular would reveal some sensible reason for her aunt's death, but she came up blank. *How could someone who took care of their health, got an annual check-up, took no medications, and seemed to be in excellent health suddenly die,* she pondered. Brie wasn't without understanding that sometimes people can have a heart attack or a massive stroke and it happens with no warning. *So is that what happened to Aunt Millie,* she wondered.

Sabrina wished she had thought of having an autopsy performed, realizing she may never know what took her aunt's life. She had no explanation of the events that now plagued her life. How was she going to find the answers? *I have to know,* she told herself.

Chapter 18

Tidying up the mess she had made on the desk, Brie decided to do some investigating around the house, perhaps going through nightstands and closets might reveal something. Since she was already in the master bedroom, she started by going through the three drawers in the armoire, then the nightstands and last the walk-in closet, but nothing sparked a clue.

Sabrina got down on her hands and knees and looked under the bed, finding two long flat plastic bins. Pulling them out and popping off the tops showed them to be full of clothes. Nothing was hidden between skirts, sweaters, and blouses. Brie slid the bins back in place. Where to search next?

She dragged a chair over to the armoire and standing on it, peered over the top. Brie thought she might find something there, but disappointed to see only a thin layer of dust. She stood in the middle of the room and looked around feeling foolish. What did she expect to find, a clue to the cause of her aunt's death, a clue to why she was having strange encounters, a clue to the dreams that were haunting her? *Alright, so I didn't find anything yet, but I will,* she reassured herself. She wasn't giving up.

Believing she had exhausted the search in this room, Sabrina went down the hall to her bedroom and then to the third room across the hall which was her aunt's craft room. Having no luck, she would start again in the morning. With the house well lit, Brie went to bed early and had a fitful night.

The next morning, Sabrina dressed in jeans and a pink fleece pullover, ready to face another day of sleuthing. She ran down the stairs to put on a pot of coffee, anxious to begin and feeling confident that today would be the day she would make a discovery. There had to be a clue in this big house.

After eating a bran muffin with coffee, she went back upstairs ready to tackle each room with a newfound enthusiasm. Looking through everything still left her without evidence. The morning went by in a fury of determination and she was feeling discouraged by noon. She went downstairs and made a sandwich for lunch taking it on a tray into the den, finding comfort in this room where she and her aunt had spent so many hours. It brought back many wonderful memories.

She continued to remain in the chair, curling her legs underneath her and staring into the fireplace. The only sound was the occasional crackling of the wood. Feeling somewhat defeated, Sabrina shifted her thoughts to the mysterious occurrences since the funeral. Closing her eyes and resting her head back on the chair, Brie replayed the initial conversation when Sophie phoned with the news. She began categorizing each detail including where she was when experiencing this unknown phantom voice. *I can't believe I'm actually trying to process something so completely abnormal. Who in their right mind hears voices,* she questioned.

How could she go back to work in less than three weeks if she didn't solve this first? Rather than be rattled about the whole affair, Sabrina took it on as a challenge. She couldn't envision the rest of her life shadowed with this uncharacteristic behavior and was certain that whatever was going on wasn't going to vanish and leave her alone.

After taking the tray to the kitchen, Brie took pad and pen from one of the drawers and returned to sit in the den. She meticulously jotted down in columns of time, place, and occurrence everything she could remember. Where was she when these events took place and was she awake or dreaming? Brie wrote exactly what was said by her aunt and the phantom voice.

After filling in all the details and rechecking the time order, Brie carefully studied the words she had written. She was sure to find the answer somewhere on this paper. She simply needed to figure it out. So far, even Sophie seemed to be oblivious to any strange matters of the unknown kind.

Sabrina was used to doing things on her own, so this wasn't any different. Believing she had made some progress, she smiled to herself tapping the pencil against her chin. She was confident a resolution was forthcoming.

Brie put the notepad on the table to give herself a mental break and get out of the house. She needed to pick up a few grocery items, and maybe afterwards stop by to visit with Bella. Rushing upstairs to change into her favorite cream-colored cashmere sweater and matching corduroy slacks, she added a touch of makeup and brushed her hair back into a ponytail. Brie was never one to spend a lot of time in front of a mirror, but then she didn't need to, she and Sophie were blessed with a natural beauty.

Sabrina was hit with a blast of cold air when she stepped outside. It felt exhilarating to stand on the front sidewalk, take in a deep breath of air, letting it out slowly. She loved the cold weather. Passing the bank showed the temperature to be thirty-eight degrees.

The grocery store wasn't crowded, and she made her way down the isles in no time. She waited patiently with her basket in the twenty-items-or-less checkout lane. The woman in front of her turned around to see who had come up behind her. Brie smiled and the woman returned the smile, turning back facing the cashier. Mere seconds later, she turned back around and looked at Sabrina again, but this time she spoke.

"Aren't you Mildred's niece?" she asked.

"Yes I am," Sabrina replied, politely.

"I thought I recognized you at the funeral," she continued.

"Oh, you knew my aunt?"

"Oh, indeed I did! She saved my life," the woman said.

"What do you mean? What happened?"

"I lost my husband a year ago. We had been married for forty-five years. When he died, I was lost and wanted to die too. I became depressed and didn't want to live anymore. About a month after he was gone, Mildred shows up on my doorstep one morning. I didn't know who she was and refused to open my door when she rang the bell. I didn't want to see anyone. Every single morning at the same time of day for a whole week she was at my front door ringing the doorbell. She wasn't giving up. I became so annoyed that one day I opened the door and yelled at her. I told her I didn't care who she was or what she wanted, but to get off my property and leave me alone. You know what she said to that?" the woman asked with a chuckle.

"I really can't imagine," Brie replied, dumbfounded.

"Mildred smiled at me and said, 'I'm your guardian angel and I've come to relieve you of your burden.' I'll never forget that day as long I as remain alive. She was indeed my guardian angel coming to my rescue, for surely I would have withered away to nothing had it not been for Mildred. She brought me back to life," the woman said with a smile on her face.

"By the way, my name is Annie Middleton. It is so good to meet you. You know, from that moment on, your aunt and I spent a great deal of time together, and she told me about you. She carried pictures of you and your sister in her purse. I recognized you both at the funeral, but I didn't want to bother you by introducing myself," she continued.

Sabrina didn't know how to respond. What do you say after hearing a confession like that? Annie was up at the cash register putting her items on the belt. Feeling a bit foolish but wanting to hear more of the story that concerned her aunt, Brie took the simple approach and asked.

"Annie, I don't mean to be forward, but do you think you and I could get together sometime over coffee? I really want to hear more of your story. Would you mind telling me about it?" Sabrina asked cautiously, hoping she wouldn't refuse.

Turning to face Sabrina, Annie replied with a smile.

"Oh, I'd be delighted. I came to love Mildred like a sister," she said.

"Let me get your phone number," Sabrina replied, reaching for pen and paper from her purse.

Call me anytime," Annie remarked, reciting her number.

"I'll jot mine down for you," Sabrina replied.

"Oh, no need. I have it," Annie told her.

"Thank you, I'll call you soon," Sabrina told her.

When Annie was ready to leave the store, she smiled as she told Sabrina she would be waiting for the call.

On the drive to Bella's house, Sabrina replayed the conversation she had with this stranger. Brie couldn't wait to meet with Annie again, fascinated by what she had just learned. *Was this part of Passionate Promises her aunt talked about in the letter,* Sabrina wondered. Did Annie hold the key to discovering exactly what *Passionate Promises* was all about? Brie thought she had her first, solid clue. Maybe now, she could gather some information to understanding her aunt's legacy. She had a live person to talk to. Engrossed in thought, Sabrina almost missed the turn to Bella's house.

Chapter 19

Sabrina's knock was quickly answered by a flustered Bella.

"Hey Sabrina, come on in," Bella stated heading to the kitchen.

Sabrina followed, taking her coat off as she trailed behind. Setting her coat and purse on a chair at the dinette table, she walked over to the counter to see what Bella was making.

"Have I come at a bad time?"

"Of course not, I'm having a slight problem with a new recipe. I can't seem to get the taste right on these pumpkin pies. Here, try this and tell me what's missing?" Bella asked, handing Brie a spoon full of pumpkin pie mix from the bowl.

"It's bland as cardboard. There must be a misprint in this recipe book because I followed the instructions, but I have a bowl of orange soup," Bella remarked, discouraged.

Taking the spoon and tasting the liquid, Sabrina knew exactly what it needed. She had made plenty of pumpkin pies from her mother's recipe. But first, she took a look at the recipe book Bella was following to see what she had put into this concoction.

"Bella, today is your lucky day. It just so happens I'm the queen of pumpkin pie makers," Sabrina told her, laughing.

"My hero, so tell me, Sabrina, what's wrong with my mixture?"

"Well, it's going to cost you. Salvaging a pumpkin pie is serious business," Sabrina declared, holding a straight face.

"Anything, name your price. I'll pay whatever you say," Bella replied, enjoying Sabrina's companionship.

Their bantering was such a delight for both women they couldn't contain themselves and burst into laughter. Bella drew Sabrina into her arms for a big hug. *What a delightful person Sabrina is,* she thought. She could truly understand why her friend Mildred had treasured her niece's visits.

"Let's see. Do you have another can of pumpkin? We need to thicken this up a bit," Sabrina commented, checking labels to see what spices were on the counter.

"Do you have any nutmeg and clove?"

"Coming right up," Bella answered, pulling out a three-tier spice rack from her pantry.

Spinning it around, she located the requested spices. Opening a large can of pumpkin, Sabrina went to work. Tossing in additional pumpkin did the trick to thicken the consistency. Brie wasn't one for measuring out increments when she cooked. She preferred to add what seemed like the right amount, stir, and do a taste test. Throwing in more cinnamon, clove, and lots of nutmeg brought the pie mixture to a flavorful blend.

"It needs one more ingredient. Do you have vanilla extract?" Sabrina asked, stirring with a whisk.

"I think I have some in the refrigerator."

Handing Sabrina the bottle, she watched Brie pour the extract into the mix and whipped it around, pouring a tad more. Picking up the spoon, she sampled the pie filling.

"Perfect," Brie declared.

Bella took a spoon, tried it, and then looked at Sabrina with a smile.

"Now, I'll have to pay whatever you ask," Bella stated with humor.

"That's right, and I ask for a piece of this pie."

"That's easy. We'll have pie and coffee when it's done."

Bella poured the mixture into two deep-dished pie shells, slid them on the oven rack, and set the timer while Sabrina began cleaning up the dishes. She made some sudsy water and wiped down the countertops and washed the dishes, leaving them to dry on the drainboard. With the kitchen back in order, Bella put on a pot of coffee to brew.

"Where did you learn to make pumpkin pies? You didn't measure your ingredients. How did you know if you were putting too much of one and not enough of another?" Bella asked.

"I watched my mother bake all kind of treats, and I learned everything I know from her. She never measured her ingredients, and so I do the same thing."

"Well, whatever your technique, it certainly works. If those pies taste half as good cooked as they did in the bowl, then we are in for a real treat."

"Oh, they'll be because it's my mother's recipe," Sabrina remarked, proudly.

"Let's go sit down while we wait on them to bake."

Bella placed two cups of fresh coffee along with the cream and sugar bowl on a tray and took it to the small dinette table. Brie reached for a cup and added her usual cream and sugar. The coffee was hot and delicious; a tasty Christmas blend. Shortly, the aroma of pumpkin filled the kitchen, making a wonderful holiday fragrance.

It gave Sabrina the idea of making her own pumpkin pies and she made a mental list of what she would need. Enjoying spending the afternoon with Bella while they waited for the pies to bake, she asked about her aunt helping people in the community, and Bella was delighted to talk about her best friend. She stated that on a few occasions she would go with Mildred to pick up a prescription or groceries for someone but remained in the car and waited. Neither realized they had sat for an hour talking until the oven timer went off. Bella told Sabrina she would soon have her reward.

"Bella, have you ever heard of *Passionate Promises*?" Sabrina asked, taking the plunge wanting to find out if Aunt Millie confided in her best friend.

"Yes and no. If you are referring to Mildred's activities, then yes; to the specific name then no. She mentioned a couple of times about giving a title to what she did. I don't mean like a business entity, but rather putting some kind of an identity to her services. I never questioned her. Why do you ask?"

"I came across a letter she left for me, and she wrote about doing good deeds in the community and called it *Passionate Promises*. She also implied that she was guided on this path. She wants Sophie and me to continue it. I thought you might know something about it. I didn't realize my aunt did any type of community service so, you can imagine, it was a shock to find out after her death. I'm really trying to understand all of this," Sabrina explained, feeling like she was babbling.

"Mildred was a private person. It simply wasn't her nature to reveal her personal business. However, as best friends, I can say that I did know she felt compelled to help others and mentioned to me once that she believed she was being led. We didn't discuss it because I could tell it was something private, so I never pressed the issue. Don't take it to heart, it was just her way," Bella tried to explain.

She didn't want Sabrina to have a misconception of her aunt for not sharing a very important aspect of her life. Both women fell silent to their own thoughts. Sabrina didn't want to push Bella for information she wasn't comfortable revealing. The subject was dropped.

Bella checked on the cooling pies and sliced two pieces. They enjoyed eating warm pie with a second cup of coffee. Sabrina didn't care if her pie was still too hot to eat because she loved pumpkin pie.

"This is some good pumpkin pie. You'll have to write down the recipe for me, but give me a general idea of the amount of each ingredient. I don't think I can do a pinch here and sprinkle there like you do," Bella stated with a chuckle.

"I'll jot it down and give it to you the next time I see you."

After finishing their pie and coffee, Bella walked to the counter to wrap a pie while Sabrina put the dishes in the sink.

When she turned around, Bella offered the pie to her.

"Here, take this with you."

"No, it's your pie. I'm going to make one for myself."

"You made the pies, so at least take one home with you."

"Seriously, Bella, you keep it but thanks anyway," Sabrina said softly, not wanting to hurt her feelings.

"Alright, but I can't promise there will be any left when you return."

"Fair enough."

Slipping on her coat, Brie walked toward the foyer and turned, giving Bella a warm embrace before leaving. It had been a wonderful visit with her aunt's best friend. Somehow she felt she knew her aunt a little better, and a feeling of pride came over her.

Chapter 20

Sabrina was going to make two pies and indulge in a slice every night until Christmas, her little treat for the holidays. Some people indulged in chocolate, but Brie preferred pumpkin. There were only two holidays in the entire year she could enjoy her favorite dessert. Since those ran in close proximity on the calendar, she didn't get to enjoy pumpkin pie that often.

She placed a couple of logs in the fireplace and had a blaze going, giving the room a warm glow. She reminisced about meeting Annie and the conversation with Bella. These two women helped Brie understand an aspect of her aunt's character she had not known. She retrieved her cell phone to call her sister.

"Hi Sophie, what are you doing?" Sabrina asked first.

"Brie, somehow when I heard my phone ring, I knew it would be you," Sophie replied.

"Oh really, without looking at the caller ID."

"Yes, without looking. What's new in your life?"

"You'd be amazed. I ran into a lady in the grocery store today who said Aunt Millie saved her life."

"No kidding! How did Aunt Millie do that?"

"She said her husband had passed away about a year ago and she fell into a deep depression. Aunt Millie pulled her out of it. Get this, she said Aunt Millie came to her house claiming to be her guardian angel."

"Oh my goodness, Aunt Millie called herself a guardian angel. That's really over the top, don't you think?"

"Perhaps to you and me, but Annie was serious. We didn't get to talk further because we were standing in the checkout line, but I want to meet with her and find out more."

"What is there to find out? Maybe Aunt Millie had a loose marble we didn't know about. I mean, if someone knocked on my door and said that to me, I would be shutting the door in their face."

"I can understand that. However, I went to visit with Bella afterwards, and she helped shed some light on *Passionate Promises*. She told me she knew of Aunt Millie's community services and confirmed that Aunt Millie believed she was inspired to do this."

"Wow, what a shocker!"

"I know! I want to understand what motivated Aunt Millie to go to her house in the first place, and why declare that to a perfect stranger. Why would she call herself a guardian angel?"

Apparently, I didn't know her as well as I thought I did. She is leaving a legacy I want to understand, and I don't want to walk away and forget it. This is important. I can't really explain why I feel this way, but I do. So I'm going to meet with Annie and hear her story," Sabrina stated a bit too forcefully.

"Okay. I didn't mean to upset you, Brie. I know how much Aunt Millie meant to you. If this will bring closure then by all means, see what you can discover. I know you're taking this letter personally. I'm not begrudging you for wanting to know what motivated Aunt Millie. I just don't feel the seriousness of the letter as you do," Sophie stated with a calmness she didn't feel.

She hoped Sabrina wasn't going over the edge. Not understanding any of this herself, Sophie wanted Brie to come to terms with this soon and put it behind her.

"Don't worry, Sophie. I'm not overreacting, I'm just trying to get to the bottom of these unusual events. Besides, what else am I going to do with all this free time?"

She could tell her sister wasn't into finding answers and that was okay. This didn't involve her anyway. Ending the conversation on a solemn note, they promised to talk again in a few days. Sabrina wasn't discouraged by her sister's lack of enthusiasm.

Brie went into the living room and looked out the front window. It was already dark outside, and the temperature would be dropping into the twenties. She hoped to get lucky and see a few flakes of white before returning to Florida.

Sabrina made some herbal tea and with cup in hand walked around the first floor through the formal dining room, circling the huge walnut table and six upholstered chairs. She crossed the foyer into the living room where for a moment she stared at a beautiful oil painting of a wintry scene before walking back around to the den. She had not begun searching these rooms and thought tomorrow she would tackle this area. Brie also wanted to call Annie and make plans to meet for coffee. As she was contemplating making the phone call, the house phone rang, startling Sabrina. It was the first time the phone had rung. She walked into the kitchen and picked it up.

"Hello," she answered, apprehensively.

"Sabrina, is that you?" the caller asked.

"Who is this?" Brie countered.

"It's Ben Cooper from the *Cooper Christmas Tree Farm.* I'm sorry if I spooked you. I had Mildred's phone number in our records," he said as a means of explanation.

"Ben, of course. It seems strange to get a call on the house phone."

"I would have called before now, but we stay very busy this time of year. Anyway, I was hoping to take that raincheck for coffee, if it still holds."

"Absolutely, the raincheck is good for another two weeks."

"Wow, I called just in time then. Good for only two more weeks, huh?"

"Yep, that's when I head home."

"Where would you like to go for coffee?"

"How about *The Country Kitchen* near my house. I can meet you there tomorrow around six o'clock."

"That works. So I have only two weeks to get to know you. Be prepared to do a lot of talking tomorrow night," Ben told her with a chuckle.

"Talking won't be a problem. Good night, Ben Cooper, and I'll see you tomorrow."

Sabrina had been in such deep thought over Aunt Millie that it took her by surprise to get a call from Ben. With everything that had happened recently, she had completely forgotten about him. She was delighted with the prospect of seeing him and could hardly wait until tomorrow evening. *Maybe a brief diversion would be good at the moment,* she thought.

It was late, but Sabrina wasn't sleepy so she went back to sit by the fire. There were so many thoughts racing through her mind. *How am I ever going to resolve these issues,* she mused. The house was warm and cozy and Brie enjoyed watching the wood burning in the fireplace. It was mesmerizing, almost hypnotic.

Her mind slipped into thoughts of her phantom voice and Brie realized she had not heard from it lately. That was probably a very good thing; however, it didn't help Sabrina find out who it was and why it appeared in the first place. Why were these appearances erratic? Was there something she was inadvertently saying, or perhaps thinking that brought on these occurrences? *I should be more worried about my sanity at the moment, than wanting to conjure up a vision. How weird is that?* she scolded herself.

Chapter 21

Sabrina took her time getting ready for the date, at least, she thought of it as a date. Applying a slightly darker blush and using warm tones of brown and cream eye shadows gave her a more dramatic look. She let her hair down where it skimmed the top of her shoulders. Brie placed a decorative clip on the right side pulling the hair behind the ear. She dressed in chocolate brown wool slacks with a soft beige turtleneck sweater and brown ankle boots and completed the ensemble with a soft brown tweed jacket.

She glanced at her reflection in the full-length mirror in the master bedroom. Brie liked to dress casual chic, a style that could go anywhere and feel comfortable. While looking in the mirror, she thought she saw a glimpse of a reflection just behind her to the left. Brie spun around looking into the bedroom, but no one was there. Sabrina knew she should be petrified, but again, she had no fear.

"I know you are in this room. Please reveal yourself. I'm trying to make contact. I want to understand why you're coming to me," Sabrina spoke.

Silence.

"Alright, perhaps another time," she said, nonchalantly.

Brie knew it would do no good to become upset. She would have to wait it out. *I'm talking to a vision. No one would believe me if I told them about this. They would think I've lost all my marbles*, she thought.

Brushing it off, Sabrina went downstairs to get her purse and cell phone before leaving. It was only a ten minute drive to the restaurant, and Brie was looking forward to the evening. A few hours of conversation over a good cup of coffee was plenty of entertainment for her. Basically, Sabrina considered herself a low-maintenance woman and that included her social calendar.

Brie pulled into a designated parking spot near the front door, locked the car, and walked inside. The warmth of the restaurant was inviting, along with the aroma of food cooking on a grill. Sabrina arrived a few minutes early and not seeing Ben, went toward a table near the back and slid into the booth. A waitress came over immediately with a menu and glass of water. Brie explained she was waiting for someone and would order when the other party arrived. Sipping on the cold water, she spotted Ben coming through the door and waved her hand.

"Hi Ben, right on time," Sabrina spoke first when he approached the table.

"Hello Sabrina, have I kept you waiting?"

"No, I just arrived a couple minutes before you, so good timing."

Spotting the newcomer, the waitress brought over another menu and glass of water. Handing the menu to Ben, she acknowledged his presence. Apparently they knew each other. Sabrina discovered he was a regular at the diner. They chatted for a moment, and she left to get two cups of coffee Ben had requested. It was understandable this small restaurant would be favored because the food was delicious.

"I eat here quite often when I'm making deliveries. Best place in town for a good home-cooked meal," Ben remarked.

"I think you might be right. I've had the opportunity to eat here a few times, and I haven't been disappointed yet. My weakness is the breakfast pancakes," Brie replied.

Ben made introductions when their waitress returned with the coffee.

"Dorothy, this is Sabrina Fitzgerald. Sabrina, meet Dorothy

Owens," Ben spoke politely.

"Of course, I should have recognized you when you came in. You're Mildred's niece. She showed me a picture of you. Mildred came in here often for coffee and a blueberry muffin, said it was her indulgence when she had a sweet tooth. I'm really sorry for your loss. She was a wonderful person," Dorothy told her.

"Did you know my aunt well?" Sabrina asked.

"Somewhat, she was a regular customer. One day I was complaining to one of my coworkers about mounting medical bills. I didn't realize Mildred overheard my conversation. You see, my husband had an accident at his workplace and injured his back. He had to go on disability but until that came through, the medical bills were piling up. We have three kids, one in high school and two in middle school. It was hard for us on just one income. Anyway, about a week later, I came into work one morning and there was a large manila envelope with my name written across it. When I opened it, another smaller envelope was inside with a note attached. It simply said, use wisely and signed, your guardian angel. There was a thousand dollars in that envelope. I asked my co-workers who left it. At the time, we had a young girl who had just started at the restaurant and she described the woman who handed her the envelope. I knew immediately the description fit Mildred. When I confronted her the next time she came in, she just smiled and placed her order for coffee and a muffin. She never admitted or denied giving me the money, but I know it was her," Dorothy explained, practically in tears telling her story.

"I tried to give the money back, but she said it wasn't hers to receive. I held onto it for as long as I could, but then little by little, I relied on it to pay for a prescription, or the electric bill or something. I knew it was her money, but what was I to do when she wouldn't take it back?" she continued, defended her actions.

Overwhelmed by Dorothy's story, Sabrina didn't know what to say.

"Well, if she gave you the money then she had a reason for doing so. Obviously, she meant for you to have it," Sabrina declared, stunned by yet another revelation of her aunt's life.

"Your aunt was truly my guardian angel. That money came at a time when I needed it most.I was struggling to keep my family going on a waitress' salary."

"How long ago was this?"

"Two years. My husband was out of work for almost a year. Things are back to normal now. Your aunt was a blessing to us."

"Thank you for sharing this with me," Sabrina stated.

Shocked, Sabrina sat for a moment collecting her thoughts. That was two people in two days who had a story to tell about Aunt Millie. With her mind whirling from this knowledge, Brie completely disconnected from Ben sitting across the table.

"Earth to Sabrina," Ben said, teasingly.

"Oh I'm sorry, I was thinking about what Dorothy just said. That's an amazing story."

"What? That your aunt helped a family in need."

"Yes, people don't just give a stranger a thousand dollars."

"Well, I'm not surprised. She was a very nice person, and I can actually see her helping a stranger."

"There are a lot of nice people in the world, but they don't go around handing out money."

"True, but perhaps this was your aunt's calling."

"What does that mean?"

"Maybe this is what she was supposed to do."

"I'm not following you. You'll have to spell it out for me. What are you trying to say?"

She leaned forward and crossed her arms on the edge of the table.

"I didn't come here to discuss your aunt. I would rather talk about you, but since you asked. I'm just saying perhaps she felt compelled, or had a passion to help the helpless; something along those lines," Ben defended his previous comment as he leaned back in the booth.

"What do you mean by *what she is supposed to do*? Is there something you know about my aunt that you aren't willing to tell me? If so, I would really appreciate your sharing it with me," Sabrina replied, firmly.

"No, I'm not keeping anything from you. I really can't say I knew your aunt that well. Mildred had been buying her tree from our family for years, and I spent a fair amount of time having brief conversations with her. Besides, this is a small community, people run into each other and news travels."

"Why did you think it was a passion to help people?"

"Like I said, word travels. Take Dorothy's story. When I first heard it and having known Mildred, my first impression was I was hearing compassion. She gave freely and willingly, no strings attached. In fact, it was done secretly. I think that is awesome. How many would do that today?"

"That's my point. People don't do things like this."

"Perhaps, not in the general crowd, but then again, how do we know she wasn't led to do this?" Ben questioned, again countering her statement.

"Okay. I get it now. Led by God to be a guardian angel and help the helpless and downtrodden. Sure, why not," Sabrina stated sarcastically, remembering the letter.

"Sabrina, pardon me for asking, but why does that offend you? Why is this so hard to believe of your aunt?" Ben asked, taken back by her attitude.

Remaining silent for a moment, Brie sipped her now cold coffee trying to collect her thoughts. Did she really want to explain herself to this person sitting across the table? Taking a deep breath, she decided it couldn't do any harm to give it a try. She didn't have anything to lose. After all, she could walk away tonight and never have to see him again.

"I think most of all, I'm hurt as well as disappointed that I didn't know my aunt as well as I thought I did. That doesn't sit well with me at the moment. Then to hear Dorothy's story just put me on edge. I realize I should be proud of what she did and I am, really, but it's hard for me to think of her with any kind of

132

spiritual connotation to her life. Passion, compassion, guardian angel, helping people, and all that is fine and good. I applaud it, but I'm trying to come to terms with how that fits with the Aunt Millie I've known my entire life."

"I can accept that. I believe your aunt was a special person, probably more so than she wanted anyone to know. Respect her choices and carry the love in your heart I know you have for her and let that be enough for the time being," Ben said, encouragingly.

Sabrina looked into his eyes and saw the empathy he had for her. As the words he had just spoken registered, tears welled up. She felt so ashamed. A single tear ran down her left check as she bent her head forward. Ben reached across the table, and gently with the tip of his index finger tucked it under her chin and raised her head. He quickly swiped his thumb pad across her cheek removing the droplet.

"You're absolutely right, Ben. Could we get fresh coffee and start over?" she asked, solemnly.

"You bet."

He raised his hand to catch their waitress' attention showing two fingers extended. Dorothy caught sight bringing over two cups of fresh coffee and removing the cold ones. Brie added cream and sugar and sat silently for a moment stirring her coffee. She felt awkward and didn't know quite how to continue.

"How long have you lived here?" she asked.

Sabrina wanted desperately to change the subject. She couldn't handle any more raw emotions at the moment.

"Off and on since I was ten, when my family moved here from Missouri to take over the tree farm."

"Where did you live in the off time?"

"I left long enough to go to college in Gainesville, Florida, actually, and came back to help with the family business."

"What was your major?" Brie continued, beginning to get curious about this stranger sitting across from her.

He isn't a bad looking man, she thought, studying his face.

She guessed him to be in his early thirties. Ben was much taller than she was, with broad shoulders and muscular arms. He wore his brown hair long enough to touch the top of his ears and had dark brown eyes. The shadow of a beard on tanned skin gave him a rugged look. Brie realized she liked what she saw. He was very masculine.

"Horticulture, my grandfather spent a lot of time with me. He would take me into the woods around our house and teach me about the various trees, bushes, plants, and flowers. He was an encyclopedia of information. I learned a lot from him and developed such a love of nature that it was the right choice when it came time for college. Besides, I knew that someday I would be the next generation responsible for the family business," Ben explained, proudly.

"If my memory serves me well, you are a photojournalist, right?"

"How did you know that? Wait, don't answer, Aunt Millie," Sabrina said, raising her right hand in the air to forestall his answer.

Ben tipped his head and smiled.

"It seems my aunt was a busy woman. I would visit every chance I could to relax between assignments, which was about every two or three months. Sometimes I was able to stretch my stay to two weeks."

"It's too bad we didn't have the opportunity to meet before now and under far better circumstances," he told her.

"I agree. For all the times I've been here, our paths never crossed. Of course, had I been here during the holidays, I could have very well been helping my aunt pick her tree. Then who knows what would have transpired. About my aunt, thanks for what you said earlier," Brie said with understanding.

She wanted him to know she really did appreciate his words.

"You're welcome, Sabrina. Just have peace in knowing she was a wonderful person and received pleasure from helping others. She will be rewarded for that."

"You mean rewarded in heaven."

"Exactly."

Brie didn't mean for their conversation to drift back to Aunt Millie, because she was done talking about her for the evening. Steering back to Ben, she asked him about his family.

"Do you have any brothers or sisters?" she inquired.

"No brothers, but two sisters. Sarah is the oldest. She's thirty-six, married with two small children and lives in California. Jennifer is twenty-four and going to college in Florida; Jenny wants to be a veterinarian. I know you have an identical twin who is a teacher in Orlando," Ben volunteered.

"Wow, you may know more about me than I know about myself," Brie replied a bit sarcastically.

This evening with Ben wasn't what she expected, and seemed to have gotten off on the wrong footing talking about her aunt. Hearing another explanation of Aunt Millie's life wasn't comforting, though it should have been. *Why is this putting me on edge,* she questioned.

She wasn't sure why it had that effect. How much of her and Sophie's life had Aunt Millie shared with the people in this community? She was finding it a bit unnerving crossing paths with strangers who knew about her. Perhaps under different circumstances, she might have been flattered, but this was making her feel very uncomfortable. This time Ben broke the brief silence that fell between them.

"Tell me about your family. Where do your parents live?" he asked, shifting the conversation.

"Our parents were killed in a boating accident when Sophie and I were in our freshman year at college. Mom and Dad had gone out on a boat with some friends, and they hit a huge rock in the middle of the lake. Everyone was thrown off. No one survived. Apparently, they didn't know the water level was down due to lack of rain. When they hit the underwater cluster, we were told the boat went airborne and flipped, landing back in the water upside down in two pieces," Sabrina said, quietly.

"I'm so sorry. How did you and Sophie handle something

that devastating? You must have been only nineteen when it happened."

"We had just celebrated our birthday a month before. It's bad enough to lose one parent, but both at the same time is unbelievably hard. We only had Aunt Millie after that. She came down to Florida for the funeral and stayed a few weeks to help us settle our parent's affairs."

"I can't imagine the pain associated with that kind of a loss."

"We wanted to drop out of school for a while, but Aunt Millie encouraged us to continue and we did. We had each other and our friends. Life does somehow go on, even in tragedy," Sabrina stated on a sigh.

"I'd like to get to know you better and while you're here, we can spend some time together. What do you think?" Ben asked, wondering if the timing was right.

Ben seemed to be a very nice man. It had been a long time since Sabrina had the time or inclination to date because her schedule simply didn't allow much freedom for a personal life. Brie decided to give it a try and enjoy the companionship during the holidays. *After all, it might actually be fun to see what dating felt like again,* she thought.

"Sounds like a great idea, but just to let you know, I'm only here until December 29th. I have to go to work," Sabrina explained, glad for the change in subject.

"Are you free Saturday afternoon? We could start with a walk through the downtown area. It's pretty festive this time of year, and there is usually some entertainment during the weekend and nice restaurants we could choose from for dinner."

"Perfect, why don't you pick me up around three?"

"Good. Would you like some pie with your coffee?" Ben asked, motioning for the waitress.

Dorothy came and took Ben's order for a slice of coconut cream pie and Sabrina indulged in pumpkin. Within minutes, Dorothy returned toting a large tray. For a short woman, she certainly was good at juggling, placing the two plates and fresh cups of coffee on the table with finesse.

They enjoyed the homemade pies and kept their conversation on a lighter note. When finished, each was ready to leave. Ben left money on the table to cover the check with a hefty tip before walking out together. He escorted Sabrina the few steps to her car. It was too cold to linger outside in the dark, so he confirmed the time on Saturday and they quickly said their goodbyes. Sabrina unlocked her car and climbed behind the wheel, looking up in time to see Ben disappear around the corner.

Sabrina wasn't in the best of moods when she returned home. Feelings of melancholy weren't helping her frame of mind after encountering another revealing story about her aunt and reliving the memories of her parent's death. She thought about the things Ben said. She walked into the den and lit a fire before settling in the rocker. Sabrina noticed the letter on the table. *Aunt Millie, why didn't you tell me?* she spoke aloud.

She picked up the letter and read it again. Though the reason for her aunt's desire to play the guardian angel role was becoming clearer, it still didn't explain why she withheld the information all these years. Brie had no problem with what her aunt did with her time, but it was the secrecy and the apparent fact that her aunt wanted her to continue her work that bothered her.

Even if Brie did give this consideration, she wasn't sure how it could possibly work with her work schedule. Sophie, on the other hand, would be perfect, a real social butterfly. She'd have to talk to her sister in more detail after the holidays and try to encourage her to take on *Passionate Promises*. That way the legacy would continue.

Chapter 22

In the days that followed, Sabrina enjoyed spending time with Ben. They did simple things like take walks in the park, stroll in and out of the little specialty shops, and take night drives to look at Christmas decorations. Brie had never taken the time to enjoy these simple things, nor did she ever have anyone special to do them with before now. It was never a priority in her life because she traveled so much, but it felt good to be with someone whose companionship she enjoyed.

She and Ben discovered they had many things in common. They both like the old classic movies and preferred slow dancing to hopping around wildly on a dance floor, though they had not tried that yet. Even though their time together would be brief, neither felt an urgency to rush their newfound friendship. Brie appreciated that about Ben. She liked keeping the company of someone who didn't place demands on her.

From the time she graduated from college, Brie hit the pavement running with a career that kept her in constant motion, which left no time to develop a long-lasting relationship with anyone. Sabrina was enjoying her one month sabbatical, learning there was more to life than work, inasmuch as she loved what she did. She was realizing she wanted more, much more.

And why can't I have a life outside work, she thought. She just never took the time or initiative to seek a personal life, being happy that her career satisfied her completely. Things were changing and Sabrina was discovering she wanted and needed something she was unable to identify. *Maybe Ben is part of what I need in my life. Would he be the one to fill this void I suddenly find myself experiencing,* she considered.

It was two days before Christmas, and her time was quickly coming to an end when she would have to return to Florida and onward to her next assignment. She had yet to resolve her aunt's death for her own peace of mind. Sabrina decided the only way to put an end to the uncertainty was to contact Aunt Millie's doctor and find out if she had a serious health condition that she wasn't able to detect by going through her general papers.

Brie called her aunt's doctor and asked for her medical records. The young woman answering the phone explained she would have to prove her relationship before they could release them. Sabrina told the receptionist she could bring a copy of her aunt's death certificate along with the first page of the Last Will and Testament, which signified Brie's relationship as her niece and last living relative. The receptionist stated that would be acceptable and a copy of the records would be ready for pick-up the next day. Sabrina was anxious to get this medical information. She wanted an explanation of her death that would make some sense of its sudden nature.

Sabrina drove to Dr. Webster's office first thing in the morning to retrieve the copy and then to *The Country Kitchen* for a stack of warm pancakes for breakfast. When she returned to work, there wouldn't be anymore indulging in pancakes. This was a holiday treat.

She settled into a booth in the back corner, to watch the people. It reminded Sabrina she had completely forgotten to call Annie. Making a mental note to do so, she sipped on her second cup of coffee, and when Brie looked up she saw Bella entering the restaurant. Bella spotted Sabrina and walked back to her booth.

"Hey Sabrina, you are out early this morning," Bella stated, sliding into the opposite bench.

"Yep, I had a taste for pancakes."

Sabrina didn't want to reveal she was out getting her aunt's medical records. She thought her investigation might upset Bella. Besides, it wasn't necessary to inform Bella of her actions.

"I wish it would snow for Christmas. Some winters we get snow and then others we don't. This one looks like we may not."

"My wish is to see snow. In my travels I have been in areas of the country were the snow was knee deep, but it would be special to have a white Christmas here," Sabrina agreed.

A waitress came over with a steaming cup of coffee and sat it down in front of Bella. All the waitresses were familiar with her coming in for coffee and to pass the time. Sabrina was enjoying her neighbor's company on a cold December morning in a small diner in the foothills of Asheville. She found herself liking her stay in the country, each day feeling more at home which was surprising. It was definitely a slower pace of living. Brie was beginning to desire to add this new dimension to her life. She wanted friendships and a relationship with a man, but realized in order to enjoy them she'd have to slow down her pace.

"How much longer will you be staying with us?" Bella asked.

"I leave right after Christmas."

"Well, it certainly has been a joy having you here."

"I've enjoyed being here this holiday. It never occurred to me that I would like being in the country for any length of time, but it has been good to be away from the fast pace for awhile."

"Please don't stay away. You have been a breath of fresh air."

"Oh, I've pretty much made up my mind to come back as often as my schedule allows. There is a definite peacefulness to living here. I'm not sure if it is the country air, or being in my aunt's home."

"For a city girl, you have adapted quite well to the country. Perhaps you have more country blood in you than you realize, or maybe you've reached a place in your life that your priorities have changed, but whatever brings you back, I will be glad to see you again."

"Thank you, Bella. You've been so kind to me, and I can see why you and Aunt Millie were such good friends. In many ways, you remind me of her."

"I hope that is a good thing."

"Absolutely, we both have Aunt Millie in our lives," Sabrina said with a smile.

"Don't forget my party tomorrow night."

"I wouldn't miss it for anything. Even if I was snowed in, I would find a way to be there."

"Well, I should be going. I have a few errands before heading home," Bella stated, reaching inside her purse to cover the cost of her coffee.

"Coffee is on me."

Just when Bella was standing to leave, the waitress came over with a large stack of multi-grain and nut pancakes and sat them in front of Sabrina.

"Are you going to eat all of those?"

"Probably not. I'll share. Why don't you have some?" Brie asked, beginning to cut the stack in half.

"You talked me into it," Bella replied, sitting back down.

Sabrina motioned the waitress over and asked for an extra plate and fresh coffee. Both women became self-absorbed in the enjoyment of fresh homemade pancakes.

"These sure are good. I'll miss eating pancakes when I go home, but no more once I leave," Sabrina remarked, pushing the empty plate away.

"That's too bad."

Brie pulled out her wallet, leaving a tip on the table before they walked together toward the front to the cash register, and Sabrina paid the bill.

"Thanks for the breakfast. I didn't mean to get a free meal."

"My treat."

"Don't forget my party tomorrow," Bella reminded her as they were leaving the restaurant.

"Oh, I'll be there at seven sharp!"

"Good."

Sabrina climbed behind the wheel of the car and pointed it in the direction of home. Each day that passed, she enjoyed country living more and more and knew it was going to be hard to leave when the time came. Visiting in the past was different than having lived here for a month. Not being in airports, hotels, restaurants, and driving through city limits to her scheduled destination was new to her. *Slowing down has it rewards. And here I thought I might get bored,* she thought to herself.

Chapter 23

Settling into the rocker with the medical records, Sabrina began reading each page of her aunt's visits to the doctor. Thus far, nothing appeared out of the ordinary. There were appointments for regular check ups, flu, bronchitis three years back, and allergies. No indication of any major health issue she was being treated for. The records went back ten years. Surely if she had some major disease or health concern, it would be notated in her medical chart. Brie was finding nothing to point in that direction, which was good her aunt didn't have anything serious, but at the same time, it didn't explain why she died so suddenly. Sabrina called her sister after reading through the papers.

"Hi Sophie, are you ready for Christmas?" Brie asked as soon as she heard her sister's voice.

"I can't wait. I'm as excited as a kid. Anything new going on?" Sophie asked.

"A couple of things; I've met a very nice man and his name is Bennaird Cooper," Sabrina said, whimsically.

"You go girl! I need details," Sophie told her, laughing.

"I thought you might approve."

Sabrina hadn't confided in her sister that she had been spending time with Ben. She didn't know if they would click, so no sense getting her sister excited about her dating someone until there was something to tell. Besides, she was just having fun enjoying his company during her holiday reprieve.

"Well, let's see. He's talk, dark, and handsome and the family's third generation of Christmas tree farmers. He has two sisters; one older, married and the younger in college."

"Is it getting serious?"

"It has potential. Our dates have been casual, like walks through the downtown shops, or a ride to look at Christmas lights. We've been doing things like that, which have been fun."

"Will you continue to see him when you go back to work? I mean you'd have to make more trips back to Asheville."

"I think so. Of course, that would probably depend more on Ben."

"Do you believe a relationship is blossoming?"

"I think there could be. I'm not rushing into anything or making more of our friendship than exists at the moment, after all, we've barely known each other two weeks. However, I will admit that I feel like we are moving into the initial stages of a relationship."

"I understand, but I would hate for you to let him slip through your hands if he could be your Mr. Right. Good men are hard to find these days. You probably don't realize that because you haven't been looking, but trust me, there aren't a lot of good ones left," Sophie explained, feeling she needed to look out for her twin.

"I'll take your advice into consideration," Brie said, laughing.

"You do that!" Sophie exclaimed, laughing too.

"Sophie, I called to tell you I obtained a copy of Aunt Millie's medical records from her primary care doctor and just finished reading through them. She had been going to a Dr. Morton Webster for several years, but nothing in the records revealed anything other than flu and allergies, simple things like that. No indication she was referred to a specialist for any condition. I don't know where else to consider looking."

"Maybe it was a heart attack," Sabrina explained.

"How was her blood pressure and cholesterol?" Sophie questioned.

"Perfect. By all indications, she was in excellent health which is why it is so hard to accept her death without a valid explanation."

"I agree, but there are a lot of things in life that can't be explained. Maybe we have to accept it was her time to leave us."

"I understand what you're saying, but I wanted to justify her death," Sabrina told her sister, frustrated knowing it was time to end the search.

"Let it go, Brie. We simply aren't going to know what happened to Aunt Millie, and there is nothing either of us can do about it," Sophie told her.

"I suppose so. At least I feel I tried my best and did what I knew to do."

"That's right. So don't beat yourself up because you couldn't validate the cause of her death. We have to accept the death certificate. She died of a heart attack. It's time to put Aunt Millie to rest."

"You're right. I need to let it go," Brie said, changing the subject.

"I'm going to a party at Bella's house on Christmas Eve, but I'll call you before I leave."

Sabrina felt more at ease having talked to her sister. Of course, Sophie was right. It was time to put Aunt Millie to rest in her mind and heart. There would be no explanation of what took place that morning when she stood at her kitchen sink. Sabrina and Sophie would never know the true reason they lost their last living relative.

Believing she had done everything to research Aunt Millie's death, Brie took the envelope of medical records upstairs and filed it away in the desk drawer. In doing so, she was closing the door to searching any further and accepting the cause indicated on the death certificate. What else could she do? *I'm sorry, Aunt Millie. I wanted to know what happened to you. How could you die so suddenly?* she spoke aloud.

Sabrina returned to the den and sat staring into the fireplace, watching sparks shoot off the burning wood, reminiscing about all the times she had stayed in this house. The next day was Christmas Eve. In years past, it hadn't bothered Sabrina to be alone at Christmas, but this year, it made her feel sad that she wouldn't be with family.

Perhaps her aunt knew her better than she knew herself because leaving her this house was giving her the only home she had known since her parent's death. Sabrina wished she had someone to share it with. *My aunt's death is making me realize that I am alone now expect for Sophie and David,* she thought.

Shaking the mood, she remembered to call Annie. Brie went into the kitchen to find her purse and located the piece of paper with the phone number. Annie answered on the fifth ring.

"Hi, is this Annie? I'm Sabrina Fitzgerald. We met at the grocery store," Brie spoke first.

"Of course, hello, Sabrina. I'm so glad you called."

"Am I calling too late?"

"No, not at all. I'm delighted to hear from you."

"I'd love to hear more of your story about my Aunt Millie," Sabrina requested.

"Well, there isn't much more I can tell you. She came by every other day to check on me and see how I was doing. I resented it at first, but she wouldn't take no for an answer. She pulled me out of my despair and showed me that I still had a life to live, even if my husband was no longer with me to share it. I know I would have died if she hadn't come by my house when she did. To this day, I still don't know how she knew I desperately needed an angel to save me," Annie told her.

"Somehow she did. Thank you for sharing this with me, and I'm glad my aunt was a help to you. I still would like to get together for coffee if you're available before I leave, but I don't mean to intrude. Do you have anyone visiting with you for the holidays?" Brie asked, concerned she might be all alone.

"Yes, I have friends visiting, and it's nice to have the house full of activity. I would enjoy meeting you for coffee, but it may be difficult for me to get away right now. When do you leave?" Annie asked.

"I'll be leaving a couple days after Christmas, but I understand you're busy with your company. Perhaps, when I return in the spring we can make arrangements to get together," Sabrina offered.

"That's a good plan. Be sure and call me then. You have a good Christmas, Sabrina."

"You do the same, Annie."

Annie called her an angel. She wondered what compelled her aunt to help others in the first place, and why in the capacity of being a guardian angel? These were questions Brie feared she would never have the answers to, but so desperately wanted to know.

Chapter 24

On one of the visits to Bella's house, Sabrina learned that she had been married for forty-two years before her husband died of colon cancer. They never had any children, which was a deep regret. Bella had been a widow for eight years and occupied her time with friends and belonged to a few clubs such as the botanical society, a local garden club and on a few event-planning committees.

Since Mildred enjoyed the same things, it sealed their fate as friends. She was taking the death of her best friend hard, which was one of the reasons Sabrina made it a point to visit at least once a week. Often Mildred's name would come up in a conversation, and she enjoyed hearing Bella talk about the antics that went on between them. During these past few weeks, Sabrina had learned a lot about her neighbor's life.

The holidays were coming to an end and time to leave her country home. Sabrina wondered if her absence would be hard for Bella. There were moments when Brie knew she was filling in for an emptiness she knew Bella was feeling. *Will it be twice as hard on Bella when I'm gone,* she wondered.

Tomorrow is Christmas. Sabrina only had a few more days before she returned to work. She wasn't ready to leave. It was odd to feel this way, but things had changed and she didn't want to leave her country home or Ben. Brie had found something here she had never experienced before and didn't want to give it up. She wasn't accustomed to attaching herself to anyone or anyplace. She got ready for the party, ignoring these unhappy thoughts.

Sabrina decided on black wool-blend dress slacks with a red cashmere turtleneck sweater, and black ankle-high boots. Walking into the master bedroom to check her image in the mirror, Brie was pleased with the reflection. She intentionally lingered hoping for a reoccurrence of the vision, but nothing happened. Sabrina retraced her steps to the bathroom, taking only a moment to add a touch of makeup, brush her hair, and slip a wide black leather headband on. She ran downstairs to call Sophie before leaving.

"Merry Christmas," they each said simultaneously when Sophie answered her cell phone.

"Hi Brie, I was just about to call you. I wasn't sure when you were going to Bella's party, but I'm glad you called first," Sophie spoke, excitedly.

"I'll be leaving in a few minutes. I told her I would be there at seven. What are you doing this Christmas Eve?" Sabrina asked, missing her sister.

"We don't have anything big planned. I think later we're going out to look at Christmas lights in the neighborhood and have hot cocoa and watch some of the old Christmas classic movies later. We've been watching holiday movies every night since we got here. I didn't know there were so many," Sophie explained, laughing.

"That sounds like fun. I love those old movies. Wish I was cuddled up on a sofa watching them with you."

"I wish you were here, sis. I miss not being with you during the holiday. It doesn't seem right to not be together for important times like this."

"I know how you feel. Let's make a promise to be together next year, no matter where it may be," Brie told her.

Sabrina knew whatever happened in the upcoming year, she wanted to be with family. Years past, it didn't bother her to be on assignment, but things were changing. Sabrina could feel her old lifestyle slipping away, replaced with a better one.

"That's a promise," Sophie remarked.

"I have to leave now, or I'll be fashionably late. Merry Christmas, sis, and give David a hug for me."

"Merry Christmas, Brie. We'll talk more tomorrow. Hope you have fun at the party."

Pulling into Bella's driveway a few minutes later, Brie could see the party through the front window that showed off Bella's well decorated tree. The door opened wide before she could ring the doorbell, and she was greeted by Ben. She smiled when he ushered her inside, out of the cold night air.

"Fancy seeing you here," Sabrina spoke first.

"Oh, I'm an old timer at Bella's parties."

Ben guided Sabrina into the room and began the introductions to the other guests. She counted about twenty people. Seeing Bella approach from the corner of her eye, she walked over to her.

"Merry Christmas, Bella," Sabrina whispered into her ear as she gave her a hug.

"Merry Christmas, Sabrina, I'm so glad you're here. Now, go mingle and meet my friends."

Sabrina smiled at Bella stepping away from the embrace and walked over to a long table set up with refreshments. She poured a hot cup of cocoa from a silver pot and walked over to the tree to get a closer look at the decorations. Thoughts of her aunt not being with them to celebrate the holiday made Sabrina sad.

"Nickel for your thoughts," Ben said, walking up to her.

"I thought it was a penny," she remarked with a smile as she turned her head.

"Inflation," he replied with a grin.

"Of course," Brie agreed.

"You looked so sad for a moment. I bet you were thinking of your aunt. Am I right?"

"Yes. I was wishing she was here. I miss her. I have lost my best friend."

"Mildred was one of the kindest people I have ever known,

and I've met plenty."

"Thank you for saying that."

"She developed a reputation in the community. I really like her."

"Let's go sit over by the fireplace. Some are starting up a game of monopoly, if you're interested," he remarked and took her elbow to guide Brie in that direction.

"No thanks. I'm not much into board games, but sitting by the fire sounds nice."

Ben's statement made her think of the individuals she had come across that referred to her aunt as a guardian angel. Even though they had previously discussed her aunt, perhaps he could shed more light on the subject.

"Ben, can you tell me a little more about my aunt's guardian angel activity? I promise I won't dwell on her all evening, but I'm still curious," Sabrina asked.

"I believe Mildred thought her good deeds were her little secret, but anyone who knew her figured out quickly what she was doing."

"What do you mean?"

"She would help people without wanting recognition. Often I've heard she left money, food or clothing, whatever the specific need may be, with a note that said, *from your guardian angel*. I think she thought no one knew she was the one doing the good works, but it didn't take long to figure out."

"Your aunt was indeed an exceptional woman, and I know you are missing her. You remind me of her in so many ways. You have a kind and giving heart just like her."

"How would you know that? We haven't been together long enough for you to see my bad side, that's all," Sabrina responded with humor.

"I don't think you have a bad side. When do you return to work?" he asked, changing the subject.

"I've a flight out on the twenty-ninth to Florida and leave for my next location within a couple of days," Brie told him.

She was ready to drop the subject of her aunt. Everyone in

the community knew Aunt Millie better than she, even after all the visits and the time spent with her.

"Do you know where you'll be going?"

"No, Joe, my assistant, will call me when I get home and let me know. I'm used to only a day or so notice from one shoot to the next and have adapted to being on the move with minimal notice."

"Sounds exciting, do you ever get tired of the traveling?"

"No, not really. I'm used to it. However, being on this holiday sabbatical has made me reflect on things that I never thought of before."

"What kind of things?"

"Oh, life-altering changes," Sabrina replied with a smile.

She knew Ben was teasing her and decided to tease right back.

"That sounds way too serious for conversation on Christmas Eve. Let's dance. Seems there is enough room for one more couple," Ben said, already standing and holding out his hand.

"I would love to dance."

Slipping into Ben's arms seemed so natural. The house was warm with a glowing fire. The fragrance of cinnamon and hot cocoa filled the air while softly lit candles threw shadows throughout the room. It was entrancing to Sabrina. Laying her head on Ben's shoulder, she relaxed and enjoyed the moment of shared closeness, not knowing if this opportunity would ever exist for her again.

Sharing thoughts and feelings with someone other than her sister was new to Sabrina. How can someone I barely know make me feel so safe and secure? *How am I going to be able to walk away from Ben in just a few days*, she asked herself.

It surprised Brie that she felt so comfortable talking with Ben about her life. In the couple of weeks they had spent together, a relationship was developing, and she believed he felt the same. Sabrina wanted more time to get to know him better, but that was going to be difficult. When the song ended,

Sabrina pulled away from his embrace reluctantly.

"Let's get something to eat," he offered and taking her hand, led her toward the table with various plates of food choices.

"Alright."

Handing her a plate and picking another from a stack on the table, they each selected their favorites. Sabrina took two mini chicken wings, a scoop of potato salad and a slice of pumpkin pie. Ben stacked his plate with a little of everything. He didn't want to miss an opportunity to try all the favorites.

"Are you going to eat all of that?" Sabrina asked, eyeing his plate.

"Every bit of it," he replied with a grin.

"You're going to make yourself sick."

"Nah, this is my favorite time of year. I get to indulge in all this good holiday food."

They went into the kitchen and sat at the dinette table, placing them away from the activity in the living room.

"This is really nice," Sabrina said.

"It's nice because you are here."

"Why, thank you kind sir," she responded, with a big smile on her face.

"I'm definitely going to miss you when you leave. When will you be back?"

"I'm not sure. It depends on the assignments. I hope to have enough of a stretch in between that I can make a trip in the spring."

"That's great, because I hear long distant relationships are a bear," he said, teasing her.

He wanted Sabrina to understand his feelings for her were more than a casual acquaintance for the time she was there during the holidays.

"Well, I hear carrier pigeons are faster these days," Brie countered, enjoying the bantering.

Ben burst out laughing. His laughter was contagious and Sabrina laughed, too. Leaving Ben when she was just getting to know him wasn't going to be easy. It seemed their feelings for one another was mutual. When they regained their composure, he spoke first.

"I'm not expecting promises. I understand you have a career that keeps you traveling, but I know we'll work it out."

"Yes, we will."

She was definitely enjoying the friendship with Ben and didn't want to jeopardize it. Each day day spent with him was another day closer to regret leaving. Putting their plates in the sink, they returned to the living room and briefly mingled with the other guests, but eventually slipped away to a corner to talk the remainder of the evening.

By midnight, the party grew to a close, and Bella's friends were beginning to leave. Sabrina said goodbye to everyone including Ben, who left around eleven forty-five. Brie lingered behind watching Bella say goodnight to her last remaining guests.

When she came back into the living room, Bella walked straight to the table and poured two hot chocolate drinks handing one to Sabrina. They went to sit by the fireplace, curling up comfortably in the matching overstuffed chairs.

"This was a wonderful party, Bella. I can see why you do this every year."

"I love the holidays, and it's a great time to get friends together."

"I'm so glad you're here. Mildred was always with me. We did this together, you know, she and I. In some ways, having you here is like having my friend with me."

"That's a nice thing to say. I'm very glad I came to Asheville. For reasons I can't quite explain, I felt I was being drawn back here."

"It's been good for me to have you here. You've been such a delight at a time when I needed it. Losing Mildred has been hard."

"I know. We both miss her terribly."

"So what's up with you and Ben? I saw you snuggling near

the fire," Bella asked, wanting to change the subject.

"I like him. He's a very nice man."

"Could any romance be brewing between you?"

"I hope so. I don't want the friendship between us to dissolve when I leave. In fact, that was what we were discussing."

"Ben and his family are good people. I've known them for years."

Each day that passed spending time together, Sabrina came closer to being more like a daughter to Bella. She enjoyed her companionship and believed it was mutual.

"Thanks Bella, I hope it does too. I was telling Ben earlier, I plan to come back in the spring which may be my first break. Usually, I do several assignments before having a few days reprieve, but it all depends on the length of time for each one."

"Well, I look forward to seeing you again soon," Bella remarked.

"Bella, look at the clock on the mantel. It's Christmas Day."

"Sure enough, we just talked ourselves into Christmas. It reminds me of Mildred. She always stayed just as you have, and we'd sit and talk into Christmas Day. Oh my goodness, how I miss her. I can't believe you and I have done the same thing without even realizing it. What a blessing you are, Sabrina," Bella commented, a little teary-eyed.

"Bella, I wouldn't say I'm a blessing, but thanks for the thought," Sabrina said, seeing the sadness in Bella's eyes.

"You are so much like Mildred. I know I keep saying that, but it's true. You have the same loving, caring and thoughtful nature as she did."

"That's a very nice compliment, thank you," Brie replied, humbly.

"I feel lost without Aunt Millie."

"I think we are lucky to have one another, and Mildred would be happy we do," Bella added, solemnly.

"Merry Christmas, Bella," Sabrina cheered raising her mug

to tap Bella's extended one.

"Merry Christmas, Sabrina."

"I should get home."

Sabrina rose to put her drink on the table. She walked to the front door, gathering her coat and purse along the way. They embraced before she dashed to the car that was covered in a thin layer of ice. It was very cold, so it took a moment for the car heater to blow warm
air and defrost the window.

Finally able to see out of the windshield, Brie backed out of the driveway. A quick glance toward the house revealed Bella standing in the doorway waving. Brie threw up her hand and waved goodbye. It was Christmas.

Chapter 25

Sabrina slept in on Christmas morning and upon arising went downstairs to start the coffeemaker. As she waited for it to brew, Brie looked out the kitchen window to see a soft blanket of white covering the ground. Unable to believe her eyes, she ran to the front door and pulled it open staring at white everywhere. Giddy with laughter, she walked onto the lawn in her pajamas and slippers and gathered the minute amount of snow she could scrape from the ground.

It was a beautiful sight to Sabrina as she turned to look back at the house and saw a winter wonderland of white coating the roof and trees along the perimeter of the yard. She ran back inside the house and grabbed her cell phone to call her sister.

"I have snow!" she exclaimed when Sophie answered.

"No way, that's not fair. It rained last night and everything is frozen, but no snow. I'm jealous."

"I'll take some pictures just in case it doesn't snow there before you leave."

"You better. It's awesome you got to see snow. Maybe we'll see some here, but if we don't, that's okay," Sophie declared, glad at least one of them had snow on Christmas Day.

"How was the party last night?"

"It was great and Ben was there. Bella has very nice friends, and afterwards, I stayed and we talked until one o'clock in the morning. You could say we brought in Christmas together."

"Sounds like you and Bella have become good friends and I'm glad," Sophie replied, relieved Brie had someone to spend Christmas with.

"I've enjoyed spending time with her, and she has made me feel comfortable while here."

"Well, that's a good thing."

"How is Christmas in Pittsburgh? Did Santa bring you something special?"

"As a matter of fact, he did. We were up early this morning and had a big breakfast before opening our presents. The only thing missing to make it perfect is you and the snow."

Sabrina detected sadness in her sister's voice that she wished wasn't there. She felt responsible.

"When are you and David leaving?"

"We'll be leaving on Friday. David wants to have a couple days at home before we return to work."

"I'm a day ahead of you, I leave on Thursday."

"Oh, I was hoping to see you when we all got back to Florida."

"Me too, we'll get together soon. I promise."

Finishing up their conversation, they said their goodbyes. The doorbell rang while Sabrina stood in the kitchen stirring cream and sugar in her coffee. She wasn't expecting anyone and with cup in hand, strolled to the front door and looked through the tiny peephole, recognizing Ben. She was still in her pajamas wet from the snow when she opened the door.

"Wow, aren't you a beautiful sight," Ben declared with a grin.

"You've got to be kidding. What you see is what you get."

"I'll take it!" he replied, laughing.

"What are you doing here, Ben? Why aren't you with your family this morning?"

"I've been with my family since dawn. We've already opened the presents and now we wait until the turkey is done for our feast."

"Oh, so what brings you to my doorstep on Christmas?" she asked, curiously.

"To invite you to Christmas dinner with me and my family."

"Come in Ben and have some coffee and tell me the real reason you're here."

Ben followed her to the kitchen. She handed him a mug filled to the brim. Leaning against the counter with her own cup in hand, she stared at him.

"Gosh, are you always this pretty first thing in the morning?" he asked, staring back.

"Of course."

"Will you come to dinner and meet my family?"

"You're serious; why do you want me to meet your family now? It's Christmas Day."

"I want you there. I should have asked you last night, but it didn't cross my mind. I want to spend some time with you today and thought that it would be nice for you to meet them. It's not often we get everyone together."

"Are you sure that would be alright with your mother, having a stranger included in the Christmas festivities?"

"My family is anxious to meet the mysterious woman I have been sneaking off to see," he declared with a smile on his face.

Brie knew he was teasing her again. She didn't have anything better to do on Christmas Day but sit around the house, so why not? It would give her the opportunity to meet his parents and spend more time with Ben, something she was easily becoming accustomed too.

"Alright, I'll come for dinner."

"Great, we'll be eating around four o'clock so I'll pick you up at two."

"Okay; I'll be famished."

"Good," he said, placing his mug in the sink.

"By the way, did you happen to notice the snow fairy brought you a present last night?" Ben asked, holding back a grin.

"Yes, I did, and who do I have to thank for this wonderful white blanket?"

"That would be me. I had a special meeting with him after leaving Bella's party."

"How did you know I wanted snow for Christmas?"

"Anyone who lives in Florida wants to see snow for the holidays, it's a given," Ben stated, proud for having this knowledge.

"This is true," Brie agreed, trying to stay serious.

"You're welcome."

"Thank you."

One look at each other and they simultaneously burst into laughter. It was several minutes before either could regain a sense of composure. This was the best Christmas Sabrina could remember having in a very long time. Ben made his way to the foyer with Brie following behind. She watched him walk down the sidewalk toward his truck.

Meeting a person's parents was always considered a big thing in the dating world. It was the crossroad when you knew the other person took the relationship seriously. However, Sabrina didn't want to put any specific meaning into meeting Ben's family. It was simply a kind gesture on his part to include her because she would otherwise be spending the holiday alone. Brie thought it fun to spend the day with Ben and admitted she was curious about his family.

Chapter 26

Ben's older sister, Sarah, didn't make it home for the holiday with her husband and children, but his younger sister, Jennifer, was on college break. The first thing Sabrina noticed was how young at heart and very loving his parents were toward one another. It was easy to see they enjoyed life, including the hard work involved with maintaining their family business. She understood where Ben got his good nature.

"So you are the little lady Ben has been keeping from us," John said as Ben introduced Sabrina to his father.

He was a slender man of average height with gray hair and mustache, which looked more silvery against his dark, weathered complexion from years in the sun.

"I don't know if I'm the one, or not," Sabrina teased back.

"I'm sure you are, and we're pleased you could come over today. Welcome to our family, and as you will see, we are very informal," he continued.

"Thank you," Brie replied.

"This is my wife, Melinda of thirty-eight years," John introduced his wife by putting his arm around her shoulder and drawing her close to his side.

She was also slender with black hair showing threads of gray around the hairline. Her grayish-blue eyes were her best feature. Obviously, she too, spent a fair amount of time outdoors. Small lines feathered from the corner of her eyes with deeper creased around her mouth. Even so, she was a very attractive woman.

Sabrina witnessed the mutual love and affection between them, and in that moment, standing before Ben's parents, Brie knew she wanted the same. Someday she wanted to be married to a man who was still in love with her after many years together. Smiling in return, Sabrina shook Melinda's hand.

"I'm so glad to finally meet you. Ben tells us you are a photojournalist," Melinda stated.

"Yes, I am, and I see your son has been talking about me behind my back," Sabrina teased, looking up at Ben standing beside her.

"All good things," he remarked and held up both hands, palms outward.

"My little sister is on the phone with her boyfriend, so I'll introduce her later. Come on in and have something to drink," Ben offered.

"Why don't you come into the kitchen with me while the men continue watching the game on television," Melinda interjected.

"Alright."

Ben turned and winked before leaving Sabrina behind with his mother. Brie smiled back and followed in the opposite direction.

"What would you like to drink? We have just about everything you can think of, just name it."

"Hot chocolate would be nice."

"Oh, we have plenty of that, and I think I'll have one myself. Two hot chocolates coming right up."

Sabrina went to the island in the center of the kitchen and took a seat at one of the three bar chairs. She loved the design. The island was large enough to have a built-in grill and small narrow sink, with a beautiful blue-speckled marble countertop. There was plenty of matching counter space along the perimeter of the room. Dark wood cabinets with glass-paneled doors covered the walls.

"I love your kitchen. Though, I don't usually have the time

to cook, I'd like to have a kitchen like this someday."

"Thank you. We remodeled a couple of years ago. I enjoy cooking but had very little counter space. I always wanted an island, so I talked John into making it an anniversary present. It was a mess for the longest time but worth every speck of dust."

She handed Sabrina a mug of hot chocolate and stood across the island sipping her own drink.

"Tell me about your work. Ben says you're very good and I don't doubt it. He showed us some of your photographs in the magazine, and I was impressed."

"I've been carrying a camera around since I was twelve years old when my dad gave me one for my birthday. I started in high school taking pictures for the school newspaper and yearbook and in college majored in photojournalism. While I was there, I did some part-time work at the magazine taking on small assignments, and by the time I graduated, I had a full-time job with them. Everything seemed to fall into place from there," Sabrina briefly explained.

"I can tell you love what you do."

"I really couldn't think of anything else I'd rather be doing, and I'm fortunate to have a job I enjoy and get to travel. It's perfect for me."

"Your parents must proud of you," Melinda added.

"My parents died while my sister and I were in college. It was a boating accident."

"Oh, I'm so sorry. Ben didn't tell us," she responded, sympathetically.

"It's okay. It was several years ago."

Both were silent for a moment.

"Well, let's get this meal on the table. I did most of the cooking yesterday, so everything is ready. The turkey is done, and I also have a small ham. Basically, all we need to do is transfer the food to serving platters and set the table."

"What can I do to help?"

"Let me show you where the dishes and silverware are and you can take care of the table."

Just then, Ben's younger sister walked into the kitchen. Having not been officially introduced to Sabrina, Melinda made the introductions.

"Jennifer is my youngest," she said in terms of acquainting the girls with one another.

"It's good to know my brother has good taste. He's told us you are a photojournalist. That must be an exciting career. I suppose you do a lot of traveling."

"Yes, I do enjoy my job and I admit traveling is one of the perks."

"Cool. You'll have to tell me more about it."

"Well girls, let's get the table set," Melinda ordered as she began transferring food from the cooking pots to serving dishes.

Sabrina set a formal table for five which included a beautiful Christmas floral arrangement with tapered red candles as the centerpiece. With each filled dish Melinda placed on the island, Sabrina and Jennifer took turns placing them on the dining room table. The men were called to dinner when everything was ready, and after everyone was seated, Ben's father said a prayer over the food.

It became a delightful and entertaining afternoon. They each had stories to share. Jenny talked about her studies and some of the antics that happened on campus. They drew Sabrina into the conversation asking questions about her travels, making her feel right at home.

Sabrina intended to enjoy every moment she had with Ben's family. It gave her a glimpse of what she was missing and made her think of Sophie having David. Brie didn't have someone special. She had a career. Up until recently, she was comfortable with that arrangement; however, she wasn't sure that was enough anymore. Everyone was finishing pumpkin pie and coffee, when Ben excused himself from the table and took Sabrina's hand, pulling her away as well.

"If you'll excuse us, I'm taking Sabrina out to walk off some of this food."

"Bundle up, it's cold outside," Melinda said.

Ben and Sabrina grabbed their jackets and went out the front door.

"Alone at last," Ben said with a smile.

"You have a wonderful family, Ben. Being here reminds me so much of the holidays when my parents were alive."

"I thought I noticed some sadness in your eyes."

"True. I often spend Christmas alone usually on assignment somewhere. In the past it never seemed to bother me, but this year it has."

"Well, I'm glad you were here today. As you can see, we are very causal and down-to-earth kind of people, nothing pretentious about us."

"I like them. Thank you for inviting me."

They didn't linger outside for long with the temperature in the low thirties. Ben's mother was washing the last few dishes in the sink while his dad was napping in the living room. His sister had retired to her room. Melinda had put on a fresh pot of coffee, and they gathered around the island enjoying a cup and chatting. A couple of hours later Sabrina announced she needed to go home.

"I'm going to take Sabrina home," Ben told his mother.

"Thank you for including me in your family dinner. I had a wonderful time," Sabrina told her, sincerely.

"It was our pleasure, and you are welcome anytime, Sabrina," his mother replied.

"Thank you, again. Will you let your husband and Jennifer know that I enjoyed talking with them?"

"Of course, this is the usual routine after a holiday meal. I apologize that my husband has fallen asleep, but I will let him know."

Sabrina gave Melinda a hug before she and Ben left. Pulling into the driveway, he kept the truck running.

"Thanks again for inviting me. I really had a good time."

"I'm glad. I couldn't see you spending Christmas alone, and I wanted you to meet my family before you left. They're a pretty cool bunch."

"It just occurred to me. Do you live at home with your parents?"

This was the first time she thought of where he lived.

"No, I don't live at home, but nearby. On the back acreage there is a log cabin that belonged to my grandparents. When they passed away, I inherited it. In my spare time I repaired and remodeled it, and that is where I live. There is a separate road farther down the lane to the entrance to my house," he explained.

"That's very convenient, you are close to your family and business, but have the privacy of your own home."

"This is true. We respect each others privacy, yet we work well together."

"When did you say you are leaving?" Ben asked, changing the subject.

"Not for a couple more days, and you know I won't leave without saying goodbye."

"You better not. I'll call you later," he told her and opened his truck door.

"No need to get out, Ben; I can see myself to the door," Sabrina said, touching his forearm, forestalling him getting out of the truck.

She ran the short distance to the front door, and putting the key into the lock, Sabrina turned and waved. He threw up his hand, smiling, and Brie smiled back.

It was at that moment Sabrina knew she would have a hard time leaving. *How am I going to leave him when I think I'm falling in love?* she asked herself. On that thought, she stepped into the warmth of her country home.

Chapter 27

The next couple of days were busy for Sabrina. As much as she hated to, she took down the Christmas decorations and packed them back under the staircase and threw the tree out on the curb to be picked up. It took one day to get the house in order, and the next day was spent cleaning from top to bottom. She didn't want to leave the house untidy. Taking a break, she decided to check in with Sophie.

"Hey sis, what are you doing?" Sabrina asked when she heard her sister's voice.

"I'm getting ready to go out with David's mom to do some after Christmas shopping. Not that I can buy very much, or if I do, I'd have to buy another suitcase. But you never know," Sophie told her, laughing.

"Sounds like fun. Wish I was doing some of that shopping with you."

"Me too. You know, I just realized you and I have never shopped the after Christmas sales."

"Next year for sure."

"Absolutely. I was hoping we could get together before we all have to go back to work."

"Perhaps we can over the weekend. I haven't talked to Joe, so I don't know what my next assignment will be or when I leave."

"Great, let's try to plan for the weekend. What did you do on Christmas after playing in the snow? You know, I'm still a little jealous."

"I had Christmas dinner with Ben's family and truly enjoyed myself. I didn't get to meet his older sister and her family this year, but his parents and younger sister are very nice. You would like them."

"Since you like them, then I'm sure I would too. This sounds serious if you are meeting the family. Are you ready to leave Asheville?"

"Honestly, I have mixed feelings. I didn't expect to make new friends while I was here. I enjoy visiting with Bella, and she has told me great stories about Aunt Millie. We have spent a lot of time talking over cups of coffee. I will miss Ben. I really do like him. Being here this past month feels like I have stepped into another world."

"That's a good thing, Brie. Don't sound so astonished. This may be the beginning of a whole new life for you, and perhaps Ben will turn out to be the right one. Just think you could be married this time next year."

"I know you are teasing me, sis. Neither of us is thinking in those terms at this point. We simply have enjoyed each other's company; however, we have agreed to stay in touch."

"Well, sounds to me you like him a lot, and any man you would give enough time to would fall in love with you. You haven't stayed still long enough for one to catch you."

"Perhaps, but truthfully, I've never given it much thought. It never fit with my career. Maybe there is something in this country air that affects a person's sensibilities."

"Or maybe you are starting to think of a life that includes more than traveling and working. You can have both, Brie. You don't have to choose between your career and a family life, look at David and me. I want to see you have your career and someone to come home to at the end of the day, or the end of an assignment. It's time to think about these things, and if being in the country has given you the opportunity to rethink your life, then it has been well worth the stay there," Sophie declared a bit too severely.

Suddenly the conversation had shifted to a more serious note.

"Gosh sis, I didn't realize you felt that strongly about my having a man in my life," Brie replied, too harshly herself.

"Don't go and get defensive on me, you know what I'm saying."

"Yes, I do understand and there is some truth in your statements. Right now, however, I need to get things ready here to lock up the house and get back to my real life; the one that pays the bills. This one seems more like fantasy. Enough about me, how was your visit with David's family?"

"We've had a wonderful time. His mom and I have baked, shopped, wrapped, and cleaned the entire time I've been here, but it's been fun. It was a good Christmas, but I still wish we could have been together."

"We will next year for sure," Brie reassured her.

"That's right, next year for sure. Who knows, you might be married by next Christmas and it could be a foursome," Sophie told her, wanting to put the conversation back on a lighter note.

"You're right, a lot can happen in a year."

She wasn't going to argue with her sister about the remote possibility of that happening, because she was having too much fun bantering with Sophie like old times. Besides there might be some truth to that statement, but she wasn't willing to admit it to her sister just yet.

"Brie, you haven't mentioned anything more about your mysterious visitor. Has all of that nonsense stopped?"

"No more dreams, or hearing voices. We've moved on to visual now."

"Are you telling me you're seeing things? Brie, don't scare me."

"Just the other day, I saw a double reflection in the mirror, and only one was mine. I even tried talking to this *apparition*."

"Okay, Brie. This is getting way out of hand. I don't like this at all. I thought I was rationalizing my way through these strange encounters and dreams, but this too much," Sophie told her sister.

"Oh, I agree, but what can I do? They just happen. I don't have any control over the situation. I'm trying, though. I talked to it to see if I could lure it to communicate with me. Do you know how abnormal that sounds to say such a thing?"

"This is the strangest thing I've ever heard. Does stuff like this really happen to people? Are you alright. I mean are you afraid, or worried about bodily harm? I can't believe I just asked that."

"Calm down, Sophie. I'm fine and I don't feel threatened. I don't understand what is going on, but I can assure you there is no fear associated with these mysterious encounters."

She could tell Sophie was getting upset and that was not what she wanted.

"Let's drop the subject for now, and don't worry about me. Promise me, Sophie. I'm okay, really."

"I'll try."

Sabrina wished there was a way to not have to tell her sister about these strange events because it was upsetting her, but she had to give her truthful answers. *Maybe once I leave, it will all go away,* she mused.

She would be leaving in two days and the house was secured for the winter. Sabrina hoped to return in the spring. She decided to take a drive into town to see George. Brie was walking through the front door and straight into his office since he was alone in the building. When he looked up and saw her approaching, George motioned Sabrina to have a seat.

"Hello, Sabrina. How was your Christmas?" George inquired.

"Very special, how was yours?"

"It was very relaxing, and I'd be home if it weren't for a deadline on some paperwork that needs to be filed."

"I wasn't sure if you would be in today and took a chance. I'm leaving Thursday morning and came by to ask you to keep an eye on the house for me. I plan to come back in the spring."

"Sure. I'll drive by periodically and check on things. Keep

the heat on low for the winter," he told her.

"So you're planning to come back. It must mean you have enjoyed your stay in Asheville," George continued.

"Yes, I've made some new friends.'

"I didn't mean to bother you, but I wanted to thank you for everything, and let you know I'll stay in touch," Sabrina said as she got up to leave.

"Call me if you need anything. Mildred would expect that of us."

"I understand."

George walked her to the front door.

"You might lock your door behind me, so strays don't walk in and bother you while you work."

He smiled and nodded watching her leave his office.

Next, Sabrina decided to pay Bella a visit and twenty minutes later was pulling into her driveway. She answered the door with a cup of coffee in one hand.

"Sabrina, come on in. I'll get you a cup."

"Thanks. I could use something to warm me; it's cold out there. Did you see the snow on Christmas Day? We actually got snow. I couldn't believe it when I woke up and saw everything covered with a thin blanket of white; it was beautiful."

"Yes, I did, and it made Christmas special. It never lasts long, but it does make a pretty sight," Bella replied.

"Well, it made Christmas perfect. I was hoping to see white this year, and I did."

"What about Ben? Did he help make your Christmas special this year? I'm prying, you know," Bella asked, humorously.

"Ben is part of my enjoying this holiday. I spent Christmas Day with his family and had a wonderful time."

"Could it be getting serious between you, or is that a question I shouldn't ask?"

"I'm not sure, but it's mutual that we enjoy each other's company. We plan to stay in touch. I guess time will tell."

171

"Time does have a way of giving us answers."

"I didn't want to take up a lot of your time. I stopped by to let you know I'll be leaving on Thursday, but will stay in touch. If you need to reach me, call my cell phone," Sabrina told her while she got up and poured the remainder of her coffee down the sink.

Brie walked to the front door with Bella following behind. The two women fell into each other arms for a firm hug. Once they separated, Bella was the first to speak.

"Be careful, Sabrina, and don't forget to call me," she continued, almost in tears.

"You take care too, Bella. I'll be in touch."

Bella stood in the doorway watching her leave. She sure was going to miss her. Things wouldn't be the same with Mildred gone and now Sabrina was leaving too.

Chapter 28

Saying goodbye to Ben was harder than Sabrina expected. Just the day before, they went to dinner and officially said their farewells, agreeing to stay in touch. It was a complete surprise to hear the doorbell ring on Wednesday night while she was packing her suitcases, but she was excited to have this unexpected visit from Ben when she opened the door.

"Hi Ben, what brings you here this time of night?" she inquired.

"I was in the neighborhood and thought I would say goodbye one more time."

"Well then come in and have some coffee. I'll make a fresh pot."

Quickly putting the coffee pot on to brew, she turned to see Ben sitting at the dinette table and noticed he had placed a card in the center. She approached the table and sat down.

"Is this for me?" she inquired, tapping the card lightly.

"Perhaps," he said with a grin.

"Can I open it now?"

"No! Don't open it until you're on the plane."

"Alright, I suppose I can wait until morning, maybe."

She tilted her head and looked at him with mischief in her eyes. Ben leaned forward giving her a quick kiss and settled back in his chair. Sabrina was taken by surprise. They had not kissed until now.

"That was nice," she admitted with a smile.

She got up to pour two mugs of coffee, bringing them with the condiments to the table. Stirring her coffee, she remained silent. Ben
spoke first.

"Did I leave you speechless?"

"Yes, you did but I wasn't sure of your feelings, and I didn't want to press the issue."

"Surely you know my intentions are beyond friendship. I like you a lot, Sabrina."

"I feel the same way. I'm happy when we're together."

"Good, we agree on the direction of our relationship. That's a load off my mind," he told her with a big grin on his face.

"Same here."

"I stopped by to give you the card. I know you have things to do so I'll leave you to finish packing. Remember, don't open until you are thirty-three thousand feet in the air," he remarked, tapping the envelope.

He got up and tossed the remainder of coffee, rinsed the mug, and placed it in the sink. Walking to the front door, he turned and kissed her once more, and Sabrina melted in his arms not wanting their embrace to end. She watched him drive away. Tomorrow she was leaving Ben.

She returned to the kitchen and retrieved the card placing it in her purse. Brie didn't want to accidentally forget it in her hurried state in the morning. She cleaned the coffee pot and mugs before going upstairs to continue packing. An hour later she was climbing into bed.

Unable to fall asleep, she let her mind drift to the past few weeks and how much she had come to enjoy this time in the country. Never in her wildest imagination would she have considered that spending any amount of time in a small community like Asheville would come to mean so much to her.

For the month she lived in her aunt's house, Sabrina came to terms with her death. There would simply be no conclusive evidence to define the true cause of her passing, and Sabrina and Sophie agreed to accept it as a heart attack. Brie was disappointed she had to accept it as a heart attack. She was also disappointed to not find a resolution to the figure that visited her. The infrequencies made it difficult to reach an understanding. It was frustrating, but what could she do?

Did the voice and dreams subside when she came to terms with her aunt's death, or when she began to accept living in her country home, or did uncovering *Passionate Promises* have anything to do with it? What started them and why did they cease? Brie didn't have the answer to these questions that haunted and confused her. She desperately wanted to understand the meaning behind the experience. She wished she would hear the soft angelic voice once more. *How strange is that,* she told herself.

With bags at the door, Sabrina made another trip throughout the house checking to make sure all was secure. She went upstairs into the master bedroom to sit once more on the edge of the bed. It was here Brie first heard the soft voice, and she wanted to hear it again. She sat quietly with eyes closed, just as she had done prior and waited.

Brie was practically willing the voice to speak, but there was no sound. She hoped in the quietness of the room she would hear the voice she had come to know yet not understand. Finally, Sabrina got up to leave. She couldn't delay any longer, or she would miss her flight.

She gathered her luggage to the car placing them in the trunk. Returning to the house to retrieve her purse, she stood inside the foyer for a moment. An incredible sadness washed over her while she stood in the doorway expecting to be told to stay. Brie believed she was leaving something important behind. What was she missing? *Please reveal yourself to me now before I leave,* she spoke softly.

With shoulders drooping, she locked the door, returned to the car, and gave the house one longing look. Sabrina felt the same sadness the day she walked away from her aunt's funeral. How could that be? This was totally different, and yet, it felt the same. She spent the drive to the airport convincing herself it was time to get back to the real world, where her next assignment awaited.

When the plane reached cruising altitude, she remembered the card and pulled it out of her purse. Brie turned it back and forth in her hand. It wasn't everyday Sabrina received a card. It was sweet of Ben, and the thought brought an instant smile to her lips. With the card still unopened, the lady next to her noticed she was hesitating.

"Aren't you going to open that?" the stranger asked.

"Probably," Sabrina replied, irritated.

Brie put the card on her lap. She didn't want the stranger reading it over her shoulder, so she decided to wait. Perhaps the lady would fall asleep. Sabrina waited.

A short time later, she slipped the envelope open and pulled out the card which instantly made her smile. The front showed a gray kitten next to a flowerpot of yellow daises with a single tear under his eye. The card read, *I miss you already, Love, Ben.*

It brought tears to Sabrina's eyes. What had she been missing all these years? A career can't send you a card, or make your heart skip a beat. He signed it *love. I think I love you too, Ben. How can I feel this way about someone I've only known two short weeks,* she thought.

Sabrina placed the card back in the envelope and tucked it away in her purse. Leaning her head back, she closed her eyes and thought of Ben. She was already missing him and they hadn't been apart a day. She must have fallen asleep because she was startled when the lady nudged Brie to fasten her seat belt, they were about to land. This happened to be a nonstop flight to Orlando and Sabrina was grateful there were no layovers. She wanted to get home.

Brie retrieved her luggage and was finally on the Beeline. For the first time in all her traveling, she felt alone. There would be no one to greet her when she walked into the condo. Brie was already wishing she was back in the country.

Chapter 29

Sabrina arrived home late in the day and left the chore of unpacking until morning. She called Sophie to let her know she had arrived safely. Next, Brie made a cup of hot tea and stepped out on the balcony for a moment, watching the waves come to shore, but not in the mood to linger, she went back inside.

Roaming around the apartment didn't give Brie the peace it normally did after a long absence, leaving her disoriented. Deciding to retire early, she took a quick shower and went to bed.

She sat on the balcony the next morning with a fresh cup of coffee and watched the early morning joggers below. Sabrina felt better for the good night's rest and called Joe to report she was ready for an assignment. They briefly chatted about their holidays, and he informed her to be prepared to leave within a few days. He would check the schedule and call back with the details.

Sabrina unpacked the luggage, started laundry, and began cleaning the apartment of the thin layer of dust that had accumulated. Afterwards, she decided to go to the grocery store and pick up a few items for the weekend. Dressing causally in beige cotton slacks and a navy turtleneck sweater, she pulled her hair into a ponytail and headed out the door. It felt good to have the cool air on her face even though it couldn't compare to the cold in Asheville. There were only a handful of days in Florida that could be considered comfortably chilly with temperatures in the low fifties.

While waiting her turn in the checkout line, Sabrina thought of Annie and wondered how she was doing. She reminisced that it was only a couple of weeks ago she had been standing in a grocery line in Asheville talking to a stranger about her Aunt Millie. Now she was in a different store in a different state, thinking about Annie, which turned her thoughts toward her aunt, which only deepened her melancholy.

When she returned home, Brie grilled a steak along with a foiled baked potato and with supper cooking, casually looked through the closet. Until she knew where Joe would be sending her, she couldn't begin organizing her clothes. She thought of going to the mall to do some shopping, but it seemed like too much of an effort, and besides she wasn't in need of clothing. She had accumulated a complete wardrobe for every season.

Sabrina ate the home cooked meal on the balcony while observing people on the beach below. She missed the short-term life she had established in the country. *There has to be a way to enjoy the benefits of traveling and have a relaxing slower pace to life as well. Surely it was possible,* she thought.

Joe called the next morning informing Sabrina she was flying to Hawaii to record a beekeeper's colony in Haleiwa. The magazine was doing an article on the decline of the bee population in the country, and this particular piece would appear in the spring issue. It was a quick assignment that would take only a few days, and from there Joe would let Sabrina know in what direction he would send her next. She packed both suitcases, prepared for warm or cold climates. After checking the equipment bag, she called Sophie.

"Hey Sophie, I'm heading to Hawaii on Monday."

"Hawaii, that's not fair. You get to see all these wonderful places, and all I have to look forward to is grading papers."

"I wish you could come with me. Besides, you know I don't pick the places."

"Of course, I know that. I'm just coming down off a high of holiday bliss and not ready to go back to work, too much fun and I got accustomed to lazy days."

"I know what you mean. I feel the same way. I'm sorry I didn't get over this weekend, but I'll stop by when I return."

"I knew you were probably busy getting ready for your next trip. How long will you be gone?"

"I don't know, but Hawaii shouldn't take more than a couple of days, and I have no idea where I'll be going from there, but will keep you posted."

"We'll be back in school to the usual routines."

"It'll feel like we never had the time off. I'll call you from Hawaii."

"Have fun, talk to you soon."

Sabrina was ready to go back to work; after all, this was her life and she loved her profession. Each photo shoot took her to uncharted territory, which was a big part of the appeal. It was never mundane. She spent the remainder of the weekend finishing small projects around the apartment, rechecked her list of clothing, and made sure everything was in order in case she didn't return for several weeks.

Brie went to bed early Sunday night knowing she would be up at four-thirty to catch an eight o'clock flight. With two layovers in route to Hawaii, it was going to be a very long day in the air.

Chapter 30

The assignment in Hawaii was a brief three days and Joe was now sending her to Colorado in the dead of winter to capture a pack of wolves. Why wolves she wondered, but didn't question the shoot. She simply did as she was instructed. Joe had informed Sabrina to expect a call from a ranger named Trevor Fletcher who would be her escort into the mountainous areas.

Her flight arrived on time in Denver at five o'clock in the evening. Sabrina knew Joe had arranged for a shuttle van to take her to the hotel. As the plane was nearing the ground, Brie peered through the tiny window to see a thick blanket of snow everywhere. It was a beautiful sight and made her think of the thin layer she experienced at Christmas. Of course, that made her think of Ben, and she felt a pang of longing to be with him again.

There was a message from the ranger waiting for Sabrina at the hotel registration desk. She called Joe and Sophie, as usual, once she settled into the room. Next, she phoned Mr. Fletcher, and they agreed to meet in the morning in the dining room of the hotel for breakfast to go over the itinerary.

Sabrina was prepared for the cold weather, remembering to pack long john underwear to wear under her jeans. She ordered room service and while waiting for the meal to arrive, unpacked her clothes. This would be her home for the next week or so.

Brie turned on the television and found an old movie to

watch as she ate dinner. Afterwards, while getting ready for bed, Brie heard the weather forecast predicting snow flurries with a high of fifteen degrees. *It will be mighty cold in the mountains,* she thought before slipping into bed.

The next morning Sabrina met with Trevor Fletcher as scheduled. He spotted Brie when she entered the dining room and stood to motion her toward his direction. Trevor was a big, husky man sporting a new growth of beard, dark, leathered skin, shoulder-length jet black hair, and eyes as dark as coal. He appeared to be American Indian. However, Sabrina wasn't familiar with the culture enough to identify his heritage, and she didn't want to ask.

She shook his hand and sat in the opposite chair. He had a cup of coffee Brie noticed was half-empty. The waitress came to the table and Sabrina ordered a cup. When the waitress returned with the coffee, she refilled the one sitting there. They chose breakfast from the menu, both declining the breakfast bar.

"So you are Sabrina Fitzgerald, the famous photographer," Trevor stated a bit sarcastically.

"No. I'm not famous, that is," Sabrina countered.

If Sabrina didn't know better, she would have sworn there was an irritation in his voice indicting he didn't approve of her. Thinking she initially misread him, she spoke next.

"I understand you will be my guide into the mountains; I'm anxious to begin. When could we get started?" Sabrina asked, letting him know she accepted his position of authority.

"I'll let you know," he answered too quickly.

Sipping on her cup of coffee, Sabrina wondered what she had done to displease this man who didn't even know her, because he was definitely being antagonistic, but why?

"That's fine; however, I'm on a schedule. Is it the weather you are considering before we leave?" she asked, carefully.

"Let's get something straight since we'll be spending some time together. I don't approve of bothering nature, and that especially includes photographing the animals. They shouldn't be exhibited in magazines. These wolves are free and belong in the wild with no trespassing of man into their habitat," Trevor declared too strongly.

"Then why are you my guide if you feel this way?"

"Not by choice, I assure you. I happened to be the only mountain ranger qualified to track the wolves."

"I see, so you're stuck with a job you don't want to do. Why not refuse?"

"It's not that simple. If I don't take you into the mountains, then some wet-behind-the-ears forest ranger will and that can cause a lot of problems, especially for the wolves," Trevor explained, somewhat less harshly.

"Look, I'm sorry to be interfering in the lives of theses wolves, but I have a boss and he sends me to take pictures of animals. It's what I do for a living. I don't want to jeopardize the wolves or any other animal's habitat. I take pictures of animals by choice because I enjoy being around them. They are unique creatures we share this planet with," Sabrina stated in defense of her profession.

At that moment, the waitress brought over a tray and set their plates on the table. An unspoken truce was called while they ate in silence. Sabrina never had to battle with someone about taking pictures of her subjects, and she didn't want to get into a verbal altercation with this man. In some ways, she understood the position he held regarding the wolves; however, she had an assignment to do. It was her job to get it done. Brie intended to call Joe the first opportunity to explain the situation she had encountered.

This is why she has an assistant to make the arrangements and clear the path about legalities so she could drop in, take the photos, and leave. The assignment was starting off on the wrong foot, and it appeared it wasn't going to get any better. Sabrina was the first to speak after finishing breakfast.

"So, where does this leave us? I need a guide to do my job, and you don't want to be it, so now what?" she asked.

Sabrina didn't want this assignment to fall through.

"I will take you to the wolves, but only one trip. There will be no trekking back and forth for days. It is going to disturb them to have man in their territory, so I want to be as unobtrusive as possible. You have to take whatever pictures you need when we're there, and when I say it's time to leave, we leave with no questions."

Well that was blunt, Sabrina thought. She knew she couldn't ague with him. Brie could only do as he instructed and make sure to get the best shots possible with the time given. It was better than nothing. Sabrina didn't want to cause any hardship by going over his head to his immediate supervisor.

"Alright, but understand I no more want to disturb the wolves than you want to take me to them. You sound as though I am going to do them physical harm," Brie declared a bit short-tempered.

"You will be doing them harm; that's the point. They will know your presence even if you are a mile away, and this will make them edgy. They settle with their young in packs, like a family."

"I don't want to disturb their home. How close can we get without them knowing our presence? I have very good lenses for my cameras and can capture subjects from quite a distance. Maybe we won't be getting as close as you think," Sabrina reassured him.

"I'll take you close enough and still be safe for them; your camera will have to do the rest. It also depends on the weather to what day we leave. I'll give you a call this afternoon when I decide."

That's fine," Sabrina confirmed.

He picked up the check the waitress had left on the table and offered to pay for her breakfast when he saw Brie pull out her wallet. Rising from the table, he left her sitting alone. Sabrina felt deflated by the conversation and pulled out her cell phone to call Joe at the office.

"Joe, it's Sabrina. Apparently, the guide you arranged for me doesn't believe in taking pictures of wild animals. He has made it quite clear he is doing this begrudgingly," she told him, detailing the conversation.

Joe had been with the magazine for almost as long as Brie. Sabrina was already an established prominent photojournalist when he was given the position as her assistant and he was delighted to work with her. Joe was a young, studious man who spent his free time playing in chess tournaments, being totally addicted to the game. He would play practically every evening with various partners within the chess club he belonged to.

"Sabrina, I don't know what to say. I made all the arrangements with the Colorado Director of Forestry. He never expressed there would be a problem with the shoot. Do you want the magazine to cut this article in case you may not get the required photos?" Joe asked.

"No, let me try first. He is allowing me one trip at photographing them. I'll do what I can, but at this point, I don't know how close we can get. My camera's lens will have to stretch to get anything decent, so let's hope it works."

"I called to give you a heads-up on the circumstances here. Mr. Fletcher is not a happy person right now. Hopefully, this will go smoothly, and I can leave quickly," Brie continued.

"I'm sorry you're having a hard time. Let me know if I should call the director and make him aware of the difficulty his employee is giving you."

"I'll keep you posted. Right now I'm waiting for him to decide what day he will take me into the mountains. It depends on the weather at this point,"

"Okay, stay in touch."

Sabrina returned to the room, not accustomed to free time while on an assignment. She found herself with nothing to do. She had to wait for the call. She couldn't call Sophie knowing she would be teaching, so Brie sat staring out the window at everything covered in white. It made a beautiful picture but was not appealing enough to entice Brie out in the cold to check some of the specialty shops nearby.

She felt alone and her mind drifted to Ben, wondering what

he might be doing at this very moment? The holiday rush for Christmas trees is over, so how was he spending his time? She thought about calling him, but what would she say? Should she make the first move, or wait for him to call her?

Sabrina reminisced about the time spent in Asheville. It was a short one-month reprieve, and yet she was finding life she begun there seem more real than the one she lived daily. *How is that possible,* she wondered. How could a place and people she barely knew come to mean so much to her?

She believed she had left something important, something unfinished. Brie tried to ignore the thought, but invariably when she had a quiet moment they surfaced to haunt her.

Trevor called three hours later stating he would take her hiking in the morning. A big snowstorm was forecasted for later in the week, and he wanted to do this now before there was too much snow to even consider the trip into the mountains. Sabrina agreed to be in the lobby at seven sharp per his instructions.

Chapter 31

This had to be the worse assignment she ever encountered. The drive into the mountains was treacherous even for a four-wheel drive truck. Snow was compressed on either side of the road about mid-height to the doors. After more than two hours of driving upward, they reached a forestry cabin and parked the vehicle. Trevor announced the rest would be on foot. *Lovely,* Brie thought. Pushing hard to get the passenger door open against the snow, Sabrina climbed down from the cab and standing in place, did a 360-degree panoramic turn. The scene was pristine white; nature untouched. It was mesmerizing to see the beauty of the snow-ladened trees with the mountains in the background.

Sabrina grabbed the equipment bag from the truck floorboard, pulled out her favorite camera, the Canon EOS, and began snapping shots in all directions; it was breathtaking and exhilarating to witness such beauty. She lowered the camera looking around for Trevor. He was nowhere in sight, but she could see the trail his footprints left in the snow; it appeared he was heading toward the cabin. Sabrina started in that direction only to find he bypassed the building and was walking toward the thick forest.

Following a considerable distance behind, she kept to the path his footsteps made traveling upwards into the thick mass. Sabrina knew there was only one chance to capture the wolves, and she really wanted to get what she came for. She noticed

Trevor never turned around to see if she was behind him. Slowly, Brie made her way to the end of the path where he had stopped. When she reached him, he made the announcement they weren't going any farther. She looked around, but didn't see anything.

"So where are the wolves?" Brie asked, cautiously.

"Probably about another quarter-mile, or so up the mountain," Trevor replied, pointing toward the north.

"Can we get any closer?"

"This is as far as we go, take it or leave it. You've got one hour and we head back. There's more snow coming in, and I don't want to be in the mountains then," he declared, sternly.

Sabrina found herself in a maze of huge pine trees so tall and thick that when looking upward, she couldn't see the sky. Brie looked around but didn't have a clue what direction to start her search. She prayed her claustrophobia didn't kick in.

"If it's not too much trouble, could you give me an idea what area I should concentrate on," Sabrina asked as politely as possible.

"Probably best to focus on that region over there," Trevor stated, pointing his finger to her left.

"Thanks."

This wasn't going to be easy she thought as she set her equipment bag on the snow and pulled out the Canon EOS again and adjusted the lens. Looking through the viewfinder, she scoped out the scene by maximizing the zoom, but there was no movement, not even a rabbit. Brie continued to concentrate in that general area, slowly scanning the forest area leading up into the rocky mountainside. She could faintly detect entrances along the sidewall and assumed there were wolves living in them, but that wouldn't do her any good if they didn't make an appearance within the next forty-five minutes.

Crunching down on her belly in the snow, Sabrina held the camera at eye level and viewed the entire area from left to right and back again. She was feeling the cold through her clothes, but was determined to be still and wait. She wasn't leaving without these shots. Taking a quick glance over her shoulder, she spotted Trevor leaning against a pine about a hundred feet back. She didn't have anything to say to him and apparently, he was a man of few words. *Just as well we don't communicate,* she thought.

Glancing at her watch, Brie had thirty minutes left. She knew it wouldn't do her any good to ask to be taken farther in, or to another location. Brie could just about hear the answer in her head. She would wait it out. Sabrina stayed focused, keeping a diligent watch through the viewfinder, and even though she was freezing, she didn't dare move and miss an opportunity.

"Times up," Trevor announced, too eagerly.

Brie ignored him and remained stationary. Did the remaining thirty minutes escape her that quickly?

"Miss Fitzgerald, I believe I told you one hour. Now we leave," Trevor announced sternly, pushed himself away from the tree, and turned toward the path backtracking out of the forest.

Sabrina gave a quick glance over her left shoulder to see him leaving her behind. That didn't bother her because she knew he wouldn't actually leave her in the woods. Looking through the camera once more, she spotted movement. Sabrina wasn't sure what it was, but something was moving at the base of the mountainside. Brie zoomed in for a closer look and spotted a large wolf staring back at her. She was caught by surprise and momentarily forgot to snap the picture. Checking again, he was still focused in her direction, but surely it would be impossible for him to know she was there, or would it?

Brie began snapping shots as rapidly as the camera would click. She hoped to get more than one wolf, but so far, he was the only one to make an appearance. Perhaps Trevor was right, and they can sense your presence even from a couple miles away. It was as though the wolf knew she was there and was standing guard, protecting his family. Well, one wolf was better than none, and that was all she had time for. Sabrina was alone among the trees when she took one last look through the viewfinder. She snapped several more shots before packing it up.

Disappointed she couldn't capture an entire family, she was at least grateful for the single wolf she did get. Sabrina brushed the snow from the front of her clothes, grabbed the camera bag, and started back out of the maze, following the path Trevor had made. When she got close to the truck, she could see him behind the wheel, and he didn't look too happy. She climbed in, and dropping the bag on the floorboard, she buckled up, refusing to make eye contact.

"You don't take directions very well," he complained as he turned the ignition.

Sabrina ignored the sarcasm and looked straight ahead. She couldn't wait to leave the company of this man. How was she going to endure a two-hour drive back to civilization with him?

Trevor returned Sabrina to the hotel, and she politely thanked him for his time before walking inside. *He was a strange man,* she mused. They didn't carry on a conversation the entire drive up or back down from the mountain and probably for the best since he didn't like her presence in Colorado to begin with.

Sabrina peeled off her clothes and took a hot shower, feeling her skin thaw under the warm water. Then she called Joe to explain the photos were of a single wolf, all that could be captured with the hour she was given, and would email them shortly. After concluding the conversation, she called Sophie to inform her she was returning home for a few days.

"Great, come by for dinner."

"Alright, we did say we would get together after the holidays."

"You bet. David is cooking, and he'll have something special for you."

"He doesn't have to go to any trouble, a sandwich will be fine."

"David doesn't do sandwiches," Sophie replied with a giggle.

"Of course not. My plane comes in at four, and I should be there around five o'clock. It'll give me plenty of time to get across town."

"Time is not important, just get here."

"By the way, how was the wolf assignment?"

"Thirty pictures, one bad wolf."

"Oh, I bet that was disappointing. I know how serious you take your job."

"Well, I suppose every shoot can't be perfect. I would have gotten more pictures if I wasn't limited to one hour; however, that was my time frame. I propped myself in the snow waiting and practically froze to death."

"We'll catch up on your excursions when you get here. You have to give me the details of your bee adventure too."

"That's right. I haven't shown you my souvenir, two bee stings. I can't wait to share them with you. See you tomorrow," Brie told her, laughing.

Brie decided to have room service again and ordered dinner from the menu left on the nightstand. While she waited, she packed her clothes. She was glad to be going home. Taking pictures of bees wasn't a thrill, nor was the battle she went through to get a few photos of wolves.

She wasn't anticipating the next assignment and that was unlike her. Sabrina didn't understand the melancholiness she was experiencing and was trying hard to smother thoughts of Ben, Bella, and Aunt Millie. Perhaps it was time to stop suppressing these thoughts, reevaluate her life, and make some serious changes. Brie never had a reason to ask herself what she really wanted out of life before, but now it nagged at her.

Joe booked an early flight to Orlando, and Sabrina was ready to be on it. She looked forward to seeing her sister again. Sophie was always a good listener and right now, she needed one.

Chapter 32

Sabrina was glad to be in Florida arriving at her sister's house. Sophie always knew the moment Brie arrived and ran out the front door to greet her. They hugged, holding onto each other for an extended moment. Then walked arm-in-arm into the house, continuing into the kitchen where David was standing over a large pot on the stove. When he heard the commotion behind him, he turned toward Sabrina with open arms, giving her a warm hug.

"What's in that big pot on the stove, David?" Brie smiled as she pulled away from the embrace.

"A cow's behind," David remarked with a grin.

"Hum, rump roast!" Sabrina exclaimed, laughing.

"You guessed it!" he confirmed, laughing too.

Sabrina walked over and looked into the pot. There were so many trimmings of potatoes, carrots, and onions she couldn't see any meat in the pan.

"Are you sure you put meat in this meal, because all I see is a pot of vegetables?" she quizzed David.

"Yes, I'm almost positive I put the meat in there too. In fact, it's ready, so if you girls will have a seat, I'll bring this monster of a pot over to the table. I also have some rolls in the oven," David commented, opening the oven door and pulling out a pan.

Sophie and Sabrina pitched in by setting the table and pouring three glasses of iced tea. Sitting down to enjoy a meal with them, which she had done so many times before, brought to surface an   aspect to Brie's life she was definitely missing. Sabrina wanted some one to share her days with who would be there when she came home from a shoot. Her world had tilted and things were changing, and she knew it began in the country.

They chatted during the meal, and as usual, when finished, David stayed behind to clean up the kitchen leaving the sisters to wander into the living room to chat. Curled up on the sofa, Sabrina began her tales starting with Trevor and how that particular assignment left her discouraged.

"Don't let it get you down. This is probably the first job that didn't go exactly as you had expected. It's bound to happen eventually."

"I realize that, and for reasons I can't explain, these past two shoots haven't been rewarding for me. I've never been dissatisfied with an assignment before. I've changed, wanting more, I suppose," Sabrina confided.

"What is it you want?" Sophie inquired, thinking she already knew the answer.

"I'm not sure."

"Have you talked to Ben since you left Asheville?" Sophie asked, wondering if this was the source of her sister's somber mood.

"No. I thought about calling him, but changed my mind. I'm waiting to see how long it takes him to call me, if he does at all," Brie answered.

"Oh, he'll call. I'm sure he has a good reason for not contacting you yet. Maybe he doesn't want to bother you while you're working."

"Perhaps, but it would be nice to talk to him. Maybe now that I'm home for a few days, I'll call him."

"That's a good idea. There's no rule that says you have to wait for his call first."

David brought three cups of coffee on a tray and placed it on the table in front of the sofa. Brie reached out and took one cup already prepared with cream and sugar the way she liked it.

"David, I'm so spoiled. I want a husband just like you someday." Sabrina told him with a smile.

"Wow, that's the nicest thing anyone has ever said about me. She wants one just like me. How cool is that?" he replied, winking at his wife.

They talked for well over two hours with each relishing stories of the past couple of months, starting with Christmas to present day. Sabrina told them of her month in Asheville while David and Sophie expounded on their trip to Pittsburgh. She also detailed the discouraging time she had in Colorado again for David's benefit. Sophie and David were always such good listeners and gave Sabrina sound advice when she needed it.

"Speaking of Asheville, have you had anymore encounters of the unknown?"

"Actually no, not since I left the house. It seemed to be most prevalent when I was there. No further dreams, either. Maybe whatever it is has stopped; however, my instinct doesn't think so. I know we first thought it was all stress induced, but I know it isn't that. This is way too real."

If I never have another episode, how will I ever know what it all meant?"

"Well, maybe you can put that experience behind you. Whatever it was," Sophie declared, changing the subject.

"Tell us more about Ben."

"Not much to tell at the moment. He is a very nice man and I was glad to meet his family. I told you I had dinner at their house for Christmas, didn't I?"

"Yes, you did. Do you think there can be a serious relationship in the making?"

"I think it has strong possibilities."

"If you really like him, Brie, don't let him get away."

"I know what you're saying. I felt very comfortable with him and his family. He is the kind of man I could fall in love with."

"What do you think, David?" Sophie inquired of her husband, who had been sitting quietly listening to the exchange between them.

Sophie filled him in on Sabrina's mysterious voices and dreams so he wasn't surprised to hear the subject come up for discussion.

"I agree with Sophie. There could be several legitimate reasons why you haven't heard from him. Maybe he is giving you some space, but it wouldn't hurt to call," David said, thoughtfully.

They talked about everything imaginable, and believing to be up-to-date on each other's news. She had enjoyed an evening of good food and conversation with her two favorite people, but it was late and time to leave.

She thanked David for his fabulous meal and promised Sophie a day of shopping soon. Sabrina was glad to have some free days giving her time to think through some of the emotions she was experiencing.

While she drove straight east to the beach, she let her mind drift to thoughts of Ben as it seemed to do more and more each day that passed without hearing from him. Maybe Sophie was right and she should give him a call. At least it would be a way of finding out why he didn't contacted her in the weeks since she left Asheville.

Chapter 33

Sabrina spent her first day at home unpacking and doing laundry. She decided to stop procrastinating and call Ben, feeling a bit nervous. She dialed the phone number he had given to her before she left. Walking around in circles in the living room, Brie anxiously waited, and when she thought it was going to voicemail, he answered.

"Hello, this is Ben," he said, a bit out of breath.

"Hi Ben, it's Sabrina. Am I catching you at a bad time?"

"Sabrina, hello, no, not at all. How's my girl?"

Those words melted her heart. He called her *his girl.* Sabrina's self-imposed fears instantly dissolved.

"I'm well. I'm home in Florida for a few days between assignments. How have you been? Have the trees been keeping you busy?"

"Better now, hearing your voice. It's been very hectic. You wouldn't think that would be the case after the holidays."

"What do you do throughout the year until the next season?" Sabrina asked, never giving any thought to how Ben spent the preceding eleven months.

"Oh, you'd be amazed how much work goes into a tree farm. We do crossbreeding for new tree typing, fertilizing and sample checks of the immature ones to make sure they have no diseases or bugs trying to embed in their trunk. Things like that."

"Who would have thought."

"Exactly. I'm glad you called. I think of you often and planned to call when things settled down a bit. So tell me, what's new and where have you traveled?"

"I went to Hawaii to take pictures of bee colonies and from there to Colorado to photograph wolves, and now I'm home for a few days until they decide where to send me next," Brie replied, nonchalantly.

"Do I hear a tone of dissatisfaction, or am I misreading your voice?"

He believed he knew Sabrina well enough to detect the change in her mood. She didn't sound like the exuberant person he knew her to be.

"I'm experiencing some disenchantment which isn't like me. These past two photo shoots haven't been as enjoyable as I expected," she admitted with a sigh.

"That's surprising. Perhaps it's just getting back into the groove after time off. I'm sure you'll feel better about the next one," Ben said, trying to cheer her.

He could tell she seemed a little down.

"You're probably right. It's always hard to get back into a routine after a break. However, I'm rethinking a few things. I'm not sure I'll accept the next assignment."

Brie couldn't believe she had spoken her thoughts aloud. Depending on the next shoot, she was considering tactfully passing it. She was giving a great deal of thought to returning to her country home sooner than the spring. There was an invisible pull she couldn't explain. *I can't let it go without understanding what it means*, she reasoned with herself.

This had to do with Aunt Millie's crusade of *Passionate Promises*. Brie knew she would be fooling herself if she considered otherwise because thoughts of it inevitably wandered to the forefront of her mind. Sabrina couldn't shake the idea that she was to do something with *Passionate Promises* even though it didn't fit her lifestyle, nor did she have any experience, or actual desire to follow in her aunt's footsteps.

It had to be resolved and simply forgetting about it didn't appear to be an option to Brie. Her conscience and curiosity wouldn't let her get away with that. Besides, somehow she knew this was important. She couldn't do anything about the fact that her sister wasn't connected to these unusual occurrences. *It probably would have been easier to handle had she been,* she thought.

"I'm not following you. What will you do if you don't take the next assignment?"

"I don't know yet. My career has always been very important to me. It's been my life, and I've loved every minute of it, but something has changed recently, and I'm not sure I even know myself what I'm wanting."

"Does this mean you could be returning to Asheville sooner than you had planned?"

"Possibly. I'm giving it some serious thought. I feel I have unfinished business with Aunt Millie. I'm sorry, Ben. I'm rambling and you don't know what I'm talking about. I realize I'm not making a bit of sense."

"I like where this is leading if it means you are coming back to Asheville. How long would you be staying this time, or do you know yet?"

"I don't know. It all depends on my next assignment and whether I take it. Also, I'd have to make arrangements with my job. I'm basically thinking aloud; nothing that can be written in stone."

"I understand, sounds like some new year's resolutions in the making."

He didn't want to encourage Sabrina in a direction she wasn't ready to take.

"I'll keep you posted on what I decide to do. What's going on in your world? How is your family?" Sabrina asked, wanting to change the subject.

"Everyone is good. You'll see them again when you return. Is there anything you need me to do at the house while you're gone?"

"No, everything is secure, but thanks for asking. It was good talking to you."

"You may not believe me, but I was going to call you in the next day or two. I didn't want to bother you while on the job. I've missed you."

"I've missed you, too. I'll keep you informed."

"You take care, Sabrina. If I don't hear from you within the week regarding your plans, I'll call. I do miss you."

Sabrina felt all warm inside. Ben called her *his girl* and that he *missed* her. She really was new at this dating thing. It was nice to hear the words, and she believed Ben meant them. Maybe she did want to go back to the country to see Ben, more than she was willing to admit to herself. *I've fallen for a man I've only known two weeks,* she realized.

Chapter 34

Four days had passed before Sabrina heard from Joe with the next assignment. This particular photo shoot was to capture the return of wild geese to the marshes in Louisiana, and any other time would be appealing but now only seemed mildly entertaining. Wading along the dense swampy marshland in bayou country simply didn't hold the fascination it should have.

"Sabrina, your next assignment requires about a week, possibly two depending on the rate of return of the geese. The magazine needs photos of them in flight as well as on the ground. Can you be ready to go next Monday?" Joe asked, already knowing the answer.

He always asked the same question each time he sent Brie on a new assignment.

"Joe, can I get back to you shortly with my answer?" Sabrina asked, cautiously.

Though Joe was her assistant and theoretically worked for her, she always referred to him being the one in charge because he would scout out specific shoots he knew would be appealing to her. Sabrina's seniority with the magazine gave her some leverage when they handed out the assignments.

Besides, the editors usually knew who they preferred to do the photographing for each article. That was the reason Sabrina bounced from place to place virtually without a break, because she was very good at capturing the essence of nature in the raw.

She was always in demand.

"Sure, but this is a first. Are you seriously thinking of refusing an assignment? You've never missed a photo shoot. What's up?"

"I have some unfinished business in Asheville, and I'm thinking perhaps I should go back for a short time," Brie offered.

"Well, I won't pry into your personal life, just let me know what I should do."

"I'll call you tomorrow with my decision."

Now what, she thought. She could press forward and take this assignment, and see if the last two photo shoots were simply a fluke, or take up the reins and make a change. She decided to call her sister. Sophie would know how to advise her.

"Hi sis," Sophie answered.

"Sophie, I need to get your opinion."

"Wow, sounds serious. Since when do you need my opinion on anything? You are the independent twin," Sophie replied with laughter in her voice.

"Be that as it may, I do need some sisterly advice. Joe called with my next job which happens to be in Louisiana shooting geese."

"Shooting geese as with a camera, not a gun."

"Funny, sis. I'm thinking of refusing this assignment, because I've been contemplating going back to Asheville."

"Are you feeling alright, Brie? You never turn down an assignment. In all the years of being a photojournalist, I do not recall one single time you have declined a shoot, this is huge. Why are you thinking of not doing this one?"

"I have unfinished business at Aunt Millie's house. There is something drawing me to return. I know this sounds crazy, but I can't seem to shake the compelling need to go back."

"I thought you weren't hearing voices anymore."

"I haven't, but I still feel I'm expected to do something with Aunt Millie's *Passionate Promises.* I need to pursue this."

"I didn't know you were seriously giving it any thought. Surely you don't expect to do anything with that; I mean, what can you do? Aunt Millie did this in her spare time to give some significance to her life. But Brie, this is not the time to go chasing after Aunt Millie's leftover dreams and leave your career in the lurch."

"Sophie, I know how this must appear to you, but I need to go back. I'm not sure what I'll do when I get there, but I can put my career on hold for a few weeks until I figure it out."

"Brie, does this have to do with Ben? Perhaps it is Ben you want to see and that is perfectly okay. In fact, I would be delighted for you and Ben to get serious about one another, and I haven't even met the man and given him my seal of approval."

"As much as I'd like to give you a thrill and say it does, I'll have to disappoint you. This has nothing to do with Ben. Yes, it will be great to spend more time with him; however, he is not the main reason for my return."

"Well, that is a bit disappointing. All I can say, as far as advice goes, is follow your heart. If you feel the need, for whatever reason, to return to Asheville, then go back and explore those issues. The magazine shouldn't fault you for a little time off after all the years you've devoted to them."

"So you don't believe I'm being foolish to return after only a few weeks back on the job?"

"No. I want you to be happy. If it means returning to the country and exploring Aunt Millie's *Passionate Promises*, by all means, do so. I can't say that I truthfully see you crusading for the downtrodden, but stranger things can happen."

"If I pursue this, would you be willing to give it a try also?"

"Gosh Brie, I don't know. I'm not the crusading type. I believe in helping my neighbor or giving a couple of dollars to the guy standing on a street corner, but this is completely different. I doubt I could do it, to be perfectly honest."

"That's okay. But I do believe I'll return for a few weeks. That should give me the time I need to figure this out. Please try to understand where I'm coming from. If I don't do this, it will nag at me the rest of my life. I know it will, and I don't want regrets."

"So you will be returning soon?"

"Yes, I think so. Thanks for the help, sis. It was good talking this through with you. Funny as it may sound, last December at Christmas, I belonged in the house and the community. Who would have thought I could ever feel this way about small town living? I've always been directed by my job and the projects rather than taking charge and making my own decisions. It's hard to be approaching thirty and realize I've missed some very important things like friendship and love. I need these. So I'm taking some time off to reevaluate and take charge of my future," Brie explained.

"I applaud you, Brie. I'm so happy to hear you say that you want other things in your life besides work. Yes, your career is great and I'm proud of your accomplishments, and you know that. But it excites me to hear you talk about wanting relationships and love. I've always wanted you to have that special someone in your life, and I'm hoping Ben is that person for you. It's good to do some soul searching. Maybe Aunt Millie knew something we didn't, because she sure thought you would want to live in the house, and believed you would take over her crusade. There's no reason why you can't blend your fast-paced lifestyle with some downtime country living. Whatever changes you need to make to achieve it, I want you to have a life that is completely fulfilling. Just be happy, Brie."

"I know you do. Things many not be the same as during the holidays, but I'll find out. I'll call you when I book my flight."

"You know I support whatever your decisions are."

"Thanks sis."

Having talked to Sophie only confirmed what she felt all along in her heart. She really didn't need her sister's approval, but rather, wanted to let Sophie know of her plans to return to Asheville. Brie felt better for the conversation knowing her sister understood and didn't fault her for her decision. She had to put a final resolution to her aunt's legacy, and for her future as well. *Somehow, I know there is a connection between the two,* she pondered.

Chapter 35

Comfortable with the decision, Sabrina called Joe.

"Hi Joe, I'm planning to go back to Asheville for a few weeks and would like you to verify that someone else can cover the Louisiana assignment. If no one is available, I will certainly do it. Next, please convey I want to take a few weeks off on personal leave with the understanding I remain available for any upcoming photo shoots if I'm needed."

"I understand. I'll get back with you."

Sabrina didn't want to cut herself off from her work, or jeopardize any opportunity for a good assignment should one appear on the horizon. Taking a few weeks for personal business didn't seem out of line considering all the years she had remained available and devoted to the magazine. Surely this gave her some leverage. Having put her thoughts into action, she was excited with the idea of returning to her country home.

She went into the bedroom and rummaged through the closet to see what she would need because it was still cold in North Carolina. Pulling out her wool slacks along with her corduroys and favorite jeans, she lined them across the bed and matched pullovers and sweaters. Sabrina spent the remainder of the day focusing on the wardrobe, and her enthusiasm escalated as she collected items to pack.

Sabrina didn't want to make flight arrangements until she heard from Joe. She didn't foresee any problem; however, Brie needed to be prudent where her career was concerned. Not once in her plans did she consider in her return to the country she would also be returning to Ben, but when the thought entered her mind, it put a smile on her face.

It was several hours later, around five o'clock in the evening, when Joe called to report Sabrina was officially off duty. The magazine had a large year-to-date wall calendar in the conference room marked with the prospective schedule of photo shoots, and written in each day block was the assigned photographer. On the opposite wall was a blackboard listing the names of those off on vacation, medical leave, and such. Brie's name was added to the list of not available.

"Sabrina, the Louisiana shoot is covered. Tony just finished an assignment and agreed take it. Also, the calendar is marked that you are 'out of the office' for a month. I'm sure that can be extended if necessary, but I put in for four weeks. I hope that was the time frame you were talking about."

"Perfect, thanks Joe. Was there any backlash in my asking for some personal time off?"

"No one had any objections as long as you remained available if needed. I assured the editors that wasn't a problem. They did ask why you needed the leave of absence since you just had a month off in December, but I think it was more out of curiosity. They wanted to make sure you had no health issues, that sort of thing."

"Gosh, I didn't think my requesting time off would cause anyone the need to know, or consider my health. I hope you put them straight on that subject."

"Trust me. I assured them you're in perfect health and planned to return to Asheville to take care of unfinished business. I hope it was okay to tell them that."

"That's perfect, Joe. I'd have said the same thing. Now I can book my flight. The clock is officially ticking. I'll stay in touch, and let me know if anything comes along that I might be interested in, or should know."

"Of course, have a good trip."

"Talk to you later."

Without wasting any time, Sabrina dialed the airline and booked a late morning flight. Accustomed to leaving on a moments notice, there wasn't much she needed to do to prepare for the trip except pack the outfits that were sorted on the bed. She debated whether to call Ben and let him know she was flying in tomorrow afternoon but decided to surprise him instead.

Next, she went through her bills and important papers to make sure nothing was overlooked that needed immediate attention. Two hours later, she was ready to leave and called her sister to let her know.

"Hi Sophie, I'm officially on personal leave from work for the next four weeks, so I'll be flying out in the morning."

"Wow, that was fast. I take it everything went okay at work?"

"No problem. I did leave myself available should an assignment come up they wanted to send me on. I didn't want to completely shut the door to anything for the next month."

"I'm glad that worked out so well. So by this time tomorrow, you'll be back in the country. Do you want me to take you to the airport, so you don't have to leave your car in the parking garage for a month?"

"I appreciate the offer, but I don't want to inconvenience you. The long-term parking fee isn't expensive. The longer your car is parked, the less your rate-per-day."

"I hope everything goes well for you. I'm certain you'll find what you are searching for."

"Thanks for understanding."

"Good luck, Brie, and call me when you get there."

"Talk to you then."

Packed and ready to leave, Sabrina took a quick shower and went to bed early. Tomorrow would be a busy day and she couldn't wait for it to begin. She was excited to be returning so soon.

Chapter 36

Sabrina fell into a deep sleep and dreamt she and Aunt Millie were sitting in a beautiful park surrounded by a garden of rose bushes with every color imaginable. She knew each rose bush has only one color, and yet these bushes had assorted colors. One rose was dark pink, another red, another purple, another peach, and so forth, all stemming from the same bush. *That can't be,* she thought.

Brie sat on the wooden bench not recognizing the scene being any place she had ever been to before. Everything around her was pure in color and texture with the sun glistening on the leaves and grass, making them sparkle like diamonds. *Where am I, and why am I sitting with my aunt, who is dead? Or am I dead too,* she questioned.

Her aunt sat quietly with her face turned upward toward the sun and her eyes closed, with a smile on her lips. Sabrina stared at her profile, but didn't say a word. *What did this mean?* She looked around and noticed they were completely alone, no other person or animal to be seen, not a bird in the sky or a squirrel in a tree. No bees buzzing near the rose petals; everything was perfectly still. Startled to hear her aunt's voice, Sabrina whipped her head around to face her aunt, who stared straight into her eyes. Something was different about Aunt Millie. Her eyes sparkled with life and vitality. Brie sat stunned, not knowing what to say.

"Sabrina, my dear, it's good to see you," Aunt Millie stated, looking deeply into Sabrina's eyes.

"Aunt Millie, you can't be here. You passed away nearly three months ago," Sabrina declared, shocked to be having a conversation with her dead aunt.

"Of course I did, dear, but did you think I would leave you?" she asked, softly.

Sabrina turned from her aunt and stared straight ahead. Surely her mind was playing tricks on her. *This is a dream. This isn't real,* she reminded herself.

"Aunt Millie, you aren't real."

"Well, that all depends. Yes, you're right, I'm deceased in your world; however, I live in another now."

"What do you mean? Are you telling me that we both are alive but living in different worlds? If that is true, then how can we be together like this?"

"Only for a short time am I allowed to meet with you in a place such as this. Once our time is up, I can never return."

This did not make any sense to Sabrina. She enjoyed being with her aunt again, however, it was simply too farfetched for even her imagination. Can you be dreaming and while in the dream, believe yourself to be dreaming? She was beginning to question her sanity, and that certainly couldn't be a good thing. *What is happening to me? This is too weird,* she thought.

"Okay, Aunt Millie. If we can sit here and talk to one another, what does this mean? Why are we brought together like this? Why am I the only one to be experiencing this?"

"I know you have many unanswered questions, and this seems very unreal to you. Do you believe in angels?"

"Yes, I do. Not that I've met one lately, but I do believe they exist."

"Good, then you believe in a heavenly place."

"If you are asking me if I believe in God and heaven, then the answer is yes, but you already know that. Just tell me what is going on?" Sabrina asked, confused, and yet, spellbound to every word her aunt spoke.

"What did you think of my letter?" Aunt Millie asked.

She continued to gaze into Sabrina's eyes.

"Actually, I didn't know what to think. I was shocked at first and hurt that you didn't tell me what you were doing. You had plenty of opportunity to share your guardian angel activities with me when I came to visit you, but you didn't, so discovering this aspect of your life after you died was hard to take."

"Have you learned anything since my death? Do you understand what I was asking of you and Sophie when I left the letter?"

"I don't know what reaction you are expecting from me. Obviously, you think there is a lesson to be learned with *Passionate Promises*. I haven't thought it through, or that I'm the right candidate to continue with your crusade. Why is it so important I do this, anyway?"

"You're right, there is a lesson, but you have to learn it for yourself. I cannot define it for you, otherwise the meaning and significance will be lost," Aunt Millie stressed.

"Great, I'm no closer to understanding any of this than before," Sabrina mumbled, uncertain of the direction the conversation was taking.

It didn't seem she was about to get any help from her aunt in understanding *Passionate Promises*.

"Sabrina, dear, don't be upset. You will come to understand very soon, I assure you. When it was revealed to me, I was just as confused as you are now. It will change your life, my love."

Sabrina stared at her aunt, dumbfounded by her words.

"You are scaring me, Aunt Millie. What was revealed to you that will soon be revealed to me? Why can't you simply tell me instead of us dancing around the subject?"

"Darling, it is meant that I guide you, but I cannot instruct you any further. It must be your decision, your choice."

"So it won't do me any good to ask you what I'm supposed to be making a choice about."

"I know you will make the correct decision."

"So you have that much confidence in me, or do you know

know how this is going to turn out?"

"Both," her aunt replied with a smile.

"By the way, after your funeral I was experiencing some strange occurrences. Was that you whispering to me?"

"What kind of strange occurrences?"

"Well, for one, while at your funeral the odd feeling that a presence was next to me, but there was no one physically there, and for another, I kept hearing a soft voice whispering in my ear. This happened often while in your house. Was that you?"

"No, my dear, it wasn't me."

"Do you know who it was, or what it means?"

"I cannot give you the answers you seek. Our time is limited, Sabrina. Know that I love you very much and want you to have a life of contentment and a heart full of joy that is everlasting. Don't be too quick to dismiss the works that are set in motion. If you give it a try, I believe you will be surprised at the outcome. I know I certainly was. I must leave you now, but remember, Sabrina, fill your heart with good deeds that will be with you for eternity," Aunt Millie stated, before fading away in front of Sabrina's eyes.

Jumping up from the bench, Sabrina twirled around searching in all directions calling out her aunt's name, but she was gone. Saddened that she didn't get to say goodbye for the second time, she dropped back down on the bench, put her face in her hands, and cried.

Brie woke suddenly with tears streaming down her cheeks. It was only a dream, yet it felt so real. How much more could she handle? Just when she thought it was behind her, here comes another dream, and now everything was more vivid than ever before.

Sabrina didn't understand matters any better. What would happen if she didn't do anything with *Passionate Promises*? Would it be the end of her life? Sabrina didn't believe that. But why so much importance put on helping the helpless, and why was Aunt Millie asking her about angels and heaven? What was that suppose to mean? Sabrina remained in bed, pulling the covers over her head, crying until there wasn't a tear left to shed.

She threw back the covers and rolled over glancing at the clock on the nightstand, reporting two-thirty in the morning. Much to early to get up, she tried to fall back to sleep, but her mind kept replaying the dream. There was so much she wanted to say to Aunt Millie but it would never happen now.

She was living through her aunt's death a second time, and it was more than her heart could handle. It seemed like yesterday when she looked upon her aunt's face while she lay at rest. Memories flooded her mind, leaving Sabrina heartbroken once again.

Chapter 37

Not knowing what time she fell asleep, Sabrina managed to get a few more hours under the covers. Waking up in a mental fog, she dragged herself to the bathroom. Her melancholy mood was somewhat alleviated by a long shower. She slipped on a pair of dark blue corduroys with a pale blue turtleneck sweater and finished her hair and makeup with plenty of time to spare before leaving for the airport.

She thought about calling her sister and conveying the dream, but decided against it. David and Sophie would be getting ready for work anyway. It was a strange dream and she tried to convince herself that was all there was to it, but in her heart, she knew better. The dream had a significant message that Brie could not ignore.

Sabrina felt like whining *why me* but refused to have a pity party. She was far too mature, or so she hoped. After securing the apartment for a month, she grabbed her bags and walked out to the car. This was the routine she often did on autopilot. Refusing to allow her mind to replay the dream for the hundredth time, she focused on what she planned to do once arriving home. Now that was a thought; *I'm going to my country home,* Brie told herself. With spirits lifted, she drove onward, anxious to get on that plane.

Sabrina parked the car, checked in luggage, and made it through the security line with forty-five minutes to spare. She thought to grab a sandwich and iced tea at a nearby food stand knowing it would be her only meal until arriving in Asheville. She had a few minutes to leave a voicemail message on Sophie's phone, but to her surprise she answered.

"Hey, I thought you would be on a plane by now."

"I'll be boarding soon. I had a few minutes and figured I would leave a message. I didn't expect you to answer. Aren't you in a classroom?"

"I'm at recess duty on the playground. Teachers take turns and this is my week. Are you still excited about making this trip?"

"Yes, I'm doing the right thing," Brie replied, debating whether to tell Sophie about the dream.

She decided against it for the moment because neither had the time for details. *I'll tell her later,* she thought.

"I believe you'll find what you're searching for, and I do understand about *Passionate Promises*. I know you need to resolve it in your mind one way or another. I can't fault you for that. Brie, whatever the outcome, find contentment too."

How unusual that her sister would use the same terminology Aunt Millie said in the dream.

"Thank you, Sophie. I need your support."

"So what is the first thing on your list?"

"I'm not sure. Maybe just sit in the house and think. I really don't know yet."

"I want to know if anything strange occurs. You know what I'm referring to. I'll be thinking of you often."

"Don't worry about me. I'm not going off the deep end, just retracing my steps back to the country for a few weeks, that's all."

"Alright, have some fun with Ben while you are soul searching. I've got to run. It's time to call the kids into class. Have a good flight, Brie."

"I'll call you later."

It was time to get in line for boarding. Sabrina couldn't wait to be back in Asheville. Just a few more hours, she consoled herself.

During the flight Brie thought about the dream. The visit with her aunt was so unbelievably vivid. It stayed in her mind so absolute, like she had actually lived in that scene. She remembered every detail and wondered if it was a vision. *But that can't be because I know my aunt is dead. There is no mistake about that,* she reminded
herself.

Telling her sister about this was going to put Sophie over the edge, and she didn't want to scare her anymore. However, there simply was no way to leave Sophie out of the loop. *She would never forgive me if I did that,* Brie admitted to herself. She needed to discuss this additional encounter of the weird kind.

Chapter 38

Sabrina went straight to the grocery store from the airport, still able to make it to the house before the sun set, which was good timing. After bumping up the thermostat to produce more heat, Brie brought in the groceries first and then the suitcases, placing them by the stairs. The house warmed quickly while she walked through the downstairs flipping on lights and checking each room.

She took the luggage one piece at a time upstairs and walked down the hall toward the bedroom she always occupied. Brie made a quick decision and continued the short distance to the master bedroom, placing the suitcase beside the bed. Looking around the room for a moment, she felt comfortable in claiming this room; after all, it was now her home. Sabrina unpacked clothes, hanging them in the closet next to her aunt's things, and cleared a couple of armoire drawers, putting her remaining clothing in them. Her aunt's items went into one of the storage bins under the bed.

Satisfied everything was in order, Sabrina backtracked to the kitchen to make dinner. She made a salad along with steamed vegetables. Brie placed the meal on a tray and took it into the den to sit by the fireplace that was already adding a nice warmth to the room. Sabrina sat quietly in the chair listening to any sounds the house might make, but the only noise came from the crackling wood. She thought about being in Asheville instead of sitting in a hotel room in Louisiana. *Did*

I do the right thing? she questioned.

Resting her head on the rocker, she closed her eyes and relaxed knowing this is where she was meant to be. It felt right. Shortly, she returned to the kitchen retrieving the cell phone from her purse and called Sophie.

"Hi Sophie, I'm here safe and sound."

"Good, now I don't have to worry. Is everything okay in the house?" she asked.

"Yes, just as I left it. I stopped by the grocery store and have already unpacked and had dinner. It didn't take long to settle in," Brie told her sister.

"So what is on your agenda for tomorrow?"

"I'll start the day by having pancakes at *The Country Kitchen,* and then stop by to visit Bella to let her know I'm back."

"I know you'll find the answers you're looking for."

"Something tells me I will."

"What do you mean? Has anything else happened?"

Sophie recognized the change in the tone of her sister's voice.

"You could say that. I had a dream last night that I was visiting with Aunt Millie."

"Oh dear, here we go again. I thought the dreams were over. What happened in the dream?"

"We sat on a bench and talked. She wouldn't answer my questions about *Passionate Promises,* but instead asked me if I believed in angels and heaven. She said I needed to make a decision,."

She didn't want to make Sophie upset again so she kept the discussion short.

"But don't worry. It was just a dream, like you always tell me."

"What is the decision?"

"I think she was referring to my accepting her legacy."

"What are you going to do since having this dream?"

"That's what I'll be giving serious thought to."

"You know Brie, this is getting way out-of-hand."

"I know. My sentiments exactly, but what can I do? I didn't ask for this."

"This whole thing is annoying me. I hate that you're going through something so strange. I'm sorry to say this to you, Brie, but this can't be normal."

"Believe me, I agree, but enough talk about it. I'll call you in a couple of days. Take care, sis, and don't worry."

"I know what you're doing, Brie, and don't you dare. Don't pull back and withhold information because you don't want me to worry. That's worse than my worrying. I'm telling you right now that would hurt my feelings and you know it. So please don't push me away. I'm your sister and your twin, we go through this together," Sophie declared, getting angry.

"I'm sorry, Sophie, if I gave you the impression I was pulling back. True, it's been on my mind that the weird dreams and such are abnormal, and I can tell they are scaring you. You're already stressed over this, and I don't want you to be. But you're right, we go through this together, twins all the way, always," Sabrina agreed.

"I promise I won't withhold anything strange from you."

"Thanks, Brie. I have to be there for you. It's in the genes."

They never could be mad at one another. It simply wasn't in either sister's personality.

"We'll talk tomorrow."

"Okay, talk to you then. You take care, Brie."

Sabrina went upstairs to the master bedroom and for a long time stood in the doorway and studied the interior, observing every intricate detail. She examined her aunt's clothing in the walk-in closet. Aunt Mille had very nice clothes and Sabrina wished she could wear them, but unfortunately, her aunt was two sizes larger.

She walked into the bathroom and recognized the plush light blue robe hanging on the back of the door. This was her aunt's favorite robe. She often wore it in the wintertime.

The bathroom had a vanity of beige granite countertops and

porcelain sinks with gold-plated faucets to match the light fixtures that hung above. The entire wall above the vanity was mirrored which reflected the lights. On the opposite wall was a deep-set shower stall. Taupe-colored ceramic tiles wrapped around the walls with an inlayed pattern using colors of rust and green. The show door was made of opaque glass.

Brie peeled off her clothes and stepped into the power of double shower heads. The force of the water took her breath away, but she slowly began to relax under the spray and stood for a long time. Drying quickly, she grabbed for the robe, and though it was too large, slipped it on. It felt soft and warm against her skin as she enveloped herself in it. Tiptoeing into the bedroom, Brie went to the armoire searching for a pair of flannel pajamas.

Sabrina didn't feel sleepy so she went to sit by the fire and let her mind drift back to the dream. What did it mean? What did any of this mean? *Who would have thought such things happened over the death of a loved one? It doesn't seem to involve Sophie. Why can't she hear voices and have dreams? Why am I the chosen one?* she thought.

Brie hoped now that she was back in her aunt's house there would be another appearance. She didn't know what else to call the apparition that visited her. She wanted that connection again. *It is the only way to put an end to all of this,* she reasoned. Brie could practically *feel* a presence and knew she wasn't alone. She believed the answers she was seeking would be found here.

"Okay, I came back, so show yourself. I want to know why I'm a target of interest to you," Sabrina spoke.

I'm really losing it now, she thought.

Sabrina was reconciling herself to the fact that she was trying to conjure up an invisible being. She was glad there was no one around to witness her behavior, especially her sister. There wasn't a sound in the house, and no one made an appearance before her.

"I thought you'd be glad that I've returned. I'm hoping you

will make yourself known soon."

Sabrina was actually disappointed that her invisible *being* wouldn't show itself. *The sooner it did, the sooner she would come to know what was going on,* she mused. But nothing happened, so Brie gave it a rest for the moment. Leaning her head back, she drifted off to sleep with these very concerns racing through her mind.

Chapter 39

"*You must stay, Sabrina,*" the voice whispered softly in her ear. Sabrina woke with a start, jumping out of the chair. Brie knew she wasn't alone in the room.

"Okay, where are you? I know you're here. I can *feel* your presence," she spoke.

There was silence, not a sound in the house.

"I'm getting annoyed with this hide and seek routine. Whoever you are, if you have something to say to me, get on with it," Sabrina demanded in agitation.

The house remained quiet. Brie knew she should be afraid, but instead, found herself very irritated. This had gone on long enough. Voices, dreams, and now a vision. She was determined to get to the bottom of it, but she didn't know how.

She accepted the invisible pull drawing her back to the house. Though Sabrina believed herself to be made of tough stuff, it was fraying her nerves, and she was quickly losing patience. Brie extinguished the fire and went upstairs to bed, exasperated with the entire ordeal. She hoped she wouldn't dream.

Sabrina slept fitfully anticipating voices and fearful of dreaming so by the light of day she was exhausted. She went downstairs to brew a pot of coffee and threw an English muffin in the toaster. While standing at the sink and looking out the back window, she was surprised by the sound of the doorbell and cautiously went to the front door, peering through the peep hole to find Bella waiting on the step.

"Bella, how did you know I was here?"

"I drove by and noticed smoke coming from your chimney, so I decided to investigate."

"Come in and have a cup of coffee with me."

"I'd love to."

Sabrina took two mugs from the cabinet and poured the coffee, taking it along with the cream and sugar to the table. She placed the English muffin on a plate and put another one in the toaster before retrieving the butter and orange marmalade from the refrigerator. Brie offered the muffin to Bella.

"Don't mind if I do," Bella remarked, accepting the muffin and buttering it. Sabrina did the same, and they sat for a moment enjoying a simple breakfast.

"When did you get in?"

"Last night. I was planning to stop by and let you know I was in town."

"I have to say, I'm curious what has brought you back so soon. I didn't expect to see you for a few months."

"I didn't think I'd be back this soon, either."

"Well, it is good to see you again. Will you be staying awhile?"

"I took a short leave from work for a few weeks. Perhaps I'm simply trying to recapture the good times I had during the holidays."

Sabrina wasn't ready to talk about the unusual experiences. Sophie and David were the only ones who knew, and Brie thought it best to keep it that way.

"Could it be Ben is the reason."

"No, I wouldn't take a sabbatical from work to pursue a relationship with a man."

"I know it's none of my business, anyway."

"That's okay. Being here will obviously give me the opportunity to spend more time with Ben, and I'm looking forward to that. However, I need to resolve a few things, and this seemed like the best places to do some thinking."

"Sounds serious."

"It could be."

"Thanks for the coffee and muffin, but I need to get home. Be sure to stay in touch while you're here."

Bella could tell something was bothering Sabrina, but she wasn't going to press for information. She figured most likely it had to do with Mildred, and the country was always a good place to find peace and solitude when one wanted to search their heart.

"I will and thanks for stopping by," Sabrina stated, giving Bella a hug before she left.

Sabrina felt a peace about returning to her country home. She quickly cleaned the dishes and went upstairs to the desk in the corner of the bedroom to retrieve the letter she had placed in the drawer before leaving. She read its contents again while sitting on the edge of the bed. Did the answer lie within the words on this slip of paper? Somehow, Sabrina was beginning to believe it did. She simply needed to concentrate and surely it would come to her. In the dream, Aunt Millie asked Brie if she had read the letter. Was she trying to give her a clue?

Chapter 40

Brie placed the letter on the table beside the chair she always occupied. She wanted a minute to simply enjoy the beauty of her backyard before getting down to the business of *Passionate Promises*. She rocked, staring out through the French doors beyond the wooden deck to the perimeter where the lawn ended and the forest began. Never in her wildest imagination did Brie think she would be the owner of something so beautiful and it was because of Aunt Millie's love for her.

Sabrina felt compelled to repay her aunt for this wonderful gift. She realized Aunt Millie gave to her all that she dearly loved, her home and a legacy, which she was yet to understand. She needed answers before she went any further with her life in auto-mode.

Remembering the dream of Aunt Millie and reading the letter once again put Sabrina in a quandary. Reflecting on the things they had talked about, Brie thought of her aunt's statements. *What did she mean it would be revealed to me soon? What would be revealed? What choice would I have to make,* she asked herself.

Exasperated, Brie turned her thoughts toward Ben. She thought of calling him, better yet, perhaps she would drive by the farm to see him. Sabrina went upstairs to apply a light touch of makeup, pulled her hair into a ponytail, and ran down the stairs to retrieve her purse and cell phone.

The farm was twenty minutes away. Brie didn't see anyone

on the grounds when she drove up close to the building, but heard the sound of a saw coming from the entrance. She stepped inside and recognized a few employees busy at woodworking, making flower boxes. The employee closest to the door noticed her entering and stopped working to walk toward her.

"Hello, can I help you?"

"Yes, I'm looking for Ben. Is he around?"

"Ben is in the field but should be back around three. By the way, my name is Sam. Can I help you with anything in his place?"

"Could you give him a message and tell him Sabrina is in town?"

"I'll let him know," he replied with a smile.

"Thank you."

She glanced at the acreage all around the outer perimeter of the yard. There were trees as far as the eye could see organized in designated rows. Leaving the farm with no place to go, Brie went home.

Now what to do, she asked herself. She took a notepad and pen from a kitchen drawer and went to sit at the table. Where to begin to solve this mystery surrounding her life? Sabrina thought back to her stay during the holidays and detailed on paper what had occurred, beginning with finding Aunt Millie's letter. She added meeting Annie and Dorothy, the waitress, and thought of George with his comments and even Ben's remarks.

Brie added each name and to the right of their name, the comments made about her aunt. She included statements Bella had made as well. Putting this on paper helped Sabrina to organize and detail her aunt's life which she was discovering since the funeral.

With a clean sheet of paper, again, she wrote down each dream, listing the individual encounters and where she was at the time. Sabrina was hoping that if she continued to log the sequence of events, eventually it would begin to make sense to her. It was all Brie knew to do at the moment.

Sabrina was aware that not all occurrences happened in her aunt's house; some took place in the condo and others in a hotel room. Hearing voices and dreams wasn't limited to one particular place, making it seem that location had nothing to do with this, but rather the focus was strictly on her. She was back at the beginning. Someone was trying to get her attention, solely, and if the most recent dream was any indication, it wasn't her aunt.

Putting some semblance of order to the past few months on paper gave Sabrina an outline of events she could study. Writing things down always helped to streamline her thoughts. Even if she wasn't any closer to understanding, at least Brie felt she was moving in the right direction. She wondered how many people Aunt Millie had helped and how she could find them.

She had the idea of placing an advertisement in the local newspaper, but discounted it for fear of receiving unsavory responses. Sabrina didn't want to be plagued with individuals wanting someone to listen to their misfortunes so she dismissed that idea.

Remembering the signed guestbook at her aunt's funeral, Brie ran upstairs to retrieve the book from the desk drawer, where she had placed it along with the other important papers from the funeral. Returning to the table, she sat reviewing the signatures. Who were all these people, and did they hold the answers to understanding her aunt's crusade? It was time to become a detective, because she only had four weeks to unravel this mystery. Sabrina thought there had to be a connection between the mysterious voice and *Passionate Promises*. *What is the voice and my aunt trying to tell me?* she wondered.

Chapter 41

Sabrina was excited and ready to set her plan in motion. She would stop by Bella's house in the morning with the guestbook and ask for her help in identifying the signatures. Brie could look up the names in the telephone book, but that would be a long process. Besides, Bella would be excited to participate. Feeling much better, Sabrina made dinner and while she waited for it to cook, called her sister.

"Hi Sophie, what are you doing?"

"Hey Brie, I just got home. How is everything in the country?"

"Well, since it's only my first day, I would say things are as expected. Bella stopped by this morning when she noticed smoke coming from the chimney."

"I forgot it's still cold up there."

"With all the traveling I do, cold days come and go for me."

"Does Ben know you're back in town?"

"I stopped by the farm earlier today, but he wasn't there so I left a message."

"Have you decided what you're going to do?" Sophie inquired, still wondering what her sister had planned.

"I'll be doing a little sleuthing. I'm taking the guestbook from Aunt Milli's funeral over to Bella in the morning to see if she can help me with the names. I thought of contacting some of them and find out if they could reveal anything about Aunt Millie's guardian angel activities."

"I'm not sure how that will help, but I suppose it can't hurt, either."

"I thought it was worth a try. I'll let you know how it goes. How is everything there?"

"We spend our evenings like two couch potatoes curled up in our separate corners grading papers, the work never ends," Sophie commented with humor.

"I'll call in a few days, or sooner if something comes up. Take care and give David a hug for me."

Sabrina was determined to find out why she was still being annoyed with dreams and the same voice again after practically three months. There had to be a logical explanation, and she was willing to employ the help of Bella to find the answers. While she sat quietly eating her dinner, the doorbell rang. She recognized Ben through the peephole and with a smile on her face, swung open the front door.

"I came over as soon as I got your message. I had to see for myself that you're really here," Ben stated and pulled Brie into his arms for a warm embrace.

There was no doubt in Sabrina's mind that he missed her. The look on his face told her everything she needed to know. Standing back at arms length, she stared into his eyes with a wide grin on her face.

"If I didn't know better, Ben Cooper, I would think you missed me," she said teasing him.

"Only a little," He smiled back.

"Come on in. Would you like some iced tea or coffee?"

"Coffee would be good if you have some made."

"Only takes a minute. I'll crank up the coffeemaker."

"I didn't mean to interrupt your dinner, finish eating. I'll fix my own coffee."

"Takes only a few seconds."

She walked over to the table and sat down across from Ben while the coffee brewed.

"I'm sorry, I don't have any extra chicken to offer you. I could make a salad and put another baked potato in the oven."

"Not necessary, but thanks anyway. I didn't stop for a meal. I wanted to see you."

"Well, I'm glad you did."

"So what brought you back to the country ahead of spring?" he asked.

"It has to do with unfinished business concerning Aunt Millie."

Sabrina wasn't ready to reveal the experiences she was encountering since the funeral. She didn't know what he would think about such a thing, and for that matter, she didn't know what Bella or anyone would think of her for declaring such ridiculous events. For the moment, her secret remained safe with Sophie.

"Do you mean legal matters?" Ben inquired with renewed curiosity.

"Oh no, nothing like that. Aunt Millie's attorney took care of everything. This is more of a personal thing."

She wasn't trying to be evasive, but she didn't want to discuss it. Brie got up and poured two cups of coffee and placed them on the table along with the cream and sugar.

"What have you been doing?" Sabrina asked, wanting to change the subject.

"I've been very busy which is why you haven't heard from me. I had to go out of town a couple times to meet with an architect about building another greenhouse on the back west corner of the property," Ben explained.

"What will you use the building for?"

"We're thinking of expanding the business to include seasonal plants and flowers such as poinsettias, Christmas cactus, orchids, ferns; things like that. We need a special house to grow them in and protect them from the cold weather."

"That's a great idea, like one-stop shopping to buy all your holiday greenery," Brie stated, excited for Ben.

"We've been giving it some thought for the past couple of years and finally decided to invest the money and do it. Should it not work out as planned, we can always use the building for something else. It won't be a wasted investment."

"When do they begin building it?"

"There are a few more details to work out, but hopefully by early spring. We want to have it completed in plenty of time to place the plants and grow them before our winter season," Ben told her.

Now Sabrina knew the reason Ben hadn't called her in the month she was gone. David was right. He had a logical explanation, and knowing this put her heart at ease.

"It's getting late and I should be going. Do you want to go out to dinner Friday night?"

"Yes, I'd love that. What time should I be ready?"

"I'll stop by around six o'clock and make reservations for seven at a new Italian restaurant that just opened in the downtown area. Do you like Italian food?"

"I love Italian food, and I'll be ready at six sharp."

Ben took his cup to the sink and spilled out the remains, and they walked together to the foyer. He opened the door to leave, and turned to brush a quick kiss on her lips and grinned when he saw the surprise in her eyes. He pulled her against him and kissed her passionately. Sabrina wrapped her arms around his neck, pressing her body into the embrace.

"Told you I missed you."

"I see that," she said, smiling up at him.

"See you on Friday. Dream about me," he instructed, leaving her standing in the doorway.

Sabrina felt like she was going to melt into a puddle right on the spot. *Oh yes, I will indeed enjoy dreaming about you, Ben,* she thought.

Obviously, he came over as soon as he got the message because he was driving the company truck with the familiar logo on the side doors.

Chapter 42

Hurrying with her morning routine, Sabrina was anxious to drive to Bella's house with the guestbook but not feeling the need to call first. She got out of the car, noticing Bella standing in the opened doorway. Apparently, she heard her drive up.

"Sabrina, you are out early. I just made a pan of biscuits. We'll have breakfast together," she insisted as they walked into the kitchen.

"Thanks Bella, am I too early to be visiting?"

"Nonsense, you come over anytime you like."

She set two mugs of steaming coffee on a tray along with the usual condiments and put them on the table. Bella pulled out the pan of homemade biscuits, still warm in the oven, putting a few on a plate, inviting Sabrina to have one with butter and jam.

Brie took a large flaky biscuit and smothered it with strawberry preserves, chewing it slowly to savor every morsel of flavor.

"This biscuit is delicious. What's your secret?" Sabrina asked before she took a second bite.

"Buttermilk and honey, a lot of buttermilk and a little touch of honey; it is a recipe that has been in my family for years. I'll write it down for you."

"Thanks, I'd love to try making them."

They ate in silence, and afterwards Bella cleared the table and quickly straightened the kitchen. She noticed Sabrina had a book with her and inquired about it when Brie put it on the table.

"I brought the guestbook from Aunt Millie's funeral. I thought maybe you could tell me who some of these people are," Brie stated, pushing the book toward Bella.

She opened it and looked at the names, admitting there were a few she recognized.

"There are names I know. Here's Katherine Thompson, Jeffrey Smith, and Sarah Logan," she said as she ran her finger down the page. There were about a dozen names from over a hundred signatures that Bella recognized. That was wonderful to Sabrina. All she needed was a handful of people to talk to. She took out a small tablet and pen from her purse and jotted down the names while Bella called them aloud, and when she counted, there were fourteen people to contact.

"Thanks, this is great."

"So what will you do with these names?"

"I knew you would ask me that. Remember during the holidays, we talked about my aunt helping people in the community. I want to find out more about it and thought by talking with individuals who where at the funeral, they might be willing to tell me about their relationship with Aunt Millie."

"You think this will help."

"Yes, I need to understand the legacy and why it was so important to her. I'm hoping by talking with these individuals it will help me understand why she felt the need to be their guardian angel."

"Well, that certainly is one way to find out. I did go with her on occasion when she needed to pick up an item for someone, but I never pressed her about it. Anything I know, I've already shared with you," Bella stated solemnly, thinking of Millie.

"Is this the reason you came back?" Bella asked, already sure of the answer.

"Yes, there is something I sense is unfinished concerning Aunt Millie."

"Knowing how close the two of you were, it's only natural to want clarity of an aspect of her life that she kept private."

"Thanks for understanding, Bella. However, I've taken up enough of your time this morning. I appreciate the help and the biscuits," Brie stated, putting the guestbook and tablet back in her purse.

Sabrina took her dishes to the sink before walking toward the front door.

"I'll write down the recipe for you the next time we meet. I wish you luck in your endeavor. If I can be of any help, you know how to reach me."

"I will and thanks, again. I'll see you soon."

Brie turned giving her a warm embrace before walking down the sidewalk to the car. Bella had become a dear friend.

Chapter 43

Sabrina pulled out the phone book and located a telephone number and address to match each name on the list, excited she had something to work with. She contacted Sarah Logan first. She listened to the phone ringing several times before someone answered.

"Weston Nursing Home, how may I direct your call?" the receptionist stated.

"Perhaps I have the wrong number, but I was trying to reach Sarah Logan."

"Yes, we have a resident by that name. Would you like for me to transfer your call to her room?"

"Yes, thank you, but before you do, why is the nursing home listed as her telephone number in the phonebook?"

"Some of our residents do have a private phone line; however, not everyone chooses to do that. Most use our main number as their personal telephone number."

The call was transferred, ringing several times before being answered.

"Hello, is this Sarah Logan?" Sabrina asked, carefully.

"Yes, I'm Sarah, who am I speaking with?" Sarah inquired in a weak voice."

"Sarah, my name is Sabrina Fitzgerald. I understand you may have known my aunt, Mildred Wilson. Your name was among the signatures in the funeral guestbook, and I'd like to talk with you about her, if I may?" Brie asked, hoping she wouldn't be refused.

"Mildred. Oh yes, indeed I knew her; what a dear person. When I heard the news, I had my daughter take me to her funeral because there was no way I was going to miss saying goodbye to my friend," Sarah replied with newfound animation in her voice.

"Sarah, would it be possible to visit with you?"

"Of course, I would enjoy that very much," Sarah replied, excitedly.

"Wonderful, when would be the best time to stop by?"

"Well, let me see. How about tomorrow morning around ten o'clock? It gets busy in the mornings, but usually things settle by then."

"Perfect. I'll stop by then, and I look forward to meeting you."

"When you come in the front lobby to the reception desk, ask for room 212."

"I'll see you tomorrow, and thank you."

She felt like dancing around the kitchen. Just maybe she had hit the jackpot on the first try, because it sounded like Sarah had lots to tell. Brie went upstairs to the desk in the master bedroom to get a legal-sized tablet and back down to the den to start a fire. She sat for a while thinking of questions to ask Sarah intending to be prepared because there were very specific things she wanted to know.

Sabrina put on a fleece jacket and walked outside for some fresh air. It was a brisk, sunny day without a cloud in the sky as she strolled in the yard inspecting the flowerbeds. Brie walked the distance to the trees that lined the backyard and paused for a moment looking back at the house. She retraced her steps to the deck and climbing the three stairs to the wooden platform, pulled the cover off a lounger and sat down. It was so peaceful. She watched two squirrels chasing one another across the back lawn.

She felt very much at home. This was so different from her apartment in Florida, or days of living in hotel rooms. There was a tranquility she had never experienced before, not even when she visited. It never felt like this, but perhaps because they were too busy to enjoy the quiet of the day. Brie was beginning to think perhaps this was the life she longed for and didn't realize it until now.

Chapter 44

Brie was ready to meet Sarah bright and early the next morning. There was a lot of activity taking place inside the nursing home when she arrived promptly at ten o'clock. Music, voices, and unfamiliar noises greeted Brie from all directions. She asked for Sarah Logan's room 212, and the young woman sitting behind a half-circular desk pointed toward a long corridor and instructed her to turn left at the end of the hallway, the rooms were marked.

Finding Sarah's room midway, Sabrina paused at the open door, cautiously looking inside to see Sarah with her back to the door. Sarah turned from the small table where she was standing to acknowledge her visitor.

"Hi, I'm Sabrina Fitzgerald," Brie stated, waiting before she walked farther into the room.

"Sabrina, hello. Come in and let me pull out a chair for you," Sarah remarked and took one out from the table and turned it around.

Sarah was a petite woman, fragile in stature and appeared no taller than five-foot one, with snow-white hair combed in a simple short style and light blue eyes. Her complexion was softly wrinkled under her powdered makeup and rosy cheeks. Brie guessed her age to be mid-eighties. She walked into the room placing her purse on the table and sat in the chair while Sarah took the opposite seat.

"Thank you for meeting with me. I was hoping to talk with

you about my aunt," Sabrina stated, getting straight to the point.

"I'm delighted to talk about Mildred. She showed me a picture of you. I would have recognized you anywhere. In fact, I saw you at the funeral with your sister, but I didn't want to impose by introducing myself. Mildred was so proud, always bragging about you being a photojournalist," Sarah commented with a smile.

"I didn't know that."

"Mildred and I became friends a few years back. I a widow, and before I came here, I had a home with beautiful flower gardens. I still miss my gardening days, but you didn't come here to discuss that. Anyway, one spring day I was planting new perennials and suddenly got this persistent pain in my chest and down my left arm, the arm which I was digging the holes in the soil. I thought I had pulled a muscle until I began to lose the use of my hand. I slumped over and that was the condition my daughter found me in," Sarah said, letting out a deep sigh.

"Heather was coming by that day to have lunch with me. She called an ambulance, and I remained in the hospital for a week and was then sent to a nursing home for another two weeks for physical therapy. The doctors said it was a stroke, and it left me temporarily paralyzed on my left side," she continued.

She was excited to have an audience.

"Then I was allowed to go home for the remainder of my recovery, and one day, Mildred came to see me. Of course, I didn't know who she was. In fact, when I answered the doorbell, I thought she was selling something," Sarah chuckled, recalling the incident.

"I don't know how she knew of my illness, but word apparently got to her, and there she was on my doorstep, asking me if there was anything she could do to help me such as run an errand, or grocery shop. She was even willing to clean my house. I remember laughing at her for the mere thought that a stranger would do such a thing and without expecting compensation," she continued, elaborating on the story.

"So what did she do?" Sabrina asked, engrossed.

"Well, I invited her in and we talked. I enjoyed the company. It was nice to have someone visit since my daughter wasn't always able to stop by when I needed something, and Mildred seemed eager to help. She would come over about three times a week for a list of things I needed, and when she returned from the errands, she stayed and had tea and we talked for hours. I can't tell you how much I looked forward to those days. I think it kept me from slipping into a depression because I was used to being very active and independent, and then suddenly it was taken from me when I had the stroke."

"How long did my aunt visit with you?"

"Perhaps three years, up until she died. I recovered from the stroke, but Mildred continued to visit since we had become friends. She was a dear person always thinking of others. I do miss her."

"I appreciate your willingness to share your story with me. I am glad you and my aunt became friends."

Sabrina's list of questions remained in her purse. They didn't seem pertinent because she was learning all she needed to know.

"You seem a lot like her. I don't know you, but then I didn't know Mildred either when she first appeared at my door. You have some of her mannerisms," Sarah remarked, noticing the intensity with which Sabrina listened.

"I take that as a compliment. You probably are aware that I came to visit my aunt often, but I've recently come to understand I really didn't know how she spent her days. That is why I wanted to meet you and learn more of what her life was about," Sabrina explained.

"I could embellish the story, but it wouldn't be fair to you or to Mildred. All I can tell you is that she was a good person and became a friend at a time when I needed one."

Sabrina was curious what condition brought Sarah to reside in a nursing home, but felt it was too forward of a question to ask of someone she didn't know. They had spent well over two hours talking when Brie realized it was lunchtime and she should leave.

"I appreciate your talking with me, but I suppose I should be going since I've taken up a lot of your time this morning."

"I'm glad to meet Mildred's niece."

"Thank you for seeing me today. I, too, am glad to meet a friend of my aunt."

Brie stood and extended her hand to shake Sarah's while she remained seated.

Sabrina made her way through the long hallway toward the entrance, and stood outside for a moment taking in a deep breath of cold air.

A bit disappointed with the story, she realized she was expecting something along the lines of Dorothy's guardian angel, mysterious and wondrous. However, Brie was glad to meet another person who had good things to say about Aunt Millie. She was able to put together the concept of her aunt's lifestyle, and it was obvious she imagined herself as an angel flying to the rescue of anyone in need. *Where did Aunt Millie come by the idea of doing such a thing?* Sabrina wondered.

Brie pointed the car toward home. She needed to think this through and decide what to do next, debating whether to continue investigating the other thirteen candidates on the list, or simply accept the fact that each person would have good things to say. Did she really need to hear every single story, and to what advantage? The conclusion would be the same; everyone would think her aunt a savior from the circumstances they found themselves in, so how would that help Sabrina to discover the reason for the voice that continued to haunt her at will?

Chapter 45

Sabrina needed to discuss this with her sister because Sophie was always a good listener with sound advice. Though Brie was accustomed to making her own decisions, she still preferred to get her sister's opinion and feedback. Besides, if she didn't Sophie would be hurt.

"Hi Brie," Sophie spoke first.

"How is everything in Florida?"

"We're doing fine, but I should be asking you that question. What's going on in the country?"

"I don't have much to report. I met another person Aunt Millie befriended. Her name is Sarah Logan; a very nice lady living in a nursing home."

"Why is she living in a nursing home?"

"I didn't ask. I figured if she wanted me to know, she would have volunteered the information."

"How did you find out about her?"

"I took the guestbook to Bella and she identified fourteen names that I could contact. Sarah was the first one I went to see this morning."

"Wow, you've been busy. So what was her connection to Aunt Millie?"

"She had a stroke, and somehow Aunt Millie found out and went to her home to help with errands, and afterwards she would stay and keep her company."

"How did Aunt Millie find out she needed help?"

"Sarah didn't know, but it's a question I wish I had the answer to."

Sabrina remembered the last dream when Aunt Millie inferred that something was revealed to her. *What exactly did that mean?* she questioned.

"Will you be seeing her again?"

"I don't think so."

"Where do you go from here?"

"I could contact the remaining names on the list, but there really isn't any reason to hear their stories because they are going to tell me the same thing in slightly different versions. What I'm trying to understand is the voice I keep hearing. I need an explanation for it, or else it needs to vanish and leave me alone."

"Is there something you aren't telling me? Have you been experiencing encounters of the weird kind again?"

"Actually, I have. The first night I arrived, I heard the voice again. Obviously someone is being very persistent that I learn something, but I haven't a clue what it is, or where to look. I tried to communicate with it, but nothing happened."

"Just when did you plan to tell me?" Sophie said with hurt in her voice.

"Sophie, don't fret over this. I wasn't intentionally keeping this from you. I guess I'm learning to live with these weird phenomena, so it doesn't seem like something out of the ordinary anymore. Besides, I would have told you when I remembered it," Sabrina explained, hoping to sooth her sister's feelings.

"You know I can't be mad at you, but it bothers me you are having these strange experiences. You have to tell me these thing, Brie."

"I positively promise I will, but I don't want you worrying over this."

"Okay. What's your next action plan?"

"Not sure. On the brighter side, I have a date with Ben tomorrow night."

"Terrific, so where are you going on your date?"

"He is taking me to a new Italian restaurant."

"Call me with the details."

"Will do."

Sabrina was glad they ended their conversation on a more normal topic. Mentioning Ben was more fun than talking about a phantom person. Sabrina knew Sophie would be on pins and needles wanting to know every minute detail of her date, which was perfectly fine with Brie because she would be equally excited to relinquish the details. With a smile on her face, Brie went upstairs to pick out her outfit for the special date with Ben.

Chapter 46

The entire day was devoted to pampering herself. Wrapped in her aunt's soft blue robe, Sabrina went to the closet rummaging through each article of clothing wanting to select something nice to wear for the evening. She finally decided on a wool-blend, brown tweed pair of slacks with a cream-colored cashmere sweater and accented the outfit with a print scarf and oval pin to anchor it around her neck. Brie was transferring a few items from her purse to a small clutch bag found on the top shelf in the closet when she heard the doorbell. She smiled when she opened the door to a very handsome man.

"Wow, look at you, stunning," Ben remarked with a grin on his face and leaned in toward Sabrina, giving her a quick kiss on the lips.

Brie felt all warm and tingly inside, catching a whiff of his cologne. It was a subtle masculine fragrance which lingered in the air, embracing Sabrina with the desire to want to curl up in Ben's arms and remain there.

"Well, you aren't too bad looking yourself, mister," Sabrina teased back.

"I made reservations for seven, if you are ready to go."

"I'll grab a coat."

Parked in the driveway was a sleek, metallic-silver Corvette. Sabrina had only seen Ben in the company truck so this was a surprise.

"Nice car," she remarked, sliding into the seat as he opened the door.

"It's my one indulgence."

When they arrived downtown, finding a parking place took three trips around the block before finally catching someone leaving a spot open. Ben took Sabrina's hand and led her into the entrance of the restaurant stepping past couples waiting just outside the door and proceeded to the podium where a young woman was taking names.

He gave his name and reservation time, and they were immediately escorted to a private table in the far corner near a window. When Sabrina was being seated, she glanced outside noticing the lights along the street making it a rather romantic setting, she thought.

"This is perfect. Did you, by chance, request this particular table, or are we simply lucky tonight?" Sabrina asked while she took off her jacket and arranged it on the back of the chair.

"I did request a table away from the crowd, so it wouldn't be too noisy. I didn't want us having to shout across the table to be heard."

"Good choice."

A young man came over with two glasses of water. He asked if they would like a glass of wine, handing a tall narrow wine menu to Ben.

"Would you like a glass, Sabrina?" Ben asked, opening the menu to peruse the list.

"No thanks, it'll only make me sleepy."

Handing the menu back to the waiter, Ben declined also. Another waiter arrived with two dinner menus stating he would be back shortly to take their order. In the meantime, while they were studying the selections, he returned with a basket of bread rolls and a dome of butter.

"What are you having?" Ben asked Sabrina.

"The stuffed tortellini shells with marinara sauce and the house salad."

"Sounds good. I'll have the three meat lasagna."

Having compared each other's choice, the waiter returned

to take their order. Ben spoke for Sabrina confirming the stuffed shells then placed his own request also asking for a glass of sweet iced tea and coffee. Brie spoke first when the waiter left.

"How was your week?"

"Busy, and it will be that way the rest of the year. When the greenhouse is finished, there will be a lot to do getting the plants set up inside."

"What have you been doing with your first few days?"

"I seem to find things to keep me busy."

"I'm curious what has brought you back earlier than you originally planned. I don't think it was because you missed me so much you couldn't stand to be apart a moment longer," he teased her.

"I will confess I missed you, but I can't say that is the reason I returned," Sabrina declared with a smile, knowing her statement would not offend him.

"I don't want to pry into your business, so if you don't want to say anything more, it's okay."

"It has to do with a letter my aunt addressed to me, and I found it to be rather disturbing. I'm trying to understand what it means," Sabrina confided, hoping she wouldn't have to explain.

She didn't want to spend the evening discussing her aunt. It seemed whenever she and Ben were together, inevitably they talked about Aunt Millie. Tonight, she didn't want to do that.

"This letter is what has brought you back?"

"Yes, the content of the letter is not a secret. We've talked about it before. It's about her leaving a legacy in the form of a mission she hoped my sister and I would carry on."

"By chance, does this have anything to do with your aunt's devotion to helping others?" Ben inquired, thinking he knew what this was about.

Besides, they had touched on the subject a few times.

"How did you guess so quickly? You've remembered our conversations," Sabrina remarked, thinking of their first date at

The Country Kitchen.

"It made me think of Mildred and the fact she was forever helping someone in a crisis. It was her nature to be where she was needed, and she never failed to come to the rescue. I can definitely see she would hope you would do the same," Ben offered his opinion.

"I was shocked when I read the letter, and she wants me and my sister to continue in her place. It seems bizarre to me."

"So what are you going to do?"

"I can't see myself repeating my aunt's lifestyle. I don't think it is in me to play the role of a guardian angel. I bet this sounds insane," Sabrina remarked and reached for the glass of water.

"It sure does," Ben said, teasingly.

"But you are definitely an angel. I can practically see your wings," he continued.

"How is my halo?" Sabrina asked, remaining serious.

"Slightly tilted to the left and there is an aura about you," he continued the bantering.

"Did you say aura, or odor?" she inquired with a twinkle in her eye.

Ben threw his head back and roared with laughter, drawing attention to them. It took a few minutes to regain their composure. Sabrina was still wiping tears from her eyes when the food arrived. They calmed down to enjoy their meal, and she smiled at Ben when he winked at her. She enjoyed his teasing nature and knew this was one of the things she loved most about him. *Love, there's that word again,* she thought. He was quickly becoming an important person in Brie's life and it wasn't her nature to let people into her private world affecting her emotional equilibrium.

"Tell me about the greenhouse plans."

Brie was completely absorbed in the moment.

"The contractor will begin construction within the next few weeks. It's going to be a mess around there for months with all the trucks coming and going, but at least they won't be pulling through the front. We have a side road they can use to haul supplies in and out."

"Will you be the one overseeing the project? Sounds like this will consume your time."

"Pretty much, trouble-shooting at best, and this is at the top of my list."

"You seem excited about it. I'm sure a lot of planning and preparation goes into a project of this magnitude," Sabrina commented, wanting to understand how it worked.

"All part of keeping up with the increasing expectations of the consumer and meeting their needs."

Both fell into a brief silence while they finished their meal. The plates were removed and dessert was ordered with coffee. Neither was ready to leave their cozy private corner just yet. Sabrina chose raspberry cheesecake, while Ben selected the triple chocolate-layered cake.

"This was a great choice for dinner. The food is delicious, especially this cheese cake," Sabrina confessed as she forked another bite.

"I can see that. You cleaned your plate and still had room for dessert."

"What can I say, I love Italian food," Sabrina admitted with a smile.

"I'll remember that."

Ben paid the waiter when he returned with the check, and they reluctantly gave up their private corner to walk out into the night air. It was too cold to walk along the sidewalk, so they opted to take a drive instead and with the heater on in the Corvette were nice and warm in minutes. Ben drove out of the city limits toward the open country area.

During the drive, they talked about everything they could imagine from the stars in the sky to their college days, to comparing classic movies they each had seen. Each expounded on their teenage years with Sabrina asking Ben what it was like growing up with two sisters. He, in turn, asked her about being a twin. He made a big loop around the city bringing them back to Sabrina's house about an hour later.

Walking quickly toward the front door, Ben continued through the house following Brie toward the kitchen where she tossed her things on the counter.

"Do you want another cup of coffee?"

"No, I drank more than my daily quota," he replied with a smile.

Sabrina noticed he was always smiling, grinning, or teasing her and realized he had a wonderful sense of humor, a quality she truly admired. Ben seemed to take things in stride and Brie thought that was a great way to handle life's circumstances.

"It is getting late and I should be going, but truth be told, I don't want to leave. I hope you know, Sabrina, you have a special place in my heart. We haven't known each other for very long, but every time I am with you, I feel even more certain we are meant to be together. They say when you meet your soul mate, you know instantly. I believe there is truth in that because that is the way I have felt about you from the beginning."

"I know what you're saying. I feel the same way, something clicked for me too, and besides, I can see it in your eyes. It must be true that the eyes are a window to the soul. When I look into yours, I see contentment and happiness which is a wonderful place to be in life. I've never been one to give any thought to the meaning behind finding your soul mate, but if this *wholeness* I feel when I'm with you is what it feels like, then I don't want to ever lose it," she told him.

"Look a little deeper into my eyes, what else do you see?" he asked, blinking his eyelids.

Sabrina stood directly in front of him staring intently into his dark brown eyes before stepping back with a smile. She was going to cross the line and say the 'L' word and why not, he asked her? This newfound relationship with Ben was progressing rapidly for her, and yet she wasn't compelled to slow it down. Sabrina was having a wonderful time letting herself be mesmerized by him. Believing they were soul mates made everything perfect.

"I see love when I look into your eyes. There's love for life, love for your family, love for your business."

"Wow, you see all that. What else do you see?"

Wrapping his arms around her waist, he pulled Brie into an embrace. He was having fun teasing her.

Tilting her head upward toward his face, Sabrina couldn't help but grin. She was falling head over heals in love with him, and there didn't seem to be any brakes to apply to her feelings. She had never felt this way about anyone before because she never took the time in her career to stop and enjoy a relationship. *Is this what I have been missing all these years,* she asked herself.

"I see you are going to make me say it. Alright, I see love for me as well. Perhaps a speck in a recessed corner of your heart," Sabrina declared, boldly.

"My dear girl, look closer. It's more than a speck," Ben announced with a big grin on his face.

Sabrina smiled back. Though she knew he was stringing the conversation along, she understood the words he spoke were very serious. Their feelings had grown strong, quickly. He kissed her gently on the lips then pulled back, looking into her eyes.

"I'm going to have to confess something to you, Ben Cooper. I, too, have a speck," she said teasingly, hardly able to hold back laughing.

"Soul mates for sure."

They pondered their confessions for a split second and laughed. Ben hugged her tightly for a moment, then took Sabrina's hand leading her to the foyer and kissed her once more before opening the door to leave.

"I'm so glad we have that straightened out. I'll call tomorrow," he told her smiling, before walking toward his car.

Sabrina stood in the doorway watching and didn't close the door until she could no longer see his taillights. Though it was late, Brie couldn't wait until morning to call Sophie and share the details of her date. This news was too important, and besides, she knew Sophie wouldn't forgive her for postponing until tomorrow.

Chapter 47

Sabrina retrieved the cell phone from her handbag and went to sit in the den. After starting a fire, she sat with legs curled underneath and called her sister.

"Hi sis, is something wrong?" Sophie asked as soon as she answered.

"No nothing is wrong, perhaps everything is right. I know it's late, but I thought for a Friday night you guys might still be up."

"We're watching a movie. So why are you calling this late? Oh, wait a minute, you had a date with Ben tonight. Okay, give me all the details and don't leave anything out," Sophie demanded with a giggle.

"I knew you'd want to know. We went to a new Italian restaurant and the food was delicious. I think we must have stayed over two hours savoring everything."

"Does that mean you both were savoring each other, too?" Sophie asked, laughing.

"We couldn't keep our eyes off each other, and I can't wait for you to meet him. I know you and David will love him."

"Wow, you are actually talking about us meeting a man in your life. This is serious stuff, sis. You have never wanted us to meet anyone you were dating."

"I know, but this is different. Ben and I really care for each other."

"You've fallen for him. I take it the feeling is mutual or you wouldn't have called me. Does this mean I'll have a brother-in-law by Christmas?"

"I don't know if by Christmas, but a brother-in-law, perhaps?"

"Oh my gosh, you aren't kidding, are you? Brie, this is wonderful. I'm thrilled you have found your Mr. Right," Sophie gushed with tears of joy welling up in her eyes.

She always wanted her sister to find someone and settle down. Sophie felt so blessed having David; she wanted the same for her sister. Perhaps it was finally going to happen, and she couldn't be more excited.

"Has he spoken the 'L' word yet?"

"Yes, in a manner of speaking. We played with the word."

"How do you play with the word, love? Either you say it, or you don't."

"I thought it was rather romantic how he brought up the subject. He actually made me come to the realization like opening a present. First, you take off the bow, then the ribbon, and carefully remove the wrappings. That is how he revealed he loved me."

"I don't get it. You're going to have to explain this one to me."

"It started with Ben telling me that I held a special place in his heart, and I believed him because I could see it in his eyes and told him so. He told me to look closer, so we played this little game until I admitted to seeing the love he had for me through his eyes."

"That certainly is an original. I don't think I've heard of love being expressed quite like that before, but it's romantic."

"It really wasn't so much romantic as comforting, kind of like slowly sliding into the realization of something wonderful and then floating there. I couldn't wait to tell you."

"I'm so glad you called."

"We can talk more later," Brie told her.

"What's the latest on contacting the people on your list," Sophie inquired, before they finished their conversation.

"I've only talked to Sarah, but I don't think I'll pursue the others. There really isn't a need. I could spend days listening to people tell me their tales, but it won't help at this point. It is frustrating," Sabrina admitted.

"I wish I could help you, but this is something you'll have to pursue on your own. Personally, I think Aunt Millie placed a burden by leaving that letter the way she did, because it has caused nothing but grief."

"I know, but let's not talk about it right now, okay."

She didn't want to talk about anything having to do with Aunt Millie. She was on a cloud of bliss at the moment, and that was definitely putting a damper on her feelings.

"Oh, Brie, I'm so sorry. Here you are telling me about your romantic evening with Ben, and I go and throw a wet noodle on it."

"It's alright. Not to worry, sis. I understand what you're saying. I'll resolve this soon, one way or another."

"Good. I know you will. Congratulations on finding your Mr. Right. Call me."

"Thanks, sis. I'll call soon."

Letting the cell phone drop into her lap, Brie stared into the fire. Sophie's comments made her think of her aunt's *Passionate Promises*. She had to resolve this issue. Sabrina knew it was time to decide what she wanted to do and come to terms with what this meant in her life.

Chapter 48

Ben called Sabrina on Saturday afternoon inviting her to Sunday dinner at his parent's house. She had enjoyed spending time with his family at Christmas and was excited to be able to see them again, agreeing to be there at four since they would be eating around five o'clock. She stressed to Ben that he didn't need to pick her up, she could just as easily drive over herself.

Sabrina decided to bring a camera to take some family pictures if they didn't have any objections. She was greeted at the door by Ben and led into the den to say hello to his father who was watching a golf game on television. After exchanging a few words with John, he took her hand and they walked into the kitchen where his mother was preparing dinner. Melinda looked up from chopping vegetables when she heard them enter.

"Hello Sabrina, Ben told us you were back in town. How's life treating you?" Melinda asked as she made a salad.

"Life is great. Is there anything I can help you with?" Sabrina offered, seeing there was still preparation to be done before the meal would be ready.

"Sure, I can always use an extra hand. If you don't mind, you could peel the potatoes," she remarked and pointed to a bag sitting in the sink.

"On that note, I'll leave you two alone to do woman's work," Ben winked at Sabrina before leaving the room.

"He's a funny one, woman's work," Melinda chuckled.

"I hope you know, Sabrina, he's teasing us. I didn't raise my son to be a chauvinist."

"Ben doesn't strike me that way."

They worked together for almost an hour. There was a chicken casserole baking in the oven, mashed potatoes, fresh green beans, tossed salad along with dinner rolls and iced tea. When the meal was ready, Brie set the dining room table and called the men to dinner. They started passing around the platters of food.

Sabrina felt very relaxed with his parents. They asked questions of her recent photo assignments and listened intently when she talked about the serious decline of the bee colonies in Hawaii. She also mentioned her trip to photograph wolves in Colorado. Ben and his parents were fascinated by her stories. Brie was grateful neither had asked why she was back so soon after the holidays.

Ben stepped up to help clear the table and placed the dishes in the dishwasher. Once the dining room was in order again, Sabrina slipped into the living room to retrieve the camera she had previously dropped into a chair and went back into the kitchen, catching Ben by surprise and snapping a few shots of him buried to his elbows in suds, washing the pans. He turned and grinned when he saw what she was doing. Eye still glued to the viewfinder, Sabrina focused the camera on his mother. She put her hand in front of her face, but laughingly consented.

Sabrina went into the den to see John had fallen asleep in the recliner and took a couple pictures of him. When she returned to the kitchen, Ben had finished the dishes and his mother was putting a pot of coffee on to brew. She snapped a few more and went to sit at the island counter. Ben joined her and it felt so natural like she had done this so many times before.

Melinda brought mugs of coffee with the condiments, and they talked for awhile. The mutual love and respect Sabrina witness between mother and son was apparent. It surrounded anyone who walked into their home. There was such harmony and comfort. Brie had a glimpse of what love could be like and she wanted to share that kind of commitment with Ben.

After an hour of small talk, Ben and Sabrina went outside for some fresh air but gave up the idea because it was too cold. Stepping back into the house, Sabrina declared to Ben it was time for her to leave. They walked into the living room where Melinda was reading a book.

"Melinda, thank you for a lovely evening. The meal was delicious," Sabrina stated, cordially.

"I'm so glad you came. How long will you be staying in town?"

"I'll probably be here another three weeks, less if an assignment comes up."

"I hope we see you often while you are here."

"I hope so, too."

After the farewells, Ben walked Sabrina to her car and kissed her far more passionately than he ever had before. Sabrina floated in the emotions that stirred within her. He pulled away and told her he would call. Brie threw her hand out the window waving while she drove down the road toward home.

Chapter 49

The house was lit from top to bottom. Sabrina had a habit of leaving every light on when the sun went down, not concerned it would create a whopping electric bill. She sat in the car for a few minutes staring at the house knowing this was now her home. It still didn't seem real to Sabrina that she was the sole owner of this big country estate. Once inside, Brie went upstairs to change clothes putting on a pair of flannel pajamas and her aunt's blue robe.

She stayed in the bedroom and began going through the stack of envelopes on the desk to see if there was anything that needed to be taken care of from her last visit. All the utility bills were forwarded to the condominium address and would be waiting upon her return. Sabrina sat on the edge of the bed thinking of what she would do on Monday. She hadn't heard from Joe meaning all is well at work.

She was growing accustomed to living in the country and wondered about making it her permanent residence. She tried to imagine living in Asheville all year rather than the condo in Florida and was discovering several benefits such as the fact that she loved this house, could spend a lot more time with Ben, and had Bella for a friend to visit often.

The realization she had more contact with people in the country than ever at the condominium complex made the condo seem more like a stopping place. There were people here who truly cared about her which made it a completely new experience for Brie.

It was still early enough to call Sophie because she wanted to mention the idea to her sister and get her reaction. She knew Sophie wouldn't be too happy about her moving away since it took her years to convince Sabrina to move to Florida, but she knew her sister would accept it.

"Hi Brie, what's up?" Sophie answered.

"Not much, I had dinner with Ben's parents today. They are such nice folks."

"That is twice you've been to visit them. This is serious when you start spending time with the family," Sophie said, jokingly.

"I hope so, because I sure am falling in love."

"Sophie, what would you think if I made Asheville my home base?" Brie continued, throwing the question at her sister.

"Are you serious? This is about Ben, isn't it?"

"Not really. I mean, yes, it would give us the opportunity to spend more time together, but I wouldn't move here for that reason only."

"The only other thing that would compel you to consider moving is Aunt Millie. Don't tell me you would relocate because of Aunt Millie's silly *Passionate Promises*," Sophie stated, sharply.

"That may be part of it, but I can't honestly say I'd move for that reason, either. I'm not saying I am moving, just pondering the idea. There is something here that gives me a comfort and peace I haven't experienced before. I've made acquaintances and friends and the lifestyle is so different," Brie told her sister, hoping Sophie would understand.

"What about your job?"

"Where I live doesn't change my job. Besides when I return here between shoots, I can visit with Bella and have opportunities to see Ben and his family," Sabrina explained, realizing she was trying to convince her sister of the idea.

"Well, Brie, it's your choice to make. Of course, you know how I want us living near one another, but I wouldn't talk you out of something you want to do," Sophie stated, hurt her sister didn't mention she would miss living close to her.

Sophie knew the occasions Sabrina would stop for dinner after assignments would come to an end, but wanted her sister to do what she thought best. It was her life and she wanted Sabrina to be happy.

"Like I always tell you, Brie, you should do what feels right in your heart. If living in the country gives you contentment, then you should definitely consider it. It would be selfish of me to talk you out of it," Sophie spoke, sadly.

"I haven't decided what I'm going to do; however, the idea keeps crossing my mind, so I wanted to discuss it with you."

"I'll miss you not living closer and stopping by for dinner, but I'll be happy for you, after all, you aren't moving *that* far away."

"Sophie, whether I live in North Carolina or Florida, I will always make the time to visit with you. I'm not going to let geographical location keep us apart. I promise you that and I mean it," Sabrina assured her sister.

"I hope not. Have you heard from Joe? Is it too soon to get word on your next assignment?" Sophie inquired, wanting to change the subject.

She wasn't happy with this news, but it was Sabrina's life, and she wouldn't interfere.

"No, which means everything is fine."

"What are your plans for the next couple of weeks?" Sophie asked, wondering what would keep Brie busy.

"I'm not sure, perhaps, more sleuthing, but I'll keep you posted."

"Alright, talk to you later."

"I'll call in a day to two."

Once the call was disconnected, Sabrina went upstairs and got ready for bed. She had a lot of thinking to do and expected to spend her remaining days tossing ideas back and forth in her mind. *I'm definitely in the right place for some major soul searching,* she thought.

Chapter 50

Sabrina woke the next morning from a restful sleep having no dreams haunting her subconscious. She started a fire before traipsing into the kitchen to make coffee and put an English muffin in the toaster. Sitting by the fireplace with the simple breakfast, Brie meditated on what to do regarding Aunt Millie's *Passionate Promises*. She was plagued with guilt for even considering dropping the idea. Apparently, Aunt Millie saw something within Sabrina that compelled her to leave this project for her. It didn't seem right to enjoy Aunt Millie's lovely home and throw away a legacy her aunt thought important.

She spent many hours examining a means to respect her aunt's request, but in a manner that fit her style. Brie knew she couldn't simply devote time to running errands and sitting with the lonely. That particular method of helping others was fine for her aunt, but Sabrina knew it would never work for her. However, there had to be a way she could use her skills and accomplish a semblance of helpfulness to others that would honor the legacy. Brie formulated a plan she wanted to put into action and see what kind of results it rendered.

She decided to call Sarah Logan at the nursing home to see if she might enjoy helping Brie with the idea. When the receptionist answered, Brie asked to be connected to Sarah's room.

"Hello Sarah, this is Sabrina Fitzgerald," Brie spoke first.

"Sabrina, I didn't think I would be hearing from you again. Do you have more questions for me?" Sarah asked, hopefully.

"Perhaps, but I wanted to know if I could visit again."

"Of course dear, I would enjoy that very much. Did you want to come over today?" Sarah asked, anxious for a visitor.

"That's perfect. What is a good time for you?"

"This may be presumptuous, can you have lunch with me in the dining room?" Sarah asked with excitement.

"I'd love to. What time do I need to be there?"

"If you get here by eleven-thirty, we could eat on the first lunch shift which is at noon; they do meals in shifts here," Sarah explained.

"I will be there at eleven-thirty, sharp," Sabrina assured her before hanging up.

Brie went upstairs to get ready taking her time since there was no rush. Once dressed, she went downstairs to find her equipment bag in the foyer. Sabrina checked each camera carefully and placed the bag by her purse excited to see how the next few hours would pan out.

Sabrina was walking through the doors of Weston Nursing Home with equipment bag in tow straight for Sarah's door which was closed when she arrived. Tapping lightly, she heard Sarah's voice.

"Come in," she called out softly.

Brie opened the door and stepped into the room to see Sarah sitting at the small table. When she walked in, Sarah got up approaching Sabrina with a smile.

"Hello Sabrina, it's good to see you again," Sarah spoke first.

"Am I disturbing you?" Brie asked.

"No, not at all. What is in that big bag you've got there?"

"This is my camera bag. I want to ask if I could take your picture."

"Why would you want to take my picture? What would you do with it?" Sarah asked with reservation.

"Perhaps you would like to make it a special gift for your

daughter."

"Now, there's a thought," Sarah chuckled.

"I have no objection to having my picture taken, but I still don't understand why you want to do it," she continued.

"I'd like to take yours as well as other residents if they allow me. Do you think anyone would mind if I took some candid snapshots while I'm here?"

"I don't know, but bring your camera when we go to lunch and you can ask some of them. Why take pictures of old folks living in a nursing home? I thought you photographed animals and nature, things like that," Sarah inquired, confused why Sabrina would be interested in taking their picture.

"This is true. My assignments are photographing animals in their natural habitat; however, I'd like to take some pictures of the residents for their pleasure."

Brie was uncertain, at the moment, of the final outcome of an idea she had been pondering over for the past few days. Hopefully, it would go in Brie's favor, or if opposed blow up in her face. The last thing Sabrina wanted to do was offend anyone. Some people simply did not like having their picture taken and nothing will convince them otherwise.

"Well, let's go down to the dining room and see what we can stir up while you put your camera to work. This is going to be interesting," Sarah commented with humor in her voice.

Sabrina walked alongside Sarah as they went down a maze of short hallways until they reached the entrance to a large dining room with individual round tables and five chairs to each table. The atmosphere in the room was chaotic with everyone talking. No one noticed Sarah and Sabrina enter the room walking directly to an unoccupied corner table. Sarah sat down, and offered Sabrina the chair next to her and once seated, Sarah leaned into Brie whispering in her ear.

"We fill out a menu selection form each morning checking our food choices. I added a guest to mine and selected baked chicken for you. It was that or meatloaf. Hope you like it," she said, explaining the procedure for lunch.

"I like baked chicken. Most anything is fine with me; however, my food limit is liver and onions," Brie remarked with a smile.

"I don't blame you. I wouldn't touch the stuff, either," Sarah replied, delighted to have a guest to share lunch.

Staff from the kitchen came out carrying large round trays loaded with plates of food. Sabrina wondered how they knew who was served what plate. Sarah saw the confusion on Brie's face and spoke before she could ask the question.

"We have assigned seats. That's how they know who gets what meal."

"You read my mind. I was wondering about that."

Two plates of food arrived just as three people came to join them at the table. Sarah introduced everyone to Sabrina. Sarah had such pride in her voice when she introduced Brie as her good friend, Mildred's niece. She continued to tell them that Sabrina was a famous photojournalist. Brie could tell this was definitely a highlight to Sarah's day. Realizing such, it made Sabrina feel good that merely her presence could have such an impact on someone else's life. *Interesting,* she thought.

The women at the table were very friendly and had many questions to ask Sabrina regarding her profession. When everyone had finished their lunch, Sabrina approached the subject cautiously of taking their picture and found they were elated with the idea. She reached down to retrieve a camera from the bag beside her chair.

The women started primping and fussing with their hair and pinching their cheeks to add color to their pale skin. While laughing and teasing one another, Brie snapped candid shots. Soon others in the dining room stopped talking and watched the activity taking place at the far table.

"Is the entertainment exclusive to that table?" a man yelled across the room.

"Oh, Fred, you aren't interested in having your picture taken," Sarah yelled back.

"Maybe I am. You women shouldn't have all the fun. Bring

that camera over here," Fred ordered with a smile.

Sabrina pulled the camera away from her face and looked around the room. So engrossed in her work, Brie was oblivious to having a captive audience. Suddenly, the room grew very quiet and all eyes were on her. Lowering the camera, she studied the faces staring at her and quickly put her idea into action.

"How many of you would like to have your picture taken?" Brie asked.

Hands went flying into the air, for it seemed everyone wanted to be included without exception. Some of the women asked if they had time to go to their room to apply some makeup and run a comb through their hair. Sabrina explained the best photographs were the shots taken candidly without posing for the camera. She encouraged everyone to continue with their conversations while she slipped around the room; hopefully without anyone being conscious of her presence.

Brie captured a few shots of Sarah talking with her friends at the table, and a few women wanted to pose and smile for the camera. The men in the room weren't interested in the outcome of their photo as long as they were not excluded.

She continued snapping pictures moving around quietly never letting her eye leave the viewfinder. Losing track of time, Sarah came up beside Sabrina informing her that the second shift would be arriving soon. Outside in the hall, many residents approached Sabrina asking what her intent was with the pictures and she told them to expect a surprise within a few days.

They returned to Sarah's room and chatted for a while.

"That certainly was entertaining, Sabrina. I can see why you are very good because you get so engrossed with your subject, almost like you and the camera become one," Sarah stated with pride in her newfound friend.

"Did I do to much?"

"Not at all. It was wonderful watching you work, and every one loved the attention. Besides, you are a celebrity to us."

"I didn't mean to take up so much of your time today, Sarah, but I still want to take your picture that perhaps you can pass along to your daughter," Sabrina explained, fearful her reason for visiting may have offended Sarah.

"Nonsense, I haven't had so much fun in a very long time, and I don't think many of the others have laughed that hard in awhile, either. It was great seeing them act like silly girls again. You brought laughter into many hearts today, Sabrina."

"That's a very nice thing to say, but I was having more fun than they were."

Sarah agreed to let Sabrina take her picture when she returned. Brie asked about visiting on Friday when she brought the surprise. Sarah was overwhelmed with excitement for the prospect of having Sabrina visit with her again.

"I would like that very much. Friday it is," Sarah said, beaming.

"I should be going, but I'll be back Friday morning."

Sarah walked Brie the short distance to the doorway of the room and stood watching Sabrina walk down the hallway.

"She is just like Mildred," Sarah mumbled to herself.

Sabrina left the nursing home surprised by the ease with which her plan fell into place. The thrill of seeing amusement on the faces of her subjects was rewarding, knowing she was responsible for the smiles and laughter as they teased and delightfully tormented each other. The mere prospect of continuing with her plan made Brie feel unbelievably happy. Never in all the years of photography has she experienced such a wonderful thrill. She had never applied her skill outside of her job. *This is going to be fun,* she thought.

Chapter 51

Sabrina stopped at a local photo shop to slip the memory card from her digital camera into an automatic photo developer. Adjusting the prints to her satisfaction, she ordered each developed to an eleven by fourteen and with time to spare went to check out the *Crafty Loft Art and Hobby Shop* a short distance away.

Brie roamed up and down the isles studying the frames, mattes, and other materials gleaning ideas for her project. She selected a simple black poster frame with matching pre-cut double black and white mattes for the resident pictures. She asked a clerk about speaking with the manager and was led to the back of the store into a small office and introduced to a woman sitting behind a desk cluttered with papers.

"Doreen, this customer wants to speak with you," the young clerk stated as a means of introduction.

Doreen looked up from her work.

"Thanks, Cindy. How can I help you?" Doreen addressed Sabrina.

"My name is Sabrina Fitzgerald and I'd like to speak to you about setting up an account for supplies since I may need them on a regular basis."

Reaching for the bottom side drawer of the desk, Doreen pulled out a credit application and handed it to her.

"Fill this out and return it to me. Be sure to include the credit amount you are applying for in the top right corner," she explained.

"If you don't mind, can I complete it while I'm here. I have a few minutes," Sabrina stated, anxious to start the process.

"Sure, you can sit over there at that table," Doreen offered the small desk and chair in the corner of her office.

Sabrina took the form and began answering the usual questions. When it came to her address, she wrote Asheville for the primary but underneath listed the condominium as the current mailing address. The next question asked for her occupation, and she filled in photojournalist and the name of the magazine she worked for. It didn't take long to complete the application handing it back to Doreen who had remained working at her desk.

When she perused the form reading over the name, occupation and recognizing the magazine title, she realized she had a celebrity sitting before her. Normally, it was art or elementary school teachers who came into the store requesting accounts, not a famous photojournalist. Doreen was ecstatic to meet Sabrina.

"I've read this magazine, *Nature on the Run,* and I've seen your work. I'm embarrassed I didn't recognize you," Doreen stated, fumbling for words.

"Thank you. How long will it take to establish an account?" Sabrina asked, getting back to business.

"It can be done today."

"That's great. I'm working on a project, and it helps to have an open account for supplies."

"The store will provide an unlimited credit line for your shopping requirements."

"Thank you, but that isn't necessary. I'll accept whatever limit you want to place on the account. Can I use the credit today?"

"Of course, I can give you a temporary credit slip, and we'll send an official store credit card in a couple of days. Should I mail it to your local address?"

"I would prefer you call me, and I can stop by the store to pick it up," Sabrina suggested, pointing to her phone number on the application.

Sabrina stood up and extended her hand to shake Doreen's, thanking her for her assistance. She left the office and grabbed a cart on her way to the isle that carried the frames she had previously scrutinized. After collecting the necessary supplies, Brie checked out with the temporary credit slip and placed her purchases into the trunk of the car. The prints were ready by the time she drove back to the photo shop.

Anxious to see the finished pictures, Brie pulled them out of the large envelope and spread them across the dining room table, carefully studying each one. Pleased with the animated expressions captured on the faces of the residents, she made choices according to the overall character of her subjects.

It took several hours to complete the project of matting and framing each selected photo, but when she was finished, Brie was satisfied with the results and couldn't wait to return to the nursing home and show them off. She felt good with what she was about to do and hoped it would be receptive. It cost her very little money to put this idea into motion, and Sabrina was willing to make the investment. She loaded the framed prints into the backseat of the car, being ready to go back to the nursing home early because it was important to complete this project before the lunch shifts began.

Chapter 52

Brie met with Jessica Carlson, the activity director at Weston Nursing Home on Friday morning excited to share the idea of the resident pictures, hoping she would have the same enthusiasm. Sabrina explained she wanted to hang the photos across the walls in the dining room prior to lunch so when the residents walked into the room, they would see themselves on display.

Jessica was a young, energetic woman who thought it was a great idea. Finding a hammer and nails, she got to work hanging the prints in a collage on each wall of the room. They worked diligently to finish the project just as the first lunch shift came strolling in. Sabrina and Jessica left the room not wanting to be seen, yet able to observe the reactions of everyone as they stood off from the entrance to the kitchen.

When each person came walking through the doorway, they stopped in their tracks in awe looking around at the walls and walked toward the photos examining each one carefully recognizing themselves. The residents were quick to realize that everyone had their picture taken and began checking more closely for their own image. Never would she have thought something so simple and easy to do could brighten someone's day. Watching their expressions was priceless to Sabrina.

Soon the entire lunch shift crowd was in the dining room, and rather than sitting at their assigned table preparing to eat a meal, they were walking around the room talking, laughing, and pointing at the photos. Sabrina and Jessica remained glued to their spot.

"Sabrina, this was such a wonderful thing you've done for the residents. I wouldn't have guessed they'd be so ecstatic about seeing their face in print. I can't remember a time when they have laughed and enjoyed themselves so much, even bingo night doesn't get this reaction," Jessica confessed in amazement.

"I'm so pleased they like the photos. Honestly, I wasn't sure what to expect, but I wanted to give it a try. This has been so much fun for me, as I see it is for them," she admitted, with renewed confidence in her idea.

"Well, Sabrina, you know what this means. You'll have to bring your camera and do the same for our second lunch shift. All the residents will want to have their picture on the wall. We can take the second group of photos and put them in the recreation room. In fact, I have an idea. We could do resident of the month; that is if you wouldn't mind coming back each month to take that person's photo and blowing it up to a small poster size. A good place to hang it would be at the reception area, so when guests come in the front door it will be the first thing they see. It would make each one feel like a celebrity and I'm convinced everyone would love it. What do you think of the idea?" Jessica prompted, hoping she wasn't being to forward with her expectations of Sabrina.

"It's a wonderful idea, and I'm ready to do it."

"We have an activity fund I can use. If you'll give me an estimate of the cost for printing and supplies, the facility can cover the expense. Also, let me know what your charge will be for the photography."

"Your idea with the photographs personalizes the nursing home for the residents," Jessica elaborated with enthusiasm.

"Let me work up an estimate, but as for the photography, I will donate my time."

It would defeat Sabrina's purpose if she turned this into a job. After all, it wasn't her intent to charge for her skills.

"That is very generous, thank you," Jessica responded in surprise.

The two women remained unnoticed as the second shift entered the dining room. Enthralled by the photos displaced on the walls, they took the tour around laughing at the candid expressions of their friends. Everyone wanted their picture included on the *Senior Wall of Fame,* which it was quickly tagged.

"What about me. I want my picture done," a woman shouted loud enough to be heard above the noise in the room.

"Who did this?" another asked.

"I heard there was a famous photographer visiting Sarah Logan. We need to ask her. She would know," another spoke up quickly.

"Wonderful. After lunch I'm going to see Sarah," the first woman replied.

"I'll go with you," the second woman agreed.

They finally ate lunch talking about the photos. Then the two women marched to Sarah's room to get the details. They wanted their picture on the wall. No one was going to be left out.

Sabrina and Jessica left the scene and walked back to Jessica's office.

"Well, that was a big hit and it just goes to show we all need a little attention. It's human nature, I suppose," Jessica offered her opinion.

"I'll return in a couple of days to take photos of the remaining residents, if that's alright with you?"

"Perfect. I know I'll have several residents asking me for details, and at least I can inform them when you'll be back."

Leaving Jessica's office, Sabrina went to find Sarah since she had promised to take her picture. Sarah was in her room, and Brie noticed how pretty she appeared in her soft print dress, knowing she had put extra effort into doing her hair and makeup. She smiled to herself, witnessing the enthusiasm Sarah held for having her picture taken.

Sabrina took Sarah's picture in her room using the beige painted wall as a backdrop. Low lighting softened Sarah's appearance rendering an almost flawless image. Brie was confident the photo would turn out good.

When the photo session was finished, Brie left the nursing home delighted with the simplicity of accomplishing her goal. It was a new experience for Sabrina to take on a project of her own making and found it extremely rewarding. Who would have thought she had it in her to try such a thing? When Sabrina pondered on the question, the answer came quickly, Aunt Millie.

Chapter 53

Brie couldn't wait to call Sophie and tell her what she had been doing. She wasn't sure how her sister would react, but was excited, nevertheless, to share this with her.

"Hi sis, what's up?" Sophie asked, beating Brie to the question.

"Well, I wanted to tell you about a project I was working on. Have you got a few minutes to talk?"

"When do I not have time for my favorite sis?" Sophie replied with a giggle.

"I'm your only sister," Sabrina bantered back.

"Oh, that's right!" Sophie said with a squeal.

Often they would enjoy teasing one another with Sophie being the instigator, and it always put Sabrina in good spirits.

"Remember Sarah Logan from the nursing home?"

"Of course I do, what about her?"

"I had lunch with Sarah and took her picture along with several of the residents and enlarged the prints to an eleven by fourteen, matted, and framed them. Today I took the finished photos and with the help of Jessica, the activity director, hung them along the walls in the dining room and you should have seen the commotion it caused. The residents were laughing and making comments about each other's photo."

"Wow, what gave you the idea to do this?" Sophie asked, surprised Brie would take on such an endeavor.

"I kept thinking of Aunt Millie's legacy and how important it was to her."

"I didn't think you would have the time, or inclination to carry on what Aunt Millie found rewarding to do in her spare time. That was her life and this is yours."

"I'm simply experimenting, and it was entertaining to the folks at the nursing home. It only took using my photography skills to bring a smile or laughter to someone and brighten their day."

"So are you thinking of doing this again?" Sophie inquired further, wondering what had gotten into her sister.

"I'm going back in a couple of days to do the remainder of residents, but if you're asking if I'm considering this long term, I think I might be."

"This has to do with those strange encounters, doesn't it? Have you had anymore?"

"No, however, I do believe there is a connection. It's the only thing that makes sense since everything began when Aunt Millie died. These strange encounters are somehow connected to her legacy. I know it sounds very weird, but I don't know what else to make of it."

"What exactly are you planning to do if you did take on *Passionate Promises*?" Sophie asked with concern.

"I'm thinking of going to a few nursing homes to talk with the activity director and see what kind of reception I get to the idea of photographing the residents. They can call Jessica at Weston if they want details. I may have found a way to carry on Aunt Millie's legacy by using my photography skills," Sabrina declared, speaking her thoughts more to herself.

"If you do decide to pursue this, what happens with your job?"

"I can do both. Donating my time to take pictures of residents in nursing homes doesn't require much, but it would mean I relocate to Asheville which I have been giving more thought to lately."

"You could do this in Florida, you know? There are plenty

of nursing homes here, if that is your decision. It doesn't have to be in Asheville."

"Besides, isn't this happening a bit fast? Moving there and taking pictures of people in nursing homes, this isn't you, Brie. What about your career, traveling, and your condo? Have you really thought this through?" Sophie hammered the questions at her sister.

"I'm merely playing with the idea at the moment. I would enjoy making Asheville my permanent residence and using my condo for Florida trips when I come to visit with you. My career won't be affected by the move. I stay gone so much of the time that where I park my personal things isn't an issue, really."

"If you're doing this because of Aunt Millie's letter, then you're doing it for the wrong reason. However, if you're considering this for your own personal satisfaction, then that is different. What I'm trying to say, Brie, is don't change your life based on a misguided obligation. It won't work and you will not be happy," Sophie expressed her thoughts, solemnly.

"I understand what you're saying, and I do value your opinion. You know I do, Sophie, but what I have experienced is a feeling of personal satisfaction to know I was responsible for bringing a moment of laughter and happiness to someone. It was exhilarating," Sabrina declared, feeling confident in her decision.

"You're very serious about this, aren't you?" Sophie asked, knowing it wasn't going to do any good to try and talk Brie out of her idea.

Maybe she shouldn't even try. This was Sabrina's decision to make and life choices to deal with. To often, Sophie felt like the over-protective parent with her sister, and how that role came about she never took the time to analyze it. Perhaps because she was more of a homebody while Sabrina was the adventurous one, or maybe she had more maternal instincts. Who knew? It really didn't matter.

"I am. How do you feel about my moving?" Brie inquired,

concerned for her sister's feelings.

"I want you to be happy. Whatever makes you feel content and enjoying life is what I wish for you. If moving to the country does that, then so be it," Sophie replied, already feeling sad that her sister was moving away, again.

"I know you want the best for me, Sophie. I promise if I do move here, I'll make many trips to visit you. Having my condo makes it easy to travel back to Florida. Even when I'm on assignment, I can do an excursion straight there rather than back here. I will basically have two homes to rotate living in," Sabrina reminded Sophie, wanting her to understand she was not forsaking their visits to live in the country.

"Okay enough about me, what is going on in your world? How is teaching and David?" Sabrina changed the subject.

"Things are the same; not too much ever changes in my world," Sophie stated with little enthusiasm.

"You have a world I want someday. A husband who loves you, a beautiful home, and a career. You have a good life, Sophie," Sabrina told her, hearing the sadness in her voice.

"Well, when you put it that way, of course, I do," Sophie replied, without her usual candid humor.

"Don't worry, sis, it will all work out. Give David a hug for me," Sabrina tried to comfort her before hanging up.

"Will do and keep me posted."

Sabrina tossed the cell phone on the table next to the rocker. Normally, talking with Sophie gave Brie of assurance, however, this particular conversation made her aware that Sophie didn't agree with her plans. It was her life and she was accustomed to making her own decisions, but she was disappointed Sophie didn't express the usual cheer Brie typically experienced from her sister.

Moving to Asheville felt right to her, even if she didn't completely understand everything that was happening. She was quickly coming to terms that this was where she wanted to be.

Chapter 54

The next morning Sabrina went back to Weston to complete the photography of the remaining residents and within a day had their photos hanging in the recreation room. Brie was amazed how effortlessly the project was completed. She asked Jessica for the name of other facilities in the area, intending to contact them to present her photography idea. Surprised by the positive response she received from each nursing home, Brie had scheduled three sessions within the next two weeks and hoped to get them done before she left on assignment.

Sabrina went to the *Crafty Loft Art and Hobby Shop* to purchase the necessary frames and additional supplies placing the bags in the formal dining room which had been converted into a workroom. She was elated the idea was turning into a full-blown assignment of her own making which gave Brie the encouragement to continue onward. The second phase on her list was setting up a darkroom to do the photo developing. She needed to decide what room in the house would be best suited and also what equipment, tools, and chemical solutions would be required. Brie knew who to call to get the information, her assistant. Joe could do the research to find a company for the necessary purchases, and she made a mental note to call him.

She went to sit at the table to begin outlining a plan on paper. Sabrina felt a contentment almost equal to her photojournalistic travels. Never had she considered doing such a thing. Traveling was her life with someone else planning and directing her days. Spending time with people was not a routine occurrence, so taking on a project of this magnitude was completely out of her comfort zone. It truly left Sabrina feeling awed.

She believed *Passionate Promises* belonged to her aunt even though no one in the community probably heard the term expressed. It was Aunt Millie's personal crusade to help others, and Brie now had a better understanding of how it came to mean so much to her. Performing such a compassionate and thoughtful act toward complete strangers was both challenging and rewarding.

Brie knew if she did something along the same caliber as her aunt, she could use the knowledge, skill, and experience of photography, something she knew well. She could pursue this endeavor setting her own terms and pace with a combination of art and antics to achieve her goal of lifting someone's spirit. Brie decided to call her venture *Snaps by Sabrina* because it was simple and suited her perfectly.

Locating the cell phone from her purse, Sabrina called Joe. She was ready to put phase two of her plan in motion. He answered on the first ring.

"Hi Sabrina, I wondered how long you would go before calling. So how is country living?" Joe inquired.

"Country living is pretty awesome. How are things at the magazine? Have I missed anything important?"

"All is well, and you know I'd call immediately if there was news."

"Of course. What I really called about is to get your help. I'm interested in developing film the old-fashioned way and need to locate a company that provides this type of equipment and supplies."

"I didn't know anyone did such a thing anymore, but if this company exists, then I'm the man to find it."

"Thanks Joe, I appreciate your doing this for me."

Joe never questioned what Sabrina asked of him. He simply did as instructed. Typically, she would have chatted for awhile keeping up with some of the other assignments and comparing jobs; however, she had other important things on her mind. The magazine no long took precedence in her life, and she found herself excited about beginning a new venture. This was something she had total control of.

Chapter 55

The next day Ben called, and she was happy to hear from him. Knowing how busy he was with his own greenhouse project, she vowed not to bother him.

"Hello, Sabrina. What have you been up to?" Ben asked as soon as she answered the phone.

"I've been quite busy."

"Really, why am I not surprised?" he replied with a chuckle.

"You'd be amazed how busy I've been."

"The suspense is killing me. So what has my girl been up to?" he inquired, playing along.

"Well, since you asked. I went to *Weston Nursing Home* and took pictures of the residents and framed each photo. With the help of the activity director, we hung them on the walls in the dining and recreation rooms," Sabrina proclaimed, proudly.

"Wow, impressive. What gave you the idea to do that?"

"Aunt Millie."

"Of course, your aunt's guardian angel thing."

"Yes, it has to do with the legacy she left to Sophie and me. I thought about trying to respect her wishes but do so on my terms."

"What exactly do you think your aunt wanted you to do?"

"She wanted us to carry on her crusade of helping others. Sophie has no interest, but I feel the need to do something."

After all, if she was considering making changes in her life, she wanted Ben to understand the reason for these changes.

"So let me see if I understand what you're telling me. You want to carry on your aunt's guardian angel activity, but do so in your own way."

"Exactly, I can use my photography skills."

"Would you live here in Asheville?"

"Yes. My thought is to move here, continue with my job at the magazine and when home, visit nursing homes and assisted living facilities taking photos of the residents that wish to have their picture taken. It's an idea still in the planning stages at the moment."

"How does taking pictures of people living in nursing homes qualify for the guardian angel type of help your aunt did?"

"I wouldn't be helping people in the same way she did. The intent is to bring a moment of joy and happiness to brighten their day. Seeing their picture hanging on a wall makes them feel like a celebrity of sorts. The response at Weston was amazing with everyone laughing and teasing each other over their expressions. Honestly, Ben, I don't know if this will work or not. If it doesn't, I at least feel I tried to honor my aunt's request."

"Maybe instead of trying so hard to please your aunt because you feel it's what she expects of you, you should simply do what you want. It sounds like you're trying too hard to honor her wishes, and I don't see how it can work under those conditions."

"I know. That is pretty much the same thing my sister said when I told her. This is the part I am trying to figure out. If I continue with the idea, is it to please my aunt, or am I doing this because I truly have a heart's desire."

"My advice is whatever you decide to do make sure it is for your own reasons and not someone else's."

"Good advice. Thanks, Ben," Sabrina stated, ready to change the subject.

"How is your project coming along?" she asked.

"Great, everything is right on schedule and we should be breaking ground in a couple more weeks. Looks like we both have new projects for this new year."

"We'll see if mine turns into a long-term project."

"Do you want to go out Friday night? Perhaps diner and maybe a

movie," he asked, which was his reason for calling.

"Of course, what time should I be ready?"

"How about six o'clock?"

"Perfect."

"Good, I can't wait to see you again."

It would be a week since their Italian dinner date. A week seemed like a long time, but they both were busy people these days. If this plan of Brie's panned out, she would certainly be a lady with little free time, but she was used to living on a tight schedule.

Thoughts of living in Asheville with her routine lifestyle of working her assignments, freelance photography, and spending time with Ben seemed too good to be true. Everything was falling into place. Sabrina was feeling more at ease with her aunt's *Passionate Promises*. She believed she was doing her best to acknowledge her request of helping others. It was important to try.

Chapter 56

Sabrina took a drive to her neighbor's house for a visit and as usual, was greeted by an exuberant Bella.

"Sabrina, how did you know I needed a break? Come in and have coffee and a blueberry muffin. I baked them fresh this morning."

"I"d love a cup of coffee. How have you been?"

Bella poured two cups of coffee and put them on the table with the condiments. She brought over the basket of fresh baked muffins and sat down opposite Sabrina.

"I've been busy cleaning out the kitchen cupboards. I've put the job off long enough and today was the day to get it done."

"Sounds too much like work," Sabrina said with a chuckle.

"That's the truth! I have old dishes and pans I've collected over the years and don't need anymore. It's time to get rid of all this extra stuff, and after I finish the kitchen, I'm going to tackle each room of the house and do some major spring cleaning."

"What made you decide to do a spring cleaning of your house?"

"Oh, I've been meaning to do this for some time now. What else do I have to do with my time? Enough about chores, what brings you by this morning?"

"Nothing in particular, I just wanted to stop by for a visit."

"Well, I'm always glad to see you. What've you been doing

these days?"

"I've been experimenting with an idea. I went to a nursing home took some candid shots of the residents and framed their pictures and hung them on the walls in the dining and recreation rooms. I was amazed how the residents reacted to seeing their face in print. These senior citizens laughed and carried on like kids."

"Well, I see you've been busy. Did you enjoy yourself?"

"Yes, I did. It was wonderful and so simple to do. I've made a few contacts and will be doing some photographing in other nursing homes."

"Is this something that will be permanent, and what about your job with the magazine?"

"I'm giving it some serious thought. I can do this in between my assignments."

"Would you be doing your photography here, or in Florida?"

"I'm seriously thinking of relocating to Asheville, using my condo for trips to see my sister or vacations. All I really need to do is bring some clothes and have my mail forwarded, a very easy transition. As for my job with the magazine, it isn't affected by where I hang my clothes. When I'm on assignment, I live in hotel rooms."

"Sounds like you have already made up your mind. Do any of these decisions have to do with your aunt?"

"Yes, I came back to make a decision about Aunt Millie's legacy. My sister has no interest.. However, I feel a need to pursue it because she emphasized it to me."

"It wouldn't be Mildred's intent to burden you, or your sister with philanthropic works just because she did them. Perhaps she was trying to raise an opportunity for you both to consider, but leaving the choice to you."

"Exactly, that is the way I look at it too, and I know she meant well. I've always looked forward to visiting Aunt Millie, but now I absolutely love living here. It has given me an opportunity to have friendships, which I never had the time to cultivate before."

"I think Mildred saw something in you and knew someday you would come to understand why she did what she did. You are very much alike."

"Yes, I believe that,"Sabrina accepted her comment with a smile.

"So, you'll be my permanent new neighbor. This is wonderful, Sabrina," Bella cheered.

"I should let you get back to your cleaning. I stopped by to let you know I might be hanging around for a while. Anyway, thanks for the coffee and muffin," Sabrina stated, getting up to leave.

"I believe you will truly love living here just as Mildred predicted. She was a smart lady."

"Yes, she was," Sabrina agreed.

Grabbing her purse and coat, she walked toward the front door. Sabrina turned to give Bella a quick hug.

Chapter 57

Very soon she would be back on assignment, anticipating a call from Joe at any time. Sabrina had found a way to have the best of both her worlds, a blend of city and country living. She planned to change her permanent mailing address to Asheville, keep her condo in Florida, remain on assignment for the magazine, and do freelance photography as well. This would give her the opportunity to honor her aunt's last wishes as best as she knew how. She could easily give of her time and skills to bring a happy moment to someone, uplifting their spirit.

Talking with Bella gave Sabrina the comfort she needed to know she was making the right decision. After all, Bella was best friends to Aunt Millie and would be the closest person to understanding her dilemma, even more so than her sister. She was beginning to comprehend the relevance of the whispering voice telling her to *stay*.

Now that she was, could that be why she hasn't had anymore unnatural events or dreams? Brie was disappointed to have no further encounters with this *being* since her return. It made her wonder about it.

Pushing these thoughts aside for the moment, she decided to call Sophie to let her know of her plans. Taking the cell phone to the den, she sat in the rocking chair looking out through the French doors onto the acreage behind the house, and for the first time saw the beauty and relevance in the gift given to her.

"Hey Sophie, what are you doing?" Sabrina spoke first when her sister answered.

"Hi Brie, I'm cleaning house. You know, that chore that has to be done every week."

"I know what you mean."

"So what's up?"

"I've made a final decision on what to do about Aunt Millie's *Passionate Promises*. I'm making Asheville my permanent residence and work my assignments from here. In between shoots, I'll pursue some photography on the side and am calling it *Snaps by Sabrina*. Cute, don't you think?"

"I like the name. It suits you."

"I don't have to limit my work to nursing homes. I may branch out with my photography services," Brie stated with newfound confidence.

"Well, you know I'll miss you living close by, but I've given this some thought since our last conversation, and you might be right. You should settle in your country home and start some new beginnings, and I do like the idea of *Snaps*. You may find yourself going into a full fledged photo business."

"I thought you'd be disappointed in my decision to reside here, but you don't sound too unhappy with me."

"I don't want to whine about wanting you to live closer. You'll simply have to detour on occasion and come visit David and me," Sophie commanded with as much cheer as she could muster.

"I promise you, Sophie, I will do that. I'm not moving too far away, and I'm keeping my condo for that very reason."

"Besides, I want you and David to come up here for Christmas. We promised each other to spend Christmas together this year. Let's plan now to spend the holidays here."

"Alright, I'll discuss it with David, but he won't have any objections. Will it be a foursome? I assume you and Ben will be spending the holidays together."

"If things progress with Ben as I believe they will, then yes, it will be a foursome."

"Wonderful."

"It's settled. Christmas will be at my new home," Sabrina declared, delighted to know she and Sophie would be together as promised.

"Speaking of Ben, how is he these days?"

"Ben is very busy adding a new addition to their business. They are building a greenhouse which will break ground in a couple of weeks. He has to go out of town frequently to meet with the building contractors."

"A busy man."

"Yes, he is. I can't wait for you to meet him. He and David are going to hit it off. I just know it," Brie assured.

"You have found Mr. Right," Sophie admitted, ecstatically.

"You are right, sis. I have found the man of my dreams."

"Wonderful. It will be awesome to add another member to the family. I get a brother-in-law," Sophie cheered, delighted.

"We'll see; anyway, I've got to give Joe a call and check in about my next assignment. I should be shipping out in a few days."

"Alright, I'll talk to you later. Call and let me know."

"Thanks, Sophie."

"For what?"

"For supporting me even if you don't agree. It means a lot to me, and I hope you know that."

"I will always support you, Brie. We're twins. We stick together, forever."

"Right, twins all the way," Sabrina agreed on a chuckle.

"Love you, sis," Sophie told her before hanging up.

"Love you back."

Sabrina felt relieved Sophie was okay with her moving. Brie knew she needed to spend a lot more time with Sophie and planned to do just that.

Chapter 58

Sabrina called Joe about her next assignment. It didn't bother Brie to be leaving Asheville because when the job was finished she would return here.

"Joe, any word on my next assignment? Thought I'd try to get a heads-up on where the magazine might be sending me," Sabrina asked.

"I haven't heard anything yet, but let me do some checking and I'll get back to you. By the way, I was about to call with the information you asked me to research. I found a company called *Midline Film Manufacturers* located in Seattle. They appear to be the best for what you are looking for, just call them and set up an account. They also give professional discounts. I have their phone number and address," he stated.

"Hold on a second, I'll get a piece of paper to write it down," Sabrina told him, walking into the kitchen to retrieve the notepad left on the table and jotting down the information.

"Thanks Joe. You're so efficient. I couldn't live without you," Sabrina declared, being in a good mood.

"I'm always glad to help, even if it is my job," Joe quipped with humor.

"Just call when you hear something," Sabrina said before disconnecting.

"Roger and out," Joe laughed back.

Joe was the best assistant a person could ask for, and Sabrina counted her blessings for having someone like him. He made all the necessary arrangements, and buffered any issues that manifested. No sooner had she disconnected the call with Joe, the house phone rang. It was Ben.

"Hi Sabrina, how are you?" Ben asked.

It had been several days since they last talked.

"I'm good. Very busy, just as I'm sure you are."

"That's why I'm calling. I hate to do this to you, but I need to cancel our Friday night date. It's the only day the contractor can meet with me, and I won't be back in town in time to go out. In fact, I may need to stay over and return on Saturday. We could go out Saturday night instead, if that works for you," he explained, feeling bad for canceling.

"Well, Ben, that's okay. We don't have to go out at all, ever again," Sabrina said, pleased for having the first shot.

"Is there anything else? I have things to do," she continued.

She couldn't help but take advantage of this opportunity to catch him off-guard. Brie was struggling to maintain a serious tone to her voice. There was silence on the phone, and it was all she could do to avoid laughing and ruining it.

Not able to hold back any longer, she spoke.

"Gotcha," Brie said laughing, feeling so completely in love with this man.

"Oh my goodness, you're good. You had me there for a minute. I must confess, I've met my match," he replied, before exploding with laughter.

"Ben, don't worry about it. We can go out anytime. I completely understand about taking care of business first. Saturday night is fine, or we can wait until one day next week."

"I know what it's like to juggle time on someone else's schedule," Sabrina replied more seriously.

"Good, can we move it to next week just in case I get stuck over the weekend?"

"Next week is fine."

"I see I'll have to be on guard for some good wit coming my way. I told you we were soul mates. By the way, how are things coming along with your own project?"

"Great. I've been surprised by the reception to the idea of photographing residents at the nursing homes. I've contacted a few more and they love the idea."

"How does this play into your regular job?"

"Easy, really. I continue with the work assignments, and when I have free time, I can do freelance photography. It works out perfectly."

"So, are you still thinking of moving here?"

"Yes, I've decided to make Asheville my home and keep my condo for visiting my sister."

"Wow, a lot has happened since we last talked," Ben stated a bit surprised.

"This was my purpose in coming back. I had a lot of thinking to do and decisions to make, and I'm comfortable with making the transition. I don't have to do anything but change my mailing address. Pretty much everything else remains the same," she clarified.

"Well I have to say, I for one like your plan. It gives me the opportunity to spend a lot more time with you."

"Yes, that is definitely a benefit. It's nice that I can do this without it affecting my profession. Actually, it feels like I am adding a dimension to my life."

"You are. Not so much by changing where you live, but adding the freelance photography to your timetable. That could be very rewarding," Ben stated in support of her decision.

"I think so too, and I've given myself a name. I'm calling my freelance work, *Snaps by Sabrina*. Who knows, perhaps I might consider it more in a business manner in the future."

"I'm excited everything is working out, and you'll be living close to me," Ben replied with humor.

"Me too," Sabrina agreed, pleased with Ben's reaction to her news.

"I've got to get back to work, but we'll go on that movie date next week. I'll call you when I get back into town, funny girl," he called her.

"Next week is fine, and I hope your meetings go well," she

told him.

"Thanks, I hope so, too. Have a good weekend, Sabrina. Think of me," Ben announced before hanging up.

"Ditto," Brie replied, laughing.

It seemed everything was falling comfortably in place for Brie. If it hadn't been for Aunt Millie, Sabrina would not be making all these changes in her life or considering a means of helping others. But since her return, *Passionate Promises* was on her mind constantly.

What she was doing with her photography wasn't enough but only the beginning, and Brie knew she would have to incorporate more of *Passionate Promises* into her daily routine. Sabrina wasn't sure how to do that just yet, but knew in time she would figure it all out. Maybe this was what Aunt Millie was trying to tell her when she said, *search your heart.*

Chapter 59

Cleaning the house, Sabrina was preparing to leave for her next assignment whenever she got the call from Joe. As she was upstairs dusting, the house phone rang and she ran downstairs, grabbing it on the fifth ring.

"Sabrina, is that you?" the caller asked.

"Yes, this is Sabrina. Do I know you?" Brie asked in reply.

"Of course you know me, dear. This is Sarah Logan, and I'm calling for a favor. My daughter was having lunch with me and commented about the photos on the walls in the dining room. She loved them, and when I told her who the photographer was, she was surprised we had a celebrity photojournalist among us. I mentioned to her about you taking my picture, and she wanted to know if you would be willing to do a mother-daughter portrait. I told her I would call and talk to you about the idea. So what do you think?" Sarah asked, straightforward.

"It's a wonderful idea. How soon did she want it done?" Sabrina asked, thinking she might be leaving in less than a week.

"There's no real hurry, just whenever it's convenient for you."

"What about next Monday? Where does your daughter want to have the picture taken? We can do it anywhere depending on the background she prefers. Perhaps there, or in a park," Sabrina told her.

"See, now I don't know those details. You'll have to talk to her."

"Why don't you call your daughter to see if Monday works with her schedule? We can take it from there."

"I'll give her a call right now, and I have to tell you, the pictures have been a big hit around here. Everyone is still talking about them."

"I'm so glad."

"I'll give you a call once I talk to Heather," Sarah told her before hanging up.

"Sounds good."

Brie couldn't believe it. It was impossible to contain the enthusiasm as she danced around the kitchen in a circle thrilled with the prospect of doing portrait shots; a new aspect to her photography.

Racing upstairs to continue with the chores, she whirled through the house with exuberance cleaning from room to room. For the first time in her adult life, she was entertaining ideas of starting projects of her own invention. It felt wonderful to be taking charge of her destiny. Again, she had Aunt Millie to thank for that.

Continuing on downstairs, she finally reached the laundry room which was situated off the kitchen, and stood in the small doorway studying the interior. *This would make a perfect darkroom,* she thought. It already had the required plumbing and electrical outlets and was large enough to put a long narrow worktable against the wall opposite the washer and dryer. The room was also equipped with a deep utility sink in the far corner. *It shouldn't be hard to change the lighting,* Sabrina considered. It could be accomplished with very little changes, and no drastic alterations to the house.

Sabrina went to the table where she had left the notepad with *Midline Film Manufacturer's* telephone number scribbled and gave them a call to set up an account. The customer service representative would mail a product catalog, and advised Brie to peruse it carefully because many items in the catalog were not available on their website. Therefore, she should call regarding placing an order.

While Brie sat at the kitchen table making her plans, Sarah called again to inform Sabrina Monday afternoon would be fine with Heather and they could use the garden area with the gazebo in the back of the nursing home as the backdrop. Arrangements were made for Brie to be at Weston by one o'clock.

Since Sabrina wasn't seeing Ben until the following week, she decided to take advantage of the weekend to plan out the darkroom. Having not received the product catalog, she went online to view *Midline's* website. Reviewing the equipment and supplies, she added up the cost and was shocked at the tally even after the thirty percent discount. However, she wasn't going to let that discourage her. She was on a mission to do freelance and wanted to develop the prints herself.

Brie knew there might be times when she would use the photo shop for quick digital prints, or possibly the program on her computer for touchups, but she was never completely satisfied with the quality of the print, which was the main reason she liked the old-fashion way of taking pictures with film. She could control the final outcome in the development. She needed to brush up on her skills because she had not developed film since college.

For the portraits of Sarah and Heather, she planned to use the same photo processing shop she did with the resident pictures. Hopefully, Brie could do electronic touchups to her satisfaction before running them to print. If the photos didn't meet her high standards, she'd explain to Sarah they would need to redo the shoot once she had her own processing equipment.

On Monday afternoon she met with Sarah and her daughter as scheduled. Sabrina was excited to be doing her first posed portrait shot, excluding the single one taken of Sarah.

"Sabrina, I want you to meet my daughter, Heather," Sarah

spoke first.

"It is a pleasure to meet you, Heather," Brie responded, extending her arm for a handshake.

"I was so surprised when my mother told me about you. You are the perfect person to take a portrait of us," Heather stated with a smile, accepting the handshake.

"Thanks for the vote of confidence, and I hope I meet your expectations."

"Oh, I have no doubts."

Heather appeared to be in her early forties, dressed in a navy blue business suit paired with a pale blue blouse. She had light brown hair styled in a short layered cut and hazel eyes. She wore very little makeup, rendering a pale complexion as Sabrina studied her appearance. Brie knew she would have to do some touchup to bring a softer look to her features.

On the other hand, Sarah was dressed in a soft pastel, floral dress with a peter-pan collar and long sleeves. She had pampered herself with a rosy blush on her cheeks and bright pink lipstick. She was refreshingly pretty, Brie thought.

"Have you decided where you want your picture taken?"

"Yes, the garden area out back."

"Follow me, Sabrina. I'll show you where it is," Sarah spoke up, taking off down the hall.

Heather caught up to walk beside her mother while Sabrina followed behind. On the back lawn behind the nursing home was a beautifully kept garden area with a gazebo that was perfect as a backdrop. Sabrina took her camera bag and placed it on a bench just inside the gazebo and took out her favorite camera informing Sarah and Heather to sit on the middle bench. They adjusted their position several times as Sabrina snapped off shots. Next, she asked Heather to remove her jacket because the soft blue blouse was a better match to her mother's dress and presented a flow between the two subjects in the photo.

Sabrina made necessary adjustments periodically to their positions, moving them around in the garden to capture the best backgrounds. Lastly, they went back inside the building using a plain white wall as the final backdrop. When she had clicked off a total of forty shots, Sabrina announced she was finished. Brie asked if they had a preference of wanting any prints in black and white or antiqued, and Heather and Sarah both agreed they preferred a standard color photo.

"I'll have some proofs ready to review in a couple of days. I'll call you before bringing them by."

"That would be great. Just call my mom and she will let me know. Also, I didn't ask about your fee?"

"That will depend on your choices. I'll bring along a price sheet when we meet the next time," Sabrina responded, thinking quickly.

She had not given a thought to the cost of doing the photos; however, something she needed to consider since all aspects of her freelance work couldn't be free of charge. She would need to use discernment. They returned to Sarah's room briefly before Sabrina left the two women standing in the doorway as she walked down the hallway to the front door. Sabrina was anxious to get them developed.

Brie stopped by the same photo shop she used previously and carefully scrutinized each picture, making the necessary adjustments before sending them to print, having several for them to choose from. She hoped they turned out to her satisfaction. Sabrina didn't like being limited in the ability to make specific alterations, but there was no choice in the matter. *This will change when I get my darkroom set up,* she consoled herself.

Chapter 60

Ben called on Sunday evening inviting Sabrina to dinner on Tuesday, referring to it as a make-up date. On Monday, Sabrina received a call from Joe to be prepared to leave in a few days for Nebraska.

"What could there possibly be in Nebraska to photograph this time of year? It's snowing there as we speak," Sabrina declared.

"I hear you; however, the magazine wants pictures of emus," Joe stated.

"Why do an article on emus?" Sabrina continued, not sure she even wanted to know the answer.

"There are several farms that raise these birds for their body oil. Apparently, the emu oil is used for medicinal purposes to aid in burns and skin disorders," Joe offered the information he had gathered.

"What kind of pictures is the magazine looking for?"

"I don't think the editors are requiring anything specific, just a few close-up shots of the emus to go along with the article."

"Okay, I'll be ready to fly out next Monday. Book my ticket," she ordered with a laugh.

"I'm on it. I'll call you later with details," he chuckled, before hanging up.

Sabrina made a mental note of things that needed to be done, and one was to deliver the photos to Sarah. She would be ready to leave on schedule.

Tuesday evening, Ben was at Sabrina's doorstep at six sharp. They agreed to go back to the Italian restaurant. Sitting comfortably at the same table in the corner, Brie smiled when Ben winked at her.

"You're looking prettier each time I see you," he told her sitting across the table and reaching for her hand.

He reached over and took her left hand that was playing with the stem of the water glass, and slipped his fingers between hers snuggling their hands so that their palms where pressed together tightly. Loosening the grip, he let his thumb slowly trace a circle within her palm. It sent a shiver through her body making goose bumps pop up on her skin. Brie hoped Ben didn't notice her reaction to his touch.

"Why, Ben, you'e going to make me blush," Sabrina declared in her best southern accent, attempting to distract from her reaction.

"I hope so, because I want to be the only one that puts color in your cheeks," Ben said, grinning.

She smiled back, and they continued to hold hands until the food arrived, and reluctantly Ben pulled his hand away. Sabrina was both disappointed for the disconnection and yet relieved. As much as she was enjoying his touch, Brie didn't know how much longer she could sit there with these sensations playing havoc on her body. It was driving her crazy.

Enjoying each other's company, they caught up on events with Ben talking about the meeting on Friday with the contractor. It turned out he had to stay the entire weekend. Brie informed him of the photo session with Sarah and her daughter at Weston. By the time they were eating dessert and coffee, Sabrina needed to tell Ben she would be leaving for another assignment.

"I heard from my assistant, Joe, yesterday. The magazine is sending me to Nebraska, and I'll be flying out on Monday," Brie informed him.

"How long will you be gone," he asked.

"I don't know at the moment, but I'm sure the next job will

follow from there. It could be a couple of months before I return home."

Sabrina called Asheville home. It flowed from her lips so naturally as though this was the only place she had ever lived.

"What are you photographing in Nebraska?"

"Birds, emus to be exact,."

"Sounds daunting, why emus?"

"Something to do with the body oil they produce and how it is used for medicinal purposes. Apparently, the magazine is doing an article on the subject."

"Okay, so we'll stay in touch by phone; two months goes by fast. At least when you're done, you'll be returning here."

"This is true."

"Well in that case, we need to go out every night this week. What do you think?" he asked, with a big grin on his face.

"You are absolutely correct, every single night," Sabrina agreed, excited to be spending so much time with Ben before she left.

They finished their meal and took a drive, just as they had done before, talking, laughing, and teasing one another mercifully. She loved his good nature. It would be very difficult to leave him if it meant she wouldn't return after the assignments, but knowing she would see him again in a few weeks, made leaving bearable. *I'm so in love,* she told herself.

When Ben took her home, he kissed her good night, not hanging around for coffee as he normally might have done. He would see her again tomorrow and every day the rest of the week. Sabrina was in a romantic daze as she closed the front door and slid the deadbolt into place.

Taking the cell phone out of her purse, she walked to the den and plopped in the rocking chair, pushing the speed dial button to call her sister.

"Hi Brie, what's up?" Sophie asked when she identified the caller.

"I'm in love," Sabrina practically shouted into the phone.

"Congratulations, does Ben know?" Sophie asked.

Sophie couldn't resist teasing her sister.

"I haven't said anything, and besides, he has already told me he loves me."

"But did he say the three important words?"

"Not exactly."

"So when do you think he'll be telling you he loves you, so you can reply back."

"We know we love each other, and the feeling grows stronger each time we are together. He even told me we are soul mates. It doesn't bother me that he hasn't actually said the three words yet. I'm not expecting to hear the actual 'I love you' from him anytime soon, but I know he does," Sabrina remembered the silly game they played.

"He might just surprise you," Sophie announced, thrilled for her sister.

"Anything is possible, but changing the subject, I'm going back on assignment and leave Monday morning for Nebraska to shoot emus," Sabrina declared with a laugh.

"Why emus?"

"My exact words when Joe told me of the assignment. Apparently, they produce a body oil similar to our natural skin oil which makes it a great transdermal carrier used for burns and other types of skin conditions," Brie explained, having done a little research on the internet.

"If you say so, but it's the middle of winter in Nebraska. How long do you think you'll be there?"

"Not long, if I can help it. I'm planning to drop in, take a few pictures, and leave in two days tops."

"How are things at the home front?" Brie asked.

"We are doing fine; same usual stuff. Work, grade papers, sleep and get up and do it all over again," Sophie stated, a bit disheartened.

"You love teaching, don't sound so down," Brie reminded her.

"Yes, I do, and I'm not complaining, really. So when you finish in Nebraska, are you returning to Asheville or Florida?"

Sophie asked, changing the subject.

"I'll be returning here first for a few days and then down to visit you. We never did our shopping spree. What do you think about us getting together and doing some serious spring clothes shopping?" Sabrina popped the question, knowing it would cheer her sister.

"That's a wonderful idea and it gives me something to look forward to. When do you think you'll be here?" Sophie perked up with newfound excitement.

"It may be a few weeks. I'm sure from Nebraska I'll be directed somewhere else. Hope you can wait that long," she teased, pleased to hear the enthusiasm in Sophie's voice.

"Knowing you're coming down, I'll definitely wait. We'll have a lot of fun."

"Yes, we will. Okay get back to grading papers, and I'll call before I leave."

"I'm glad you have finally found someone you love, sis," Sophie said, happy for Brie.

"Thanks, it feels right with Ben."

"I'll talk to you in a couple days," Sophie told her.

Sabrina was determined to spend a lot more time with her sister, realizing she needed to reassure Sophie of her promise to make several trips to visit. This would be the first of many excursions back to her home state, and Brie knew it would be a lot of fun for both of them. She was looking forward to it herself.

Chapter 61

Sabrina returned to *Weston Nursing Home* as planned on Wednesday afternoon with the prints. Spreading them across Sarah's small table gave Heather and her mother a chance to review each one, carefully deciding which pose and background they preferred. It didn't take either long to select the same three Sabrina also thought were the best. Narrowing it down to one would be difficult, but it depended on what they liked.

Brie waited patiently as Sarah and Heather perused through the photos. Finally, they agreed on the same pose. *That was easy,* Sabrina thought.

"My mother and I agree on this one, and I only want two prints. How much do I owe you for them?" Heather asked as she pointed to the chosen photo.

"That is all you want?" Sabrina confirmed the order.

"Yes, just one each. I'll get some frames and hang one here in my mother's room, and the other I'll take home."

"In that case, they're yours, no charge."

Heather and Sarah both looked at Sabrina with surprise written all over their faces.

"I don't understand. I engaged your services to photograph a mother-daughter portrait, and I expect to pay," Heather announced a bit strongly.

"This is true; however, it is my gift to you and Sarah," Brie offered as she looked at Heather's mother.

"How sweet of you, Sabrina, but it's not necessary," Sarah spoke up.

"Of course, it isn't necessary, but I very much want to give this to you. I enjoyed photographing you with your daughter."

"Heather, let's not argue with Sabrina. If she wants to make it a gift, then we should graciously accept," Sarah told her, seeing the determination in Sabrina's eyes.

"I feel funny not paying for your time. It doesn't seem right."

"I have a suggestion. Would you be willing to pass a few business cards around to friends, neighbors, and co-workers? I'm starting a freelance business in the area and could use some advertisement."

"Absolutely, I would be delighted. Give me a handful," Heather stated, accepting this arrangement.

Reaching into her camera bag, Sabrina pulled out about twenty cards with the logo of a camera sitting atop a tripod in the upper left corner and *Snaps by Sabrina* written across the middle of the card along with her name and cell phone number directly beneath. Brie had these printed shortly after she decided to do photography at the nursing homes, knowing she would need a calling card.

"I appreciate it, and I will have your portraits ready by Friday," Sabrina carefully collected all the photos and replaced them in the large envelope.

"I'll walk you to the front door," Sarah spoke as she preceded Brie through the doorway of her room.

They remained silent walking down the hallway until they reached the entranceway.

"That was a very thoughtful thing you did, and it reminds me so much of Mildred that it makes me want to cry. People, in general, don't do such things like you did today," Sarah spoke first.

"It was truly my pleasure, Sarah. It meant a lot to me to do this. I'll see you on Friday," Sabrina confirmed, before walking out.

Sarah remained standing in place, watching Sabrina get in her car and drive away. In some strange way, she seemed more like a daughter than a new acquaintance. *Silly,* she thought as she turned to walk back down the long hallway to her room.

Brie stopped at the photo shop to order the selected print in the correct size which would be ready within an hour. She drove to the *Crafty Loft Art and Hobby Shop* to select three special frames with appropriate mattes, one for the self-portrait of Sarah. Sabrina wanted to surprise Sarah by having the pictures already framed.

Choosing three traditional dark wood frames and light beige matting for the portraits, Brie backtracked to the photo shop to pick up the prints and went home. Sabrina was completely satisfied with the results of her first official freelance work and found it worth the experience to do Sarah's at no cost.

She discovered it to be exceedingly rewarding to partake in bringing joy to someone's life, and with something so simply as a portrait. It is the collection of special moments in our life that make wonderful memories. Brie was pleased to play a role in adding to the memories for Sarah and Heather.

Chapter 62

Sabrina was delighted to hand over to Sarah two beautifully matted and framed portraits on Friday just as she had promised.

"Are these the pictures?" Sarah stared with excitement at two brown bags Brie was holding.

"Yes, I wanted to surprise you so I took the liberty of framing them. If you and Heather don't care for my choice, you can change them to your liking," Sabrina explained.

Laying the large bag on the table, Sabrina carefully slipped out the identically framed pictures. Sarah gasped when she saw the portrait, bringing tears to her eyes.

"Sabrina, this takes my breath away, and I can't wait to call Heather and have her see these," Sarah said as she looked at Brie with moist eyes.

"We must pay you. Your time and talent should be compensated," Sarah spoke softly, feeling very emotional.

"The expression on your face is priceless to me; that is my compensation. I am so pleased you like your portrait," Sabrina told her with sincerity.

"Oh, I do. I truly do," Sarah replied, overwhelmed.

"Sarah, I have one more surprise for you," Brie said, pulling out the self-portrait from the smaller bag.

Sabrina handed the identically framed picture to Sarah. She took one look at herself in the photo and began to cry. She was to touched for words.

The joy Sabrina witnessed was causing her heart to explode

knowing she was responsible for this happiness in Sarah.

"I'm going on assignment with the magazine in a couple of days, but when I return I'd like to stop by and visit," Sabrina told her.

"Oh yes, please do. I was hoping you would stay in touch, but I didn't want to be presumptuous and ask," Sarah said, gathering her composure.

"I hope Heather enjoys her portrait, and if for any reason she is not happy with it, please let me know," she informed Sarah.

"She will love this. I'm sure of it," Sarah told her.

"Take care of yourself, and I'll see you when I get back," Sabrina stated as a means of farewell.

Brie leaned forward and gave Sarah a quick embrace.

In the visits Sabrina had made to the nursing home, Sarah had become someone she wanted to remain in contact with. Just like Bella, and perhaps Annie, these women who knew her aunt were now becoming important in her life. *Such an unusual turn of events,* she thought.

She had one more stop to make before returning home. Driving into the small parking lot of George's office, Sabrina caught him in- between clients. He was standing by the receptionist desk when she walked in the door and motioned her to follow him into his office.

"Sabrina, I haven't seen you for a while. How are you?" George asked, walking behind his desk to sit.

"I'm doing great. I wanted to tell you I'm moving to Asheville," Brie announced from her usual chair.

"What brought you to decide to relocate?"

"Aunt Millie, this is her fault," Sabrina answered, holding back a smile.

"So we are going to have a new guardian angel in the community," George accepted the banter, knowingly.

"No, I could never fill her footsteps, but my aunt was right about one thing. She believed when she left her home to me, I would come to love living here, and I do. I came by to tell you

I'm staying in the house."

"That's wonderful, Sabrina, and I'm glad for you. You're correct, Mildred believed you would be happy living here if you ever gave it a try. Remember my offer stands, if you need anything, don't hesitate to call." George told her.

"Thank you. I'll be going on assignment in a couple of days, so could you keep a watch on the house?" Brie asked carefully, not wanting George to think she was taking advantage of his good nature.

"Certainly, it's not a problem."

"Thanks, again, and I'll be in touch when I return."

Next, she drove to Bella's house. Brie wanted to let her neighbor know she would be gone for a while.

"Hey, what brings you around on this beautiful day?" Bella proclaimed.

"Hello Bella, you sure are chipper," Sabrina stated with a grin and stepped into the house.

"Always happy to see you."

"You mean I can make you feel this good just by showing up."

"Absolutely," Bella bantered back.

"How about a cup of coffee and slice of coconut cream pie, baked it yesterday."

"Sounds delicious, I never refuse home-cooked food."

"Good, so tell me what brings you over today?"

"I came by to let you know I'm going on assignment for a few weeks. I couldn't leave without letting you know," Sabrina told her.

"I appreciate that. I would have worried if I didn't hear from you."

Sharing a piece of pie and coffee, they chatted until it was time for Sabrina to leave in order to get ready for her daily date with Ben. She hugged Bella and promised to let her know the moment she returns, but informed her she could be gone for a couple of months. Having finished with the scheduled visits, Sabrina drove home and called her sister.

"Hey Sophie, what's new in your world?" Sabrina asked.

"I don't have anything new to report at the moment. What about you?" she returned the question.

"I'm leaving on Monday for Nebraska, but don't forget about our shopping spree, because when I get back I'm coming down to visit you," Sabrina confirmed her plans.

"Oh, I haven't forgotten. In fact, I'm holding you to it," Sophie commented, excitedly.

"Plan on it, sis."

"I hope you don't get snowed in. They are having some blizzards out that way," Sophie offered the information.

"Hush, don't jinx this trip," Brie told her sister, laughing.

"Never, just have fun with the birds," Sophie giggled.

"You know I have fun with all the animals," she said, teasingly.

"Of course, but now you can share time between the four-legged and the two-legged kind," Sophie bantered right back.

"This is true. Seriously though, I can't recall when I've spent so much time having conversations with individuals. I'm not just talking about Ben or Bella, but visiting with Sarah Logan, or talking with Annie. I even stayed in touch with George, the attorney. It is so different for me to want these friendships. They have become important to me. I didn't realize how much of a bubble I was living in," Sabrina confessed.

"I think this is what Aunt Millie was trying to get you to see about yourself. Something, obviously, she already knew. She wanted to draw you out of that bubble, as you call it, and know there is a whole big world. Careers are great, but they aren't everything and we shouldn't make them the center of our life. She wasn't begrudging you your lifestyle, but rather wanting you to look beyond. For that, I agree with her. I just think she had a strange way of going about it, but that is what I believe she meant with *Passionate Promises*," Sophie told her.

"I agree. Spending these two separate months in her house and meeting people because of her has caused to reevaluate my life. But *Passionate Promises* is much more than opening my eyes. There is a profound purpose to what she did and wants carried forward. It's more than a legacy of words with her hope that we feel the same way she did. When I had that last dream of meeting Aunt Millie, she implied that something was revealed to her and would be revealed to me and that I had a decision or choice to make. I didn't know what she meant, and of course, it was just a dream. But her words still haunt me," Brie confided her thoughts as well.

"In such a short time, so much has already changed in your life. You've made the decision to move into Aunt Millie's house, you're in love with Ben and probably will be engaged sooner than you think, you've made friends with Bella and others in the community, and you are starting your own freelance photography business. All of this because you spent eight weeks, relatively speaking, in the country. To me, that is astounding," Sophie stated, releasing one long breath.

"And you still have your career intact. You have done a major overhaul of Sabrina Fitzgerald with all these additional dimensions. This is wonderful and good for you, a blessing. Cherish all that you have and be grateful, Brie," she continued.

"Oh, I'm grateful. I'm grateful to Aunt Millie because without her letter, I wouldn't have known to pursue the things that have brought me to where I am right now. Realistically, I probably would have locked up the house and come back on occasion, or even sold it. I don't know. What I do know is that letter changed everything for me."

"What about the voice? You said there haven't been anymore events, but what do you think that was all about?"

"That is the one remaining issue that I haven't been able to resolve in my mind, and it's the one that bothers me the most. I desire to know who it is, and why they came to me in the first place. If I never have another encounter, it would leave a lot of unanswered questions. I'd like to have an opportunity to better understand it, but apparently that isn't an option. There have been no more since the dream."

"Well, you said the message was always the same, to *stay*. Since that's what you plan to do, perhaps whatever it was has fulfilled its purpose and nothing else needs to be satisfied."

"Yes, you're probably right. It may be something I'll never have an answer to."

"I'm so very proud of you, sis, and happy for you, too. Call me when you leave to go play with the emus," Sophie told her, ending their conversation on a lighter note.

"Thank you for helping me through this transition and being there for me, even when I know you didn't always agree."

"Anytime, sis, anytime," Sophie replied, laughing.

"I love you, Sophie. I'll call before I leave," Brie stated, ready to end the call.

"I love you too, Brie. Twins all the way, always," Sophie chanted, before hanging up.

Placing the phone on the kitchen counter, Sabrina took a tour of the house. She would be leaving in two days and was glad to have already cleaned and secured everything. On her list of things to do, she remembered to call and reschedule the nursing home resident photography session to a date after she returned. The only thing left to do was pack some very warm clothes and be ready to leave first of the week.

Returning to the den, she rocked and thought of the conversation she had with Sophie. True, so many things had happened and changed for her. She still had unanswered questions and knew she had to come to terms that she may not ever know the meaning behind everything she experienced.

Brie believed she had a better understanding of her aunt's desire to leave such a legacy, and she wanted very much now to continue with *Passionate Promises*. It meant everything to her. She wasn't doing this out of guilt, nor to appease her aunt's final request because she felt it was expected of her, but rather it was in her heart to do so of her own accord.

She could appreciate the meaning of *guardian angel* and in a very unusual way Brie realized in her heart she wanted to be a guardian angel, too. She wanted to do more than have people smile for the camera with her photography, because she saw the need to hep others in a more personal manner.

Perhaps, her brief time with Sarah, and speaking with Annie has brought her to this point. She wasn't sure when she made this decision, but there is was. *I want to be a guardian angel just like my Aunt Millie*, she told herself.

Extinguishing the fire, Brie walked through the downstairs once more turning off most of the lights and went upstairs. *Enough thinking for one evening,* she thought.

Chapter 63

When Sabrina stepped out of the bathroom after taking a warm shower, she saw a beautiful, angelic figure shadowed in a soft, white cloud appearing in the middle of her bedroom, the room where she first heard the soft voice whispering for her to stay. Not the least bit afraid, Sabrina stood spellbound by what she saw. With tears flowing down her cheeks and choking on raw emotion, she struggled to summon the courage to speak.

"You came," Sabrina barely whispered.

"You're an angel. You're the one who whispers to me, but I don't know you," she continued, almost unable to speak.

"Yes, you do know me, Sabrina," the angelic figure responded.

"How do I know you, or what you want from me?" Sabrina spoke softly to the presence before her.

"Search your heart, Sabrina, and you'll come to understand."

Sabrina stood in silent reverence, staring at the magnificent heavenly being before her.

The powerful love and peace surrounding the angel was tangible to Brie. She wanted to step closer, but was afraid if she moved the angelic figure would vanish.

"You have come to me several times since my aunt's death. Now I know it was you beside me at her funeral, but I don't understand why. You kept telling me to *stay,* and I thought it meant I should stay in this community, but for what reason? Do you have anything to do with my aunt's *Passionate Promises*?" Sabrina asked, softly.

"Yes, Sabrina, I'm aware of *Passionate Promises*."

"Please explain it to me. I desperately want to know."

"Had you not believed in your heavenly Father, I could not present myself before you. Knowing that you do with a pure heart, I have been sent to guide you to do your Father's work."

Instantly, Sabrina remembered the dream where Aunt Millie was asking if she believed in heaven and angels. She said she already knew what her decision would be. All the missing pieces of the puzzle were slipping into place. *Oh my gosh,* she thought.

"My aunt inferred that something was revealed to her and would be revealed to me. It's you. You appeared before her like you are now appearing before me."

The meaning behind the legacy was quickly slipping into place for Sabrina.

"My aunt was chosen to be a guardian angel, wasn't she? Did you tell her to call her crusade, *Passionate Promises*?"

"Yes, she was chosen to be a guardian angel. However, *Passionate Promises* was of her own making."

"Are you telling me that I have been chosen to be a guardian angel, too? Did my aunt have anything to do with this decision?"

This revelation was almost more than her heart could bear.

"You made the decision yourself. Upon this choice, I have come to now guide you. You will know what to do, because it will be in your heart. There will be no more confusion or misunderstanding from this moment forward, Sabrina. Your destiny has been established. You have a heart acceptable to your Father to do His work. You were chosen to follow in her footsteps. Yes, she knew just as she told you."

"What am I suppose to do now?"

Sabrina remembered vaguely that Aunt Millie mentioned in her letter, something about her path was guided by God and she was doing this for Him. It all made sense.

"You're the one who guided my aunt and told her who needed help. Of course, that is the only way she would've known. Did you tell her to leave this legacy to me? How was I selected to carry on in her place?"

"She believed in you."

"What really happen to my aunt? What caused her death?" Brie asked, carefully.

"I can not answer that question."

"Why isn't Sophie included?" Brie asked, wanting to know why her twin wasn't privy to this experience.

"Again, that is not for me to say."

"But she has a good heart. She should be a part of this," Sabrina explained.

"Dear one, I can not give you all the answers you seek. That is not my purpose."

"Will I ever see you again?" Sabrina asked with a desperate feeling of being alone.

"You'll never be alone, Sabrina. I will always be with you. Remember, search your heart and listen carefully," the angel told her before slipping away.

Sabrina remained still, staring straight ahead where the angel had appeared. When the power of what had just occurred hit her, she began to cry. The tears slid down her cheeks as she remained frozen in place.

Brie slowly collapsed to the floor and held her face in her hands, weeping uncontrollably. She felt her heart was going to burst with the heaviness of what she had just learned, to be found worthy and acceptable to be a guardian angel. It was a long time before she could gather her composure.

She went to sit on the edge of the bed, exactly as she had the very first time she heard the beautiful melodic voice whispering for her to *stay*. Brie remained for a long time pondering everything the angel had said. She felt like crying all over again.

Not the least bit sleepy, she went downstairs into the kitchen and made a cup of herbal tea taking it into the dimly lit den to sit and rock. She didn't know what time it was, and it didn't matter. There was no one she wanted to talk to, not even her sister. Brie felt compelled to keep this to herself. She wasn't sure how she could tell Sophie about this revelation, not knowing how she would react. Now she understood why Aunt Millie didn't say anything during her visits. How could she? *If she experienced anything close to what I'm feeling at this moment, she couldn't,* she thought.

Sabrina felt ashamed she had lived with so little faith and knowledge of God. She didn't blame anyone for this, it just was. She wondered why He would choose her when she didn't have much to do with Him throughout her life. But for reasons she didn't yet grasp, she was deemed acceptable to carry on her aunt's legacy. *I'm sure when you wrote the letter, Aunt Millie, you only hoped I would become a guardian angel, too,* she thought.

A peace and calmness came over her and she went upstairs to bed. Sabrina fell into a deep, sound sleep without dreaming. When she woke the next morning, Brie felt different and definitely knew she wasn't herself. She stepped into the bathroom to study her reflection in the mirror to see she looked the same, but inside she knew she had changed. Brie realized it was her heart.

Epilogue

Sitting in her favorite chair, looking out through the French doors upon the tree-laden acreage, Sabrina felt one with the beauty and serenity of nature. With a piece of stationery and pen, she wrote a letter to her aunt.

Dear Aunt Millie,

The love I have for you is like a daughter's love for her mother. I always felt your love, and I miss you deeply. Where do I begin to tell you that what you have given to me exceeds materialistic things and takes my breath away? I have so many new beginnings, and I can only thank you for them.

Your legacy of Passionate Promises has given a spiritual realm to my life that I have yet to imagine. Aunt Millie, I will proudly carry Passionate Promises forward, and I thank you with a humble gratitude and enduring love.

Love,

Your niece, Sabrina

When she finished, Sabrina sat with the paper and pen in her lap. Closing her eyes for a moment, she reminisced about all that had occurred in the short time she had spent living in this country home. She knew it never would have been if not for her aunt's foresight and understanding of the spirit within the niece she loved like a daughter.

Tears of joy slid down Sabrina's cheeks. Reading the letter

she had written, Sabrina folded it and walked upstairs to the master bedroom. Pulling out the middle drawer, she located the envelope and place her letter alongside her aunts and sealed it. Sabrina then placed the envelope in the far right corner of the middle desk drawer.

Farewell, Aunt Millie, she whispered.

Shadow of a Promise

A Vow

EXCERPT

Shadow of a Promise, A Vow is the sequel to *Passionate Promises, A Legacy,* which continues the story of identical twins, Sabrina and Sophie. Sabrina unveils a surprising legacy in *Passionate Promises, A Legacy* left to the twins by their last remaining relative, Aunt Millie. However, Sophie encounters her own revelation that rocks the core of her life.

Sophie's perfect world has just been shattered. Shocked when one of her newborn twins is diagnosed with a life-threatening health condition, she finds herself thrust into an emotional abyss fighting against events and circumstances that quickly escalate out of control, leaving her desperate for a resolution other than the one she is facing. Unable to accept the doctor's prognosis, she finds herself alone in her quest for another answer to her baby's medical crisis.

Sophie discovers she must deal with a secret that has haunted her for years, never considering there could be a connection between her past and her daughter's future. In her deepest, darkest hour of despair, she cries out in agony for help with nowhere to turn. Gripped in grief and frantic as time is slipping away, she struggles to make restitution, but will her efforts be enough to save her baby from an unacceptable fate?

She questions if her purposeful estrangement involving the legacy is somehow affecting her life in *Shadow of a Promise, A Vow.*

About the Author

Patricia Marlett is dedicated to writing inspirational novels for both the adult and young reader genres. With a contemporary platform, she enjoys penning plots that reflect life experiences through drama, intrigue, suspense, humor, and love. Inspirational messages are subtly woven within the endearing themes of her stories lending to heartfelt expressions from laughter to tears and always with hope and joy.

Visit Patricia at her website, www.patriciamarlett.com, to learn of her passion for writing, view her books, and for contact information.